COLD GROUND

A DCI REECE THRILLER

LIAM HANSON

CRIME PRINTS

Copyright © 2021 by Liam Hanson

All rights reserved.

No part of this publication may be reproduced, distributed, or transmitted in any form or by any means, including photocopying, recording, or other electronic or mechanical methods, without the prior written permission of the publisher, except as permitted by U.K. copyright law. For permission requests, contact author.

The story, all names, characters, and incidents portrayed in this production are fictitious. No identification with actual persons, living or deceased, is intended or should be inferred.

Published by CRIME PRINTS

An Imprint of Liam Hanson Media

ISBN-13: 979-8763879773

BOOKS BY LIAM HANSON

DEADLY MOTIVE
COLD GROUND
KILLING TIME
CHASING SHADOWS
DEVIL'S BREAD
ALL THAT REMAINS

For my wife and children

COLD GROUND

Chapter 1

He'd murdered his own mother only a few days earlier. Gripped her scrawny neck and throttled all signs of life out of her. Her eyes bulged. Tongue went blue and hung from the corner of her mouth like a cheap cut of uncooked steak. Her bowels gave way only seconds before her arthritic knees did.

It was an act of sheer impulse on his part. A lifetime's pent-up anger released like pus from a festering boil.

Mother had rarely shown him love and affection. Preferring the *comforts* provided by men who came and went while Father was busy at work.

As a boy, young Richard saw it all. Every sordid detail. It disgusted him. *She* disgusted him. Her type cared for no one but themselves. He despised each and every one of them.

When at last she left the family home, it was without prior warning or explanation. Father, for reasons he took to his grave, chose Christmas Eve as a suitable date on which to end his own life.

At the age of six, Richard bounced out of bed, eager to get downstairs and tear through toy boxes covered in colourful wrapping paper. *'Santa's been!'* he'd yelled, pushing open the glass door at the foot of the narrow staircase. But there was no shiny new bicycle propped against the plump arm of the sofa. No overfilled stocking, or tubes of jelly sweets under the tree. Only a corpse rotating on the end of an improvised noose.

He was to blame. That's what most people said. His parents were happy before he came along and spoiled things.

They took him away and put him into the care system. When he rebelled, they beat and bullied him. And in the quiet hours of darkness, a few came to deal abuse of the most wicked kind.

He'd withdrawn inside himself, learning to survive day-to-day, like a snail seeking the protection of its hardened shell. And harden he did. They were moulding a killer, though couldn't have known.

Then along came a woman unlike any other he'd previously met. Aunt Freda rescued him from the horrors of the children's home, bringing him up as her own, guiding him along the right path in life. The successes he'd enjoyed in adulthood were largely down to her.

He was crying now. Caught in the terrible memory of her death to cancer only a few months earlier. Her passing had left fewer good people in the world, the balance shifting in favour of women like Mother.

When Aunt Freda had lain on her deathbed, she'd taken his hand in hers, telling him to follow his destiny. He understood the deeper meaning in her words. He was meant to redress that skewed balance.

And so here he was, outside the home of one such evil woman, about to get started...

Chapter 2

Killing Mother had given him nowhere near the same buzz he now felt lying in wait for the unsuspecting woman. The anticipation alone sent a shot of adrenaline coursing through his body.

He'd taken no chances. Had calculated and minimised the risks. Every move was planned with a military-type precision.

The wiper blades juddered across the dirty windscreen of his Volvo with a series of squeaks, the glass not yet wet enough for their smooth operation. The noise interrupted his thoughts and irritated him. He turned off the wipers and checked the rear-view mirror for the umpteenth time. There was still no sign of his intended victim.

That wasn't an issue. He'd watched the woman arrive home more times than he could remember and knew she wouldn't be long.

The local newspapers and television channels had reported sightings of a prowler in the area. A man dressed in dark clothing, who hid and watched, but so far had done nothing more serious. Women were warned to take care and not walk alone after dark.

The media's interpretation of his actions fell well short of the mark. No one but him and the late Aunt Freda truly understood his motivation. He was no prowler. A pervert, neither. What he was doing had a much greater purpose. There was a world of difference between the two things. Even if the so-called *experts* failed to comprehend that fact.

He made another check of the rear-view mirror and saw parked cars and refuse bins, mostly.

His first victim—*The Prototype*, as he privately referred to her—would arrive on foot. Alone and on the same side of the road as he was. Then she'd cross almost twenty metres short of where he was waiting beneath the overhang of a leaning tree.

He'd have already moved by then, knowing just the place to hide and wait. He'd watch her open the low gate with an outstretched foot – an aversion to getting her soft fleece mittens wet. Then she'd use the meandering path leading to the side entrance of the house, to where the shadows were their darkest and nightmares lay in wait.

With the Volvo's engine shut down, Dr Richard Wellman collected his bag and stepped out into the icy night air.

Chapter 3

On the opposite side of the city, another hapless victim fell to his knees on a hard concrete floor, a muffled *'humpf'* escaping his bloodied lips as he landed in a heap. A bald man with a tattooed face—Billy Creed, to use his rightful name—limped in circles around him.

Three other men watched without saying anything. One carried a machete. All had deep scowls and bad intent.

'Were you part of it?' Creed asked, his thick neck straining against a button-down shirt collar. It was a question for which the gangster demanded an answer, not bullshit. 'Did they pay you to fuck up the repair on my security system?'

The CCTV engineer raised his head a few inches off the ground. Unnecessary, given they'd earlier blinded him using his own broken thumbs as implements of torture. He mumbled an incoherent response through bubbles of red spit and broken teeth. Then he lurched onto his front with a thud.

The sound had a pigeon take flight overhead. A short hop to a safer perch on a rusted tractor at the far end of the drafty barn.

The place smelled of engine oil, neglect, and fear in bucketfuls.

'Nobody could have got into my club unseen if you'd done a proper job.' Creed came to a halt with a sharp intake of breath and a foul mouth. He leaned on a polished cane. 'How much did that Gillighan-bitch pay you? Or was it that fat-fuck of a copper?' Almost three months had passed since the shooting, yet the shattered knee still plagued him day and night. 'Denny died because of what you did.' He prodded the engineer when he got no response. 'It's only right his little brother is the one to even the score.' Machete-man got his cue. 'For Denny,' Creed said over the sound of sharpened steel cleaving its way through human flesh and bone.

For Denny,' the others repeated, as though ending a prayer at church.

Chapter 4

Richard Wellman had his *Prototype* positioned on the bed upstairs; the young woman's death needing to look entirely natural, and not caused by foul play.

'You're dying,' he said, putting a hypodermic needle and empty syringe to one side of the nightstand. 'I've given you a neuro-muscular blocking agent.' As a nurse, she'd have understood the seriousness of the situation she now found herself in, and would know that she was completely helpless without him.

He lent on an elbow and filled her lungs with a few of his own deep breaths, his dry lips scratching against hers. 'You're temporarily paralysed,' he whispered. 'Dead within a matter of minutes if I were to get up and leave.'

Chapter 5

ONE WEEK LATER

Detective Chief Inspector Brân Reece clung one-handed to the exposed rafters of the old cottage, his phone gripped between his good shoulder and bearded chin. In his free hand was a roofer's hammer. He hated heights and spoke without daring to look down at the ground. 'Turn the radio off. I'm taking a call.' When his best friend didn't respond, he lobbed the hammer in his general direction. It broke a slate and went sliding down the roof and out of sight.

Yanto glared once he'd regained his balance. 'Jesus Christ. You could've killed me.'

'The radio.' Reece jabbed a finger at it. 'Hang on,' he said for the caller's benefit. 'I can't hear a word you're saying.'

'Missed me by that much, you did.' Yanto measured the distance with a finger and thumb. 'What the hell's got into you today?'

'Shut up.' Reece shifted the phone to the other ear, grinding his teeth when his shoulder complained. 'Not you, ma'am.' He sat listening for a good two minutes longer, all the while waving at the sulking Yanto, trying to get his attention and apologise. He needn't have bothered. The man was legendary for his ability to keep something like this going for days. 'I'm in Brecon, getting some jobs done on the cottage,' Reece said, before tucking the handset away in his jacket pocket. 'Right, I'm off.' He couldn't be sure his voice had reached as far as the stone chimney stack, but from Yanto's angry reaction, he guessed it must have done.

Reece began inching his way down the partially slated roof on the seat of his jeans and soles of his boots. 'Oh shit,' he muttered, stretching a leg to slow himself down. He withdrew it, repositioned, and felt for the ladder propped against the back of the building. 'Are you sure this thing's okay where it is?' He took a deep breath and went over the side, not waiting for an answer.

'I'm warning you.' Yanto was on the move. Headed for the hammer that had since come to rest in a short stretch of sagging guttering. 'Get your arse back up here.'

'I can't,' Reece shouted down the throat of the wind. 'The chief super wants me back in Cardiff a week or two early. They're short-staffed, what with Jenkins still serving a suspension.'

Yanto pointed at the gaping hole in the roof, and palettes of Welsh slate stacked on the gravel driveway below. 'And who's gonna finish this lot?'

Reece's legs were still unsteady after the ordeal of descending the creaking ladder. He made his way around the side of the cottage, coming to a halt on a frozen puddle. The ice splintered underfoot like a thin pane of glass, making *plinking* sounds. 'We've broken the back of it. Won't take you too much longer to get it finished.'

Yanto swung his leg in temper, only just staying upright on the roof's steep pitch. 'I don't have time for this,' he said in a high-pitched whine. 'There's the farm and builders' yard for me to see to.'

'Another couple of days and you'll be done.' And with that, Reece opened the car door and got in.

'Don't you dare,' Yanto called over the noise of the engine revs. He grabbed for the hammer and flung it only a few metres short of the battered Peugeot when it pulled away. *'Bastard!'*

The car's back end twitched violently as rubber sought purchase on a mix of ice and loose gravel, Reece laughing properly for the first time in well over a year. With Yanto and the cottage soon out of sight, he reached across the passenger seat and rummaged through a glovebox filled with empty sweet packets and old music cassettes. He took a Stubby screwdriver and stuck its pointed end deep inside a hole in the radio's front panel, twisting it left and right. Led Zeppelin's *Stairway to Heaven* was approaching its main solo. He turned the volume up. It was promising to be a good day.

LIAM HANSON

He dragged a fistful of dirty knuckles across the windscreen as the Storey Arms went by on the left side of the road. He saw Corn Du. Her big sister, Pen y Fan—the highest British peak south of Cadair Idris in Snowdonia—was hidden just behind.

He'd scattered his father-in-law's ashes on the taller twin's summit only a few weeks earlier. His wife's had rested there for a full twelve-months before that.

With Jimmy Page working his magic on a double-neck Gibson guitar, Brân Reece floored the accelerator en route to the University Hospital in Cardiff.

Chapter 6

THE BUILDING WAS SPREADING like an aggressive cancer left to its own devices. Opened in 1971, they'd kept adding bits, rather than starting over with something fit for purpose. The mortuary was in the bowels of the hospital, and well out of sight of most of the living.

Reece hadn't yet changed into something more appropriate for his visit, such was the urgency of Chief Superintendent Cable's call. He trudged the corridors in heavy boots and dirty jeans, attracting looks of disapproval from people who should have known better.

"Get yourself across to the morgue," was all Cable had said during their breezy rooftop conversation. *"We're moving quickly on this one. DC Morgan will fill you in when you get there."*

And here he was. At the morgue, as directed.

Ffion Morgan stood behind a tall Perspex window, doing her level best to look beyond the whirring disk of a bone saw and the mist of fine red spray that followed wherever it went. 'Boss,' she said on sight of him. 'The chief super mentioned you were on your way.'

'I've been on a roof,' Reece said when his junior looked him up and down with a quizzical eye.

'You?' She held onto the laugh, but not so the smirk. 'On a roof?'

'Take the piss if you want, but that's where I've been.' He came down the steps and took the space next to her. 'How are things back at the madhouse?'

Morgan turned and retched when the bony skullcap came away from the cadaver's head, revealing what looked to be a big grey cauliflower. 'It's just a cauli with flecks of dirt on it,' she said, trying to fool herself.

Reece chuckled. 'I'd nearly forgotten how much you hate coming to these things.'

'Doesn't everyone?' She gagged and put a hand to her mouth. When able, she asked: 'How's the shoulder?'

Reece gave it a good rub. 'Could be worse.'

On the other side of the screen was a tall and distinguished-looking man dressed in black scrubs, green plastic apron, and white Wellington boots. 'What's the rush with this one?' Reece asked. 'I normally get to view the body at the scene of the crime before you start taking it apart.'

Dr Twm Pryce, Home Office Forensic Pathologist, held the deceased man's brain in both hands, like it was a Pagan offering. On a shiny extraction table behind him was the rest of his patient, lying there like a hollowed-out canoe.

On an adjacent table was a naked old man, his skin as white as milk, except for red liver spots dotting his body like a mild case of measles. A female pathologist rummaged inside him as though picking the winning ticket from a tombola. The old man's entire alimentary canal, from tongue to rectum, rested in a large shiny bowl next to him.

'It's good to see you back at work,' Pryce said. 'Looks like the Assistant Chief Constable has been getting it in the ear from someone further up the chain of command. This prowler is all over the newspapers, and now a stabbing on the doorstep of the hospital is giving the politicians kittens.'

'That might be the case,' Reece said. 'But removing the body before the SIO gets a glimpse is a big no-no by anyone's reckoning.'

Pryce lay the brain to rest on the tray of a weighing scale. 'Your pal authorised it.'

'Pal?' Reece turned to Morgan for further explanation. 'Who does he mean?'

'DI Adams.' Morgan rolled her eyes. 'I'll explain once we get over to the crime scene.'

'You do that,' Reece said, his attention drawn to the nearest table and the body of the younger man. The mortuary technicians were in the early stages of reassembling his organs, albeit in clear plastic bags shoved into the gaping hole in his front. 'Who is he?'

Morgan shook her head. 'There was no ID found on him.'

'Nothing at all?'

'Could have been taken if the motive was theft?' she suggested.

'What have I told you about jumping to conclusions early on?' Reece said. 'Keep an open mind, remember? And don't get yourself rabbit-holed.'

'Will do, boss.'

'Where was he found?'

'Allensbank Road. Just outside the hospital boundary.'

'Not your typical venue for a gang-related stabbing.'

'I guess he could have been assaulted elsewhere. Then dumped from the back of a car – the intention being to warn and not kill him.'

'What do you think, Twm?' Reece pressed his head against the screen. 'Sound plausible to you?'

The pathologist took another brief look at the corpse. 'There are a few scuffs to the knees, hands, and left cheek. It's difficult to say for sure.'

'What about the stab injury itself?' Reece said. 'Can you give us any more detail on that?'

'Well, the blade penetrated the full thickness of the right ventricle. That's the thinner side of the heart. The poor man didn't stand a chance once his attacker withdrew it.'

'And would he have died instantly?' Morgan asked.

'They seldom do.' Pryce peeled off his rubber gloves and deposited them in a bin marked *Clinical Waste Only*. 'Victims of such attacks tend to bleed into the pericardium—the closed sac around the heart—and with nowhere else to go, the collection of blood causes full cardiovascular collapse and death within minutes, if not treated.'

'That makes sense,' Morgan said. 'The crime scene suggests he walked a few yards across the road before keeling over.'

Pryce used a foot to tap closed the stubborn bin lid. 'Sounds about right in my experience.'

'Anything else of interest?' Reece asked.

'There are no defence wounds,' the pathologist told him. 'Often, the victim will grab for the blade when it's thrust at them, sustaining terrible cuts in some instances. I've known people lose fingers when it's pulled away again through their clenched hands.'

Reece looked over to where the technicians were tucking the anonymous victim into a black bag for his night in the fridge. 'But there's nothing like that in this case?'

Pryce shook his head. 'A solitary stab injury to the chest, and that's it.'

'Could mean he knew his attacker,' Morgan said. 'He'd have no reason to defend himself if he wasn't expecting to be assaulted.'

Reece started up the steps, Morgan following closely. At the top, he held the door open and waved her through ahead of him. 'You might be right,' he said, catching her up in the corridor. 'Let's go see the crime scene.'

Chapter 7

There was a single white van carrying the South Wales Police emblem on the paintwork of its side panels, and patrol cars blocking all routes off the T-junction with the hospital. There were blue lights, but no loud sirens. Those had been reserved for the early hours of the morning. Mostly to piss off the locals.

People in hooded white coveralls, overshoes, and face masks came and went with monotonous repetition. Carrying equipment. Bagging and labelling things for the record.

Uniformed officers walked shoulder-to-shoulder along the road and pavements, their heads lowered to the ground like hungry crows in a freshly ploughed field. They were looking for the murder weapon. Hunting for the nugget that might help solve the case.

A squat yellow lorry from the council, with its equally squat driver, dealt with the drains. Objects of potential interest lay in muddy puddles on the broken tarmac for someone way down the pecking order to sift through.

Reece waved his warrant card at a confused-looking constable in uniform and ducked beneath a taut length of blue-and-white crime-scene tape that was doing its best to break free of its mooring. 'I'm the SIO for this one,' Reece said, slapping at the tape. 'Shift yourself.'

'But I thought...?' The constable left it there, not daring to take his half-hearted protest any further. He went back to what he was doing, which, to the enquiring eye, didn't seem to be anything of much use.

Reece left him to it, and without further discussion, made his way towards a blue tent billowing in the choppy wind. Had it not been for the heavy weights placed at each corner, the thing might have lifted off and deposited itself on the busy road beneath the nearby flyover.

'What are *you* doing here?' The accent was unmistakably Brummie and belonged to DI Robert Adams. *'I'm* the SIO, not you.'

'Not anymore, you're not,' Reece said, shooing him away as he would an annoying dog.

Adams stomped down the street, fumbling under his coveralls for a phone with which to call the station and Chief Superintendent Cable.

'Shouldn't you have taken a formal handover first?' Morgan asked. 'DI Adams saw the body in situ, after all. He even waited to get a second look at the crime scene after it was removed.'

Reece had no intention of doing any such thing. 'I'll get more sense from the photographs and a quick chat with Sioned Williams.'

'You're the boss.'

He leaned closer. 'What's he still doing here, anyway? He's an out-and-out halfwit.'

Morgan watched the DI disappear out of sight, gesturing like a tic-tac man at the races. 'Rumour has it, he's put in for a transfer back home.'

'Station canteen is his best bet.' Reece reached for a coverall. 'Hold on to me while I get my boot through the bottom of this thing.' Once suitably dressed and signed in with the scene guard, they went over to where the crime scene manager was talking with another woman. 'Morning, Sioned,' Reece said with his best effort at a smile.

The CSM double-took, and grinned widely. 'Brân, lovely to see you. I'd heard mutterings you were coming back sometime soon. How's the shoulder?'

'Better every day,' he lied. 'Thought I'd get the details straight from the horse's mouth. Save myself having to spend any time with numpty over there.' Adams was still walking in circles further up the road, his phone pressed to the side of his head. Reece gave him a wave just for the hell of it.

Williams caught hold of the detective's arm, forcing him to be more professional. *'Horse's mouth*, eh?'

'It was a compliment,' Reece said defensively. 'I meant, you're the go-to person, and not that you look like Shergar.' He ducked away from her. 'Not much, anyway.'

She pushed him towards the gaping tent flap before he could cause any more trouble than he already had. 'Get in.'

Inside were more people dressed in white paper suits, and an area of pavement soaked with dark blood. Reece felt his chest tighten and pushed a finger beneath his collar. When that had little to no effect, he knew he had to get out of there.

'This is where the victim fell to the ground and died,' he thought he heard Sioned Williams say.

He shut his eyes. Opened them again and saw Anwen—his dead wife—lying on that same stretch of road, bleeding to death.

Someone called his name.

Williams?

Anwen?

He really couldn't tell who.

Chapter 8

Reece was sitting on the cemetery wall next to the tent when Morgan found him. She perched on a section of damp stonework with only a small gap left between them. 'Another of your flashbacks?'

'I'm fine,' was Reece's response to her bringing it up. He nodded at a line of yellow cones meandering towards them from the other side of the road. 'So, he was stabbed over there and then came this way to die of his injuries.'

Morgan's gaze followed the short trail. 'It's in keeping with what Dr Pryce said at the post-mortem.'

Reece pressed his back against the railings and sniffed.

'You don't agree?'

'I'm on board with that,' Reece said. 'I just thought it ironic how our victim staggered towards the graveyard like he knew he should be trying to get in.' He pushed off the wall and stood. 'Let's go hear what else Sioned has to say.'

They found the CSM talking shop with the blood splatter analyst. There was lots of finger pointing and head bobbing as the couple followed the line of yellow cones.

'Feeling better for some fresh air?' Williams asked on sight of him.

'Would you agree the victim was stabbed on the pavement over there?' Reece pointed to a yellow cone marked with a black number **1**. 'Then came across the road, bleeding heavily and falling here?'

'That would be my thinking,' Williams said.

'I don't suppose the attacker was kind enough to leave the knife behind for us to find? Twm Pryce reckons it's about four inches long, with a serrated edge.'

'No such luck, I'm afraid.'

Reece clucked his tongue. 'Oh, well. It was worth a try.'

'There's no community spirit these days,' the CSM joked.

'You're telling me. This sort of thing rarely happened in my day.' Morgan rolled her eyes at the other women, all three of them familiar with the story about to be told. Reece continued, regardless. 'When we had a beef with someone, we'd meet up in the local park after school for a fight. With our fists, mind you. No knives or guns. Ever. After that, it was all forgotten. No grudges. We'd play rugby together and share a bag of chips on the way home.' He thrust both hands in his trouser pockets and moved on without waiting for a reply.

Chapter 9

Opened in 2009, Cardiff Bay Police Station was little more than a stone's throw away from the bustling multi-million-pound waterfront development.

Reece parked in his usual spot round the side and used the public entrance at the top of the steps to get in. 'Afternoon, George,' he said, marching through the empty foyer without stopping to chat. 'Thought you were cutting back this side of Christmas?' he called over his shoulder.

The desk sergeant looked surprised to see him and patted an ample belly. 'I'll have you know, I'm down a full belt hole already.'

'Dream on.'

George watched him go by; dirty boots shedding wiggle-shaped worms of dry mud in their wake. 'You look like you've been down a coal mine.'

'On a roof,' Reece corrected, and sounded quite proud of himself.

'Really?'

'Yep. Me and Yanto.'

'How is the miserable so and so?' George asked.

Reece turned and raised his arms high in the air. 'Happy as the proverbial pig when I saw him last.' He chuckled at the memory of his best mate launching the hammer at the departing Peugeot.

'Why do I find that hard to believe?' George craned his neck through the hole in the glass. 'Seriously though, it's good to see you back. Did yourself proud at the Midnight Club.'

With a quick salute, Reece disappeared into the stairwell with a squeak of its partly glazed door. He took two stairs at a time, spiralling upwards through the centre of the building, levelling off on the second-floor landing. 'Afternoon all,' he said, passing through the open-plan space that was home to the Cardiff Bay Murder Squad. He checked his wristwatch and went through to his office in search of an overnight bag kept there for such occasions.

Morgan had made her own way back from the hospital in a pool car, and was there at the station before him. 'Coffee's on your desk, boss.'

'You come by helicopter?' Reece asked with a fatherly frown. 'Or did Scotty beam you across?'

'All the traffic lights were with me.' Morgan dropped behind her desk and raised the screen of her laptop. 'You remember Ginge?' She nodded towards the lanky plain-clothes officer sitting to her right. 'He's on a secondment to us.'

'I remember him,' Reece said, rummaging through the contents of his travel bag. 'I was shot in the shoulder, not the head.'

Ginge leapt out of his seat and offered an eager hand in greeting. 'Ffion's got me working with the press department, sir. I'm putting some posters together to ID the dead man.'

'Sounds like fun,' Reece said, squeezing past the desk without shaking the outstretched hand. 'Mine are filthy.' He held one up as evidence and got as far as the door to the landing before turning to face the newbie. 'One thing I want you to know now you're on my squad. People here call me Reece, or boss, but never, sir. You got that?' He was on his way again, headed for the showers and a clean change of clothes.

CHAPTER 10

REECE SAT AT THE head end of a long table, his team assembled for a major-crime briefing. He called them to attention. 'All phones except mine should be off or on silent mode.' His gaze swept the room before settling on the paperwork in front of him. 'What we know so far is that our victim is a white male in his early to mid-twenties. Identity as yet unknown. Stabbed once in the chest with what was likely to be a four-inch blade with a serrated edge.' He searched for Sioned Williams among the group. 'I'm guessing you still haven't found it?' When the CSM confirmed they hadn't, Reece went back to reading from his briefing sheet. 'The right side of the victim's heart was penetrated, causing him to bleed out – but not before he crossed the road, which is where he collapsed and died on the pavement.'

Someone tutted.

'Poor sod,' said another. 'Tragic waste of a young life.'

'There were no defence wounds or traces of the attacker found at the post-mortem. No wristwatch, wallet, or phone on the victim.' Reece looked up. 'Maybe he doesn't carry them. Unlikely, I know. But we need to find out.'

'He was robbed by the sound of it,' Ginge said authoritatively. Morgan clipped his ankle under the table, making him wince. 'Sorry, boss. I'm getting ahead of myself.'

'Any CCTV footage we can get hold of is to be looked at.' Reece stood when his phone started vibrating on the desk. 'And I want uniform knocking on doors, asking questions. Identifying our victim is our number one priority.' He collected his phone and thumbed the *answer* prompt.

It was George, the desk sergeant. 'There's a lady with me downstairs. She says her husband's gone missing.'

'What does she expect me to do?' Reece asked.

'She's asking for you by name and won't speak to anyone else.'

Reece lowered himself onto his chair and massaged the bridge of his nose. 'Did you tell her I only deal with the dead?'

'That's just it,' George said. 'She's convinced he's been murdered.'

Chapter 11

Kath Hall caught Reece's eye as soon as he came through the door at the foot of the stairwell. She looked to be in her early-to-mid-thirties, and would have been pretty had her face not been contorted with grief. 'Hello,' he said, extending a hand in greeting. 'I'm DCI Reece.'

The woman stopped pacing and promptly burst into tears.

Reece contemplated giving her a hug, but even the thought made him feel awkward and so he looked to George for help. The desk sergeant was busy dealing with an old lady reporting a missing cat, leaving him to fend for himself. He patted the younger woman's shoulder—it was all he could manage—and led her to a room off the main foyer. He brought two plastic cups of water from the dispenser. Putting one on the table, he took a sip from the other. 'What makes you think your husband has been murdered?'

'Pete's been gone a full week,' Hall explained. 'No phone calls. No sightings of him.' She raised her head to stare at the detective through red-raw eyes. 'He'd never do that.'

'Did the two of you row before he left?'

'He didn't *leave*.' Kath Hall pressed a wad of wet paper tissues to her nose. 'That thug at the nightclub had him killed.'

Reece shifted in his seat. 'Who do you mean?'

'The *Midnight Club*, I think they call it. In the city centre,' Hall said. 'Pete worked on the security system, just before Christmas. He told the owner that patching it up in places was no good. The entire thing needed gutting and starting again from scratch.' She cleared her throat and dabbed her eyes. 'But he was having none of it.'

'By *he*, are we talking Billy Creed?'

Hall's head rose and fell. 'I told Pete not to touch the place. Had a bad feeling about it. But he was convinced Creed would give him the maintenance contracts on his other business premises. Said we'd be quids in once that happened.'

Reece finished his water and got himself a refill. 'But how do you know Billy Creed is involved? Or that anyone else has done your husband harm? People take off all the time and return once they've got their head straight.'

'There was nothing wrong with Pete when he left. Someone's got him. Got him and done something awful.'

Reece gave his head a slow shake. 'I'm sorry, but suspicion alone isn't good enough. I'll need solid evidence if you want me to look into it.'

Hall took a moment to compose herself. 'Pete got a phone call a few days before he went missing. Something about him having to pay for what happened to Denny.'

'Still too vague. It could mean anything.'

'I read the newspapers,' Hall said, tearing the tissues apart. 'I know who Denny Cartwright was. How he died. And that Billy Creed lost a knee in the shooting. That man had my husband killed, even if he didn't do it himself.'

Reece watched the woman agonise over her ordeal. 'All right,' he said. 'Leave it with me.'

Chapter 12

The patient's condition was settling. A torrential haemorrhage stemmed by a pair of skilful hands and the application of a long-nosed arterial clamp. The surgeon peered over the top of his image-magnifying eyewear, his brow beaded with a silky sheen of perspiration. He nodded at the consultant anaesthetist. 'That was a close one.'

Dr Richard Wellman studied his monitor without replying. The woman's blood pressure remained a little on the low side. Her heart-rate galloping as her survival mechanisms compensated for the sudden and unexpected fluid loss. He opened a gate-clamp on the drip-set and let the transfusion speed through, noting that all parameters displayed on his screen were slowly returning to normal.

He sat and made entries on an anaesthetic record, his own heart not so much as skipping a beat during the entire fraught event.

The atmosphere in theatre lightened after that. A middle-aged man with a moderate scoliosis cracked morbid jokes as he transferred blood-soaked swabs from a metal floor-bowl to a clear plastic bag. The surgeon called for someone to switch on the radio. *Let It Bleed* by the Rolling Stones, causing him to wax lyrical behind a light-blue face-mask.

Wellman tutted under cover of a paper drape stretched taut between two drip-stands at the head-end of the patient. Such music only encouraged loutish behaviour and promiscuity, in his opinion. He knew only too well and wore the T-shirt to prove it. Metaphorically only. He'd never worn such a thing. Jeans neither. He was strictly a suit and tie man – just as Aunt Freda had brought him up to be.

He despised his colleagues even more than he did their choice in music and company. Many had previously spoken ill of him. Brought trouble his way from the medical director. Especially the flat-chested scrub-nurse who reminded him all too much of Coco the Clown. Others had started giving him a wide berth. Most preferring to whisper conspiratorially in corridors and from behind closed doors.

He caught fleeting glimpses of Coco counting clean swabs and used needles; flirting shamelessly with the professor while surgical instruments to-and-fro'd between them. What was the woman thinking, wearing all that ridiculous make-up at work? And what were *they* thinking, allowing her to do such a thing?

She was flaunting her wares and coming close to selecting herself for punishment.

But there were those who were far more deserving of his attention. Take the young student nurse over in the corner of the operating theatre. She'd smiled at him twice. Even came to ask questions about his anaesthetic machine. She was egging him on, but would undoubtedly complain the very moment he dared reciprocate in kind. That's what they were like. That's what they were *all* like. Leaning in his chair, he couldn't quite make out what it said on her name-badge.

Later, then. He'd find out when he had a good enough reason to get close to her.

He took a newspaper from his satchel and spread it over a crossed knee, trying all the while to ignore Mick Jagger's repeated offers to lean on him. Quickly disinterested in anything the broadsheet offered, Wellman reached for a copy of *Metro* from the shelf behind him.

Knife-crime in the city was on the increase. No surprise there. It was a national pandemic, almost. Drug-crazed gangs running county lines and killing one another in frequent episodes of senseless violence.

His own *plus one* hadn't helped the bleak statistics any.

The next page brought deep lines to his face. There had been more sightings of the Night Prowler. Still, they misunderstood his intent and labelled him a *fiend up to no good*. Several reports suggested he'd been in two places at once.

If only.

Metro mentioned nothing about the dead girl. He'd got away with it. A confidence booster if ever he needed one.

Another glance at the beeping monitors had him reduce the concentration of volatile anaesthetic agent delivered to his young patient. A final entry made on the chart marked the conclusion of what had been a very complex procedure.

With that done, he took a peek over the top of the drape. The surgeons were busy closing the horizontal incision in the woman's lower abdomen – peritoneum and muscle coming together under the command of thick nylon sutures. Satisfied all was well, he chose his moment and stepped out to the anaesthetic room to liberate a full pack of Suxamethonium Chloride from the wall-fridge. Back in the operating theatre, he placed the glass vials in the fold of his newspaper, and that, into a side-pocket of his leather satchel.

Another glance over the top showed the patient's wound was now fully closed, dressings applied, and the suction bottle on the drain compressed for use.

Dr Wellman looked around the room for Smiler, wanting to get a proper sight of her name-badge before going home for the evening. She was nowhere to be seen. Lucky girl. But would that luck last?

Chapter 13

The short fabric strap hung like a stunted stalactite from the ceiling of the bus. Dr Wellman gripped it tightly and touched against the person in front of him when the vehicle rounded a bend in the road. The woman shifted her position and would have seen a man dressed in smart clothing. A man who apologised unreservedly, and without delay.

'It's like a cattle market in here,' he said. 'Every person for themselves.' He didn't often take the bus to and from work. But now and again, he liked to check on the local riff-raff.

The woman looked away without response or complaint and moved a full two inches at the very most before a human wall blocked her path.

Wellman leaned closer and breathed the scent of apple blossom in her hair. When she got off at the next stop, he studied her through the condensation on the window – tight red curls rising and falling in time with a wide and hurried stride. She knew he was watching, even though she refused to look anywhere but straight ahead.

That made him smile. Not something he did very often. Should he get off the bus and follow? Find a way inside her home and have some fun?

Yes?

No?

He decided on the latter, given she hadn't led him on. Hadn't teased him in the way women normally did. She didn't deserve to die. Not yet, anyway.

Besides, random wasn't the way he did things. Everything in his life had purpose. Each move was pre-planned to minimise omission and error. Even the embarrassing hiccup with the now-dead Harlan Miller had been dealt with efficiently.

The medical student shouldn't have used *that* laptop for the audit project. Nor should he have gone browsing through his clinical supervisor's search history without asking. And he definitely shouldn't have demanded a monthly *"expenses account"* in order to *"keep this between you and me."*

Miller had paid for his scandalous threats with his young life. His death made to look like one of the city's many fuckwits had stabbed him in a drug deal gone wrong.

With the attractive redhead well out of sight, Wellman let his thoughts settle on the next *chosen one*. Poppy. What a pretty name. And sad, some might say, that the petite blonde would not get to see her twenty-third birthday.

Chapter 14

Wellman got off the bus at the next stop and walked the rest of the way home. He was met inside the front door by a draft coming from the far end of the narrow hallway; one bringing with it the noxious tang of meat turning bad. That would have to be dealt with, and quickly, before some meddling neighbour called the environmental health team. Or worse still, the police.

'I'm home, Mother,' he called into the darkness, wiping his shoes on a mat that welcomed visitors in bold lettering. 'How was your day?' With a hand held to his ear, he listened for a reply he knew would never come.

He went through to the kitchen and rested his satchel against the legs of a wooden carver, his coat and scarf left draped over the chair's arched back. 'Tea?' he shouted and caught himself laughing at such a ridiculous suggestion.

The kettle got fresh water. A tea strainer heaped with aromatic green leaves. On the marble mantelpiece, a carriage clock announced the new hour with seven bright chimes, though Wellman didn't notice, his full attention now focused on the satchel and its ill-got contents.

The muscle relaxant had proven to be the perfect choice of murder weapon, attracting absolutely no suspicion of foul play.

Using his laptop to load a Facebook profile page he'd previously viewed a dozen times or more, he reclined in the chair and sipped his tea.

He'd selected prospective victims by listening to loose coffee-room talk at work. Eyeballing name badges on the uniforms of the most boastful ones. Young women who made no secret of the fact they were playing the field. Pretties who thought nothing of snuffing out a man's hopes and dreams with a left-swipe of a cruel finger.

There were so many to choose from: on the general wards; labour ward; main and day theatres. And that was before he'd factored in the addition of students of medicine; of nursing; of physiotherapy. The supply was almost endless.

All he needed to get started was a name like Poppy Jones, for instance. Then input some *'works at'* information on the Facebook page, and voila, there she was: the young midwife wearing a short black dress and holding a glass of what would undoubtedly be Prosecco. All her peers drank it, though Wellman couldn't for the life of him fathom why.

Poppy was at a party of sorts, draped over the thick arm of some muscle-bound moron with dental veneers. He clicked on the *Photos* tab, stopping to check for new uploads, shaking his head when he came across the beach holiday and bikini shots.

The next image showed Poppy in a different dress. It was shorter than the previous one. Likewise, the replacement thick-armed moron. She was behaving like a whore and would end up like Mother if he were not to intervene and save her from such a thing. He tore his stare away to glance at the underside of the ceiling. 'She's just like you!' he screamed through gritted teeth.

There were photographs of the girl's bedroom posted for all to see. And images of the layout of other parts of the home. None of it surprised him. Some women were stupid enough to pose right next to their front door: tits, thighs, and house-number there to be found by all manner of deviants who should never be served such things on a plate.

He leaned sideways in the chair and lifted the satchel onto the kitchen table in front of him. Reached inside and removed a small yellow-and-white box labelled Suxamethonium Chloride. He put it on the table and went rooting inside the satchel for a second time.

Sevoflurane, it said on the label of the fist-sized brown bottle. Used to incapacitate his victims long enough to position and inject them. He'd even made his own variant of a Schimmelbusch anaesthetic mask, by drilling dozens of small holes through the clear plastic surface of a standard one. The handheld device worked because the victim's own act of breathing drew air over a gauze wick system soaked with the volatile agent—picking it up in gaseous form—rendering the person asleep. The more they panicked, the faster they breathed, the quicker the effect.

He rolled the bottle in the palm of his hand; the air trapped within it forming a large bubble at its upper centre-point. Left and right, the bubble went, and always in the opposite direction to the tilt of his hand.

What he had in front of him was sufficient medicine to incapacitate and kill more than a dozen women.

Not nearly enough for what he had in mind.

Chapter 15

It was the day Detective Sergeant Elan Jenkins had been dreading for almost three months. They'd suspended her on full pay following the Belle Gillighan case and arranged the disciplinary hearing stupidly fast.

'That means they want you back as soon as possible,' her partner, Dr Cara Frost, said.

'Or that they want me gone equally quickly,' was Jenkins's less positive take on it.

Either way, here it was: Judgement Day. The beginning of fresh opportunities, or the premature end to something she'd worked so hard to achieve.

She held her head in her hands and sighed for the umpteenth time since coming downstairs for breakfast. A solitary croissant sat on a plate in front of her. A cup of coffee going cold next to it. She licked a fingertip and dabbed at a few wayward flakes of pastry. Brought the finger to her mouth and took it away again, leaving the remaining flakes untouched.

Frost came to the table and took a seat. 'You have to eat on a day like this. You'll need the energy to concentrate properly.'

Jenkins raised her head. 'I don't know why, but I've lost my appetite this morning.' She attempted a smile but didn't get anywhere close.

'It's going to be okay,' Frost assured her. 'You're an excellent police officer, with an exemplary record. There's no way they'd contemplate losing you.'

Jenkins squeezed her partner's hand. 'Thanks for the vote of confidence, but it's not me I need to convince.'

Frost took a deep breath. 'Look—'

Jenkins beat her to it. 'What I did was indefensible.' She hung her head back and closed her eyes. 'I've no idea what I must have been thinking at the time.'

'You were under immense pressure and living with a manipulative individual,' Frost said. 'Besides, DCI Reece will give you a glowing character reference. He told me as much only yesterday.'

'You saw him?' Jenkins levelled her head and looked away. 'He hasn't spoken a word to me in weeks.'

'He was at the mortuary, talking shop with Twm Pryce.'

'He's back at work then.' Jenkins gave that more thought. 'Lucky him. Maybe that's why he's not responding to any of my calls. He's distancing himself from the pariah.'

'Nonsense.' Frost dragged her chair closer and poured herself another coffee. 'He's been preoccupied, that's all. Terrible, that business with his wife.'

Jenkins wondered if Reece's presence at the hearing would do little more than hammer the last nail in her coffin. As far as she was concerned, the lid was already on, with all four of its corners screwed down. She puffed her cheeks and let the air out slowly. 'What if he gets all arsey with them and they take it out on muggins here?'

Frost leaned over and planted a soft kiss on top of Jenkins's head. 'There's no way he'd do that to you.'

'You don't know him like I do. This PTSD thing has made him so unpredictable, it's scary.' She started on the pastry flakes for a second time. Dabbing at them as though squashing an army of scurrying ants. 'As soon as they piss him off—and they will—he'll be lurching across that desk trying to chin one of them.'

Frost nibbled on a fingernail before speaking. 'Have you given any more thought to what I said yesterday?'

'I can't think about that right now.'

'We could sell this place and pool our resources. Get something with more outdoor space.'

'It's too soon.' Jenkins repeated herself with a whisper and a soft shake of her head.

Frost checked her watch against the clock on the far wall. 'Shouldn't you be in the shower right now?'

Jenkins went and disconnected her phone from its charger. 'I'm going to ring him and explain,' she said, leaving the room. 'I can't risk him being there.'

Chapter 16

There was no chance of Jenkins, or anyone else, getting hold of Reece, off-grid as he was, pounding the dirt track along the Taff Trail. So called because it followed the winding course of the river sharing its name, the full route stretched some fifty-five miles from Brecon to Cardiff Bay. He wasn't planning on doing it all. Just a six-mile section. Enough to clear a foggy head and some demons that hadn't yet pissed off and left him alone for the day.

The previous night had been a particularly bad one where sleep was concerned. He'd tossed and turned for hours on end before pacing the landing in search of peace. When eventually he did drift off, the nightmares were back to taunt him with vivid images of his wife lying face-down on the side of the road.

LIAM HANSON

He'd woken up in floods of tears, calling Anwen's name. Men don't cry, he'd kept telling himself while feeling for the pounding pulse at his wrist. The razorblade had marked his skin, but gone no deeper only because of a promise he'd made to a father in memory of a dead daughter. 'Damn you, Idris!' he'd screamed, smashing the heel of his fist against the plastic bath surround. 'Why won't you let me die and be with her?'

He'd left the house well before dawn, a daily run better medicine than anything the shrinks could ever prescribe. It gave him time to think, to focus, and besides, Anwen was with him every step of the way. He could sense her presence. And if he listened to the wind—*really* listened—he could hear her sweet voice singing to him the entire time he was out there.

He passed a man with a dog. Made way for a woman on a horse. And shared a tune with the earliest of birds.

He was crying again. Sobbing and laughing at the same time. Glad to be alive, but hating every minute of it.

Nothing made sense anymore. Not since Anwen had died and left him all alone.

And so he ran.

Ran to the beat of his own broken heart.

CHAPTER 17

Jenkins and her Federation Rep passed through the front door of the County Hall building. 'I didn't see Reece's car out there,' she said, and wondered if she should be any more or less nervous because of it.

Steve Cook held the door open for someone coming in behind them and nodded towards a reception desk situated further into the foyer. 'Make your way over there. We need to sign in and let them know we've arrived.'

Jenkins's insides were turning over. It was just as well she hadn't managed breakfast. It might have been making a reappearance right now. 'I said I didn't see DCI Reece's car out there.'

'Don't you worry about him.' Cook handed a letter to the woman staffing the desk and followed it up with the required items of ID.

Jenkins waited in silence, checking the windows for any sight of her boss. She was so confused that she didn't know what she wanted from him. Turn up. Don't turn up. She really couldn't decide.

After what appeared to be little more than a cursory check, both the letter and ID were returned. 'You know where to go,' the woman said with the look of someone who'd seen her fair share of poor outcomes. 'It's the usual room.'

Jenkins thanked her and followed Cook towards a short flight of steps that doubled back on themselves as they descended out of sight. At the top, she stopped and got the woman's attention with the wave of a hand. 'I don't suppose DCI Reece is here yet?'

The woman shook her head and looked almost apologetic. 'Hasn't confirmed his attendance, despite two requests from us to do so.'

Cook rested a hand on Jenkins's back, prompting her to advance onto the marble steps. 'You're better off without him.'

Reece broke away from the main trail and clambered up the steep slope of the mountainside as though he were being chased by someone who wanted him dead. Beyond the bare branches of the overhanging trees were shades of purple heather, mountain streams, and steep drops into the valley below. He gripped handfuls of brittle ferns and wilting saplings, battling against the ruggedness of the land with the narrow straps of his rucksack clawing at his aching shoulder as he rose and fell.

His breathing came in rapid bursts. He pulled with both arms. Pushed with both legs. Dragged himself along on the flat of his belly when the terrain demanded it of him. He was almost at the summit. A little over ten metres to go.

When at last he got there, he found himself sandwiched between the mountaintop and the wettest of low-hanging clouds. He fought back against the wind, calling his dead wife's name.

Chapter 18

'DS Jenkins.' The woman was tall and pale, Slavic in looks, and wore the uniform and rank of a chief superintendent. 'Come this way, please.'

Jenkins waited for Cook to put paperwork away in his case and gather a suit jacket he'd draped over the back of his chair. 'Here goes,' she said, doubting her ability to survive the next few hours without throwing up.

The meeting room was smaller than she'd expected, with tables set out in a U shape. Lord Justice Vaughn was seated on the bend, flanked by two other people. One was an independent member of the public. The second seat was for the vampiric chief superintendent.

Jenkins and Cook were positioned to the left of the panel, opposite the Force-appointed barrister and presenting officer.

She opened the buttons on the jacket of her black trouser-suit and took a deep breath. It didn't help.

'Water?' Vampira again. The woman's eyes were an icy blue, making her seem all the scarier.

'Not for the moment, thank you, ma'am.'

Cook took hold of the jug and poured a good measure for both of them. 'Take a sip,' he said for Jenkins's ears only.

After formal introductions and general housekeeping were out of the way, Lord Justice Vaughn read the charges: 'That you, Detective Sergeant Elan Jenkins, did, during the month of December last year, disclose sensitive and confidential information to an unauthorised third party.' The judge continued, Jenkins listening to his every word as he levelled the charges against her. 'And that your conduct, as outlined above, is contrary to the standards expected of you as a serving member of the South Wales Police.'

She thought she might puke all over him. Either that, or pass out.

'Do you accept or deny that your actions amount to gross misconduct?' Lord Justice Vaughn said.

Cook nudged her. 'You have to answer.'

'I deny the charges, Your Honour.' Her response was more forthright than she'd expected, leaving her concerned she might have overdone it.

'DS Jenkins was in a physical, as well as an emotionally abusive relationship at the time in question,' Cook said, handing out a fan of documents to support his claim.

'Are you submitting this as mitigation?' Lord Justice Vaughn asked.

'I am, Your Honour. For the record, DS Jenkins's ex-partner was an extremely manipulative and dangerous individual who'd successfully deceived the prison services in the Republic of Ireland. DS Jenkins lived in constant fear of the woman, and any information divulged at the time would therefore have been as a result of extreme threat and duress.'

'Then why didn't she report it?' the presenting officer asked. 'There are formal processes for such matters.'

'She did.' Cook again. 'To a DC Ken Ward, who, unbeknown to DS Jenkins, was a corrupt officer in collusion with the woman in question.'

'To a senior officer, I meant.'

The Federation Rep shrugged. 'DCI Reece was on forced leave. DI Adams was unapproachable; his behaviour bordering on bullying. And Chief Superintendent Cable...'

And so it continued for the next hour or more. Question and answer. Claim and counterclaim. When they pushed for more detail, Jenkins became flustered and unable to recall key pieces of information. They wanted dates and times. 'No dates, no proof,' they told her.

Fuck you! she wanted to scream, and at one point almost got up and left. But that would have been tantamount to giving in. And whatever negative labels Elan Jenkins might have picked up over the years, *quitter* wasn't one of them. She checked the clock on the wall opposite. Time was running out. *I need you here, Reece. I need you here right now.*

Then it came. A knock at the door. Vampira rose from the table and went to answer it.

Jenkins leaned to one side of her chair, unable to get a clear sight of who was out there. Snippets of voice had her believe it might be the woman from the reception desk upstairs.

The door closed with a click, Vampira waiting on her feet a few moments longer before speaking. 'Detective Chief Inspector Reece has just entered the building.' She lowered herself onto her seat and took a deep breath.

Jenkins gulped. *Oh, shit!*

CHAPTER 19

Poppy Jones was down on both knees, forcing folds of thick cardboard into a clear recycling bag—bemoaning the fact that shit like this was always left to her—when a dark shape went past the side window of the kitchen. It made no sound. Chose not to stop and knock at the door. Was likely nothing more troublesome than her own overactive imagination doing its thing again.

That's what she told herself, anyway. Mostly because it was what her housemates would have said had they been at home instead of working the night-shift at the local hospital.

All of them except Harlan Miller, that was. Poppy hadn't clapped eyes on the medical student since their drunken shag the night before last. And that stuff with his iPad – *Aw gawd*. What had she been thinking? Maybe he thought the same and was choosing to ignore her from this point onward. Could life in the household get any more awkward than it already was? Her life especially. All of them living in what she often referred to as the *goldfish bowl*.

She got up and pressed her face against the frosty glass of the window, saw nothing, and opened the back door instead. 'Hello,' she called into a night that was as black as coal. 'Harlan, is that you?' The garden gate squeaked a response, monotonously repeating itself on the command of a rising wind.

With the last of the bags knotted, and the back door left wide open, Poppy made off down the path; the cord of her dressing-gown trailing close behind on the wet flagstones.

The bin lid threw a small puddle of chilled water at her when she raised it, her right foot and its pink slipper catching most of the splash. She squealed and shook a leg like an old dog taking a pee, before bolting the gate closed. She checked it again before turning away.

Who knows what first drew Poppy's attention to the bedroom window on the return trip up the path. Or what made her stop and stare. The curtains, perhaps? Had they not been fully open when she'd stood at the gate looking back at the house only a few moments earlier? She wasn't sure now that she had to think about it.

And that sliver of a gap between them. One wide enough to let a person—a maniac—watch from the darkness beyond. Poppy stabbed repeatedly at the air with her clenched fist. 'Eek, eek, eek,' she said Hitchcock-style, and laughed at her own dark sense of humour.

Back in the kitchen and annoyed with herself for letting the house get cold, she engaged the Yale lock with a reassuring clunk of its heavy mechanism. Maniacs could stay the hell away tonight. It was time to finish that glass of chilled Prosecco and get stuck into a good book before a hot bath and then bed.

She frowned. Hadn't she left the glass on the table and not the draining board, which is where it was now? The fluid level hadn't altered. She'd moved it before going out into the garden. That was it. That's what she must have done.

The floorboards creaked overhead. They always did at this time of night. But not usually in the way they now were. 'Jordan, if that's you, I told you we're over. I'm not putting up with any more of your shit, okay?' She stared at the ceiling. Her eyes drawn slowly from left to right in sync with the direction of movement. She did her best to ignore it and threw herself onto the sofa.

There it was again. The noise. Just as loud as before, but this time moving from right to left, and no less annoying. 'What's wrong with you?' she said, tossing the paperback to one side. She went to the door at the foot of the stairs. 'You know how this always ends in the films.'

She pushed on the door and stepped into the colder hallway, her breath held deep within her chest. When the flick of a chrome light switch flooded everything around her in a soft yellow glow, she exhaled and let herself relax. 'A maniac would have cut the power,' she whispered for her own benefit. She was already more than halfway up the carpeted stairs. 'Harlan. Jordan. Stop messing about.'

She knocked on the first door on the lower landing. Stood outside and waited. 'Suba, are you home?' There was silence but for the sound of her own heavy breathing. The same was true of the next three doors. Leaving only the bathrooms and her own room to check in what had once been the attic.

Poppy inched towards the shower-curtain, her hand held outstretched, thoughts of Norman Bates *eek-eeking,* loudly in her head. She got ready. 'One. Two. *Three*,' came as something of a muted squeal when she swept the curtain aside to reveal nothing more improper than a worn bar of Imperial Leather soap, replete with a few dark hairs sprouting out of the top of it. She made a mental note to remind Harlan that the girls didn't need to be dealing with such things every time they wanted to take a bath. She was rehearsing the forthcoming telling-off when something shifted in the mirror opposite. A smudge of dark colour that was gone in an instant. 'Jordan, I'm warning you. Come on now, you're frightening me.'

And then she smelled it. Not aftershave, but a clinical odour that was vaguely familiar.

'It's time to die,' someone said. 'Are you ready?'

Before Poppy could answer, a firm hand from behind pressed a facemask over her nose and mouth.

'Breathe. Make it easy on yourself.'

She knew what that smell was now. Recognised it from the hospital. How could she have been so stupid?

Chapter 20

There was a raucous celebration going on at the Rummer Tavern opposite the castle. Built circa 1713—and until recently, a nostalgic pastiche of Tudor style—the pub was now one of a gazillion identical city sports bars.

Ginge turned his back to the crowded bar and handed Reece a drink over the heads of everyone else around them. 'There you go, boss.' After making a fool of himself by jumping to conclusions at the briefing, the newbie was keen to impress. 'Penderyn Sherrywood.' Reece's favourite whisky, distilled and bottled just up the road.

'Cheers, matey. You'll go far,' the DCI said, relieving him of the shorts glass.

Next was the turn of Ffion Morgan. Ginge passed her a glass of white wine. And then a tonic water, ice-and-slice to Elan Jenkins. 'You sure I can't get you anything stronger?' he asked. 'This piss-up is for you, after all.'

Jenkins pulled a silly face. 'Alcohol is like poison to my system. Even the smallest drop.'

'Shit.' Ginge looked like his colleague had admitted to having a terminal diagnosis.

Reece pushed between the two of them and patted her on the back. 'A final written warning, then. That's my girl.'

'It's not something to be proud of.' She took a sip of her drink and suppressed a burp. 'It's all bubbles and fizz, this.'

Reece was hunting for somewhere to sit and didn't reply. Giving up almost immediately, he said: 'Not worth the paper they're written on, those things. Gives the pen-pushers a sense of self-importance, that's all.'

Jenkins didn't look convinced. 'I appreciate you turning up today.' She stood on tip-toe, leaning forward to peck him on the cheek. She settled on the balls of her feet again when he moved out of reach. They both blushed.

'What did you expect me to do?' Reece said, ending the brief silence. 'You're going places. This daft episode won't hold you back.'

'Not for a while, I'm not,' she replied. 'There's going to be a strategy meeting before I'm allowed back to work. And even then, there's no guarantee I won't be transferred elsewhere. As far as I see it, I'm done here in Cardiff.'

Reece lowered his whisky glass. 'Over my dead body.'

'I wouldn't dare put that offer on the table if I were you. They might just snap at the chance.'

'You're not wrong there.' Reece was suddenly preoccupied again. 'Where's Ffion gone?'

Jenkins pointed towards a rowdy gathering in the far corner of the room. 'There she is. Like a man-magnet, as usual.'

'She's a good-looking woman,' Reece said, wondering if he should go over and rescue Morgan from the *roider* sporting an orange tan. 'Hang on to this, will you?' he said, trying to pass Jenkins his drink.

She didn't take it from him. 'No need. Just watch how this goes.'

When Reece next got sight of Morgan, she had the man's face pinned tight against the wall, his bulky arm drawn up his spine, fingers pulled back in an agonising pose. People gathered around them, laughing. Several using their phones to film the event for their social media reels.

'You *do* know I used to practise Krav Maga?' Morgan said when Roider had been thrown out of the pub and all was well again. 'I'm thinking about going back to classes.'

Reece turned to Jenkins. 'Did you know we had our very own Bruce Ffi on the squad?'

'I did,' she said, laughing. 'That's why I told you to let her deal with it herself.' She and Morgan high-fived. 'Girl power.'

'Was I the only one left in the dark about this?' Reece asked. He was about to say something else when he caught the unmistakable reek of stale cigarettes close by. Someone reached through the crowd and pinched the flesh of his cheek, tugging it playfully.

'And how's my favourite detective?' It was Maggie Kavanagh—local crime reporter for the South Wales Herald—Columbo-style mac; red lipstick; and beehive hairstyle. 'I heard screaming when I went past,' she said with a wet cough, 'and knew you wouldn't be far away.'

Chapter 21

Reece crossed the threshold of the crowded bedroom, watching Dr Cara Frost examine the young woman's lifeless body. She had her back to him, and to Reece's mounting irritation, was being less than forthcoming with dialogue. He shifted to one side when a crime scene investigator approached with a large black case. Again, when a second CSI followed with a battery of photographic equipment. When he could take no more of the pathologist's silence, he went closer and said: 'Find anything suspicious?'

Frost replied without turning to face him. 'Apart from the dead girl, and a duvet cover stained with dried semen, you mean?'

The doorway dance continued as more people came and went. 'Are you telling me she was raped and murdered?'

'You're putting words in my mouth, Chief Inspector. I gave you the facts only. Cause of death could be due to any one of several natural causes.'

Reece wasn't one for games at the best of times, and drinking whisky well into the small hours was giving him little reason to change any of that. 'So why was *I* called to look at this?'

Frost was on her feet, putting things away in her doctors' bag. 'All I said to plod outside was that the evidence points to there being a second person present in this bedroom—a male specifically—before, or after, that young woman died.' She smiled. Sort of. 'Either way, I thought it might prove useful if you found and interviewed him over the matter.'

Reece's irritation needle was idling somewhere between amber and red. 'Uniform called it in as a confirmed murder.'

'A misunderstanding.' Frost shrugged. 'You can't blame *me* for that.'

Reece stepped aside to let her pass onto the landing; the floorboards creaking underfoot. 'Where's Twm?' he asked. 'Why isn't he here?'

'Dr Pryce is winding down into retirement, as you already know.' Frost managed a wider smile this time. 'That means you'll be seeing a lot more of me from now on.' Pausing halfway down the stairs, she spoke through the gaps in a line of white spindles. 'Thank you for what you said at Elan's hearing yesterday. I'm told it was your testimony that swayed things in her favour.'

'And the post-mortem?' Reece asked. 'When will you be doing that?'

'Later today, hopefully.'

'Hopefully?' He watched her disappear through the front door. Heard her heels clip-clopping on the pavement outside as she made her way along the street and back to her car. 'Right,' he shouted into the busy hallway. 'Which one of you idiots got me out of bed this morning?' No one owned up to the misdemeanour.

Morgan appeared at the foot of the stairs, dressed in a grey trouser suit over a black silk blouse, and didn't look half the worse for wear he did. 'Do you want to speak to the housemates, boss, or shall I crack on?'

Reece sat down on the top step and massaged both temples. 'Is there any point until we know it's foul play for sure?'

'One of them's got a fair bit to say for herself. Claims the dead girl's been followed home from work a few times lately.'

'By our prowler, no doubt?' Maggie Kavanagh and her newspaper had a lot to answer for. If the South Wales Herald was to be believed, then most of the women in Cardiff had experienced a recent encounter with him. 'On my way,' he said, getting up with a groan.

Chapter 22

In the kitchen with Reece were three housemates, two uniformed officers, and Detective Constable Ffion Morgan. The room smelled of toast and strong coffee, suggesting the cohabitants had only recently risen from bed. There was a young woman sitting by herself at a large pine dining table. She was slight in stature and of south Asian origin. Indian, Reece decided. 'Any of that coffee going spare?' he asked, eyeballing a glass cafetière on one of the worktops.

'Help yourself,' the woman said with a dismissive wave of her hand.

'You don't mind?' he asked, wagging a piece of doorstop-thick toast at her. 'I didn't get time to eat before I left the house.'

Morgan rested her hand on the woman's shoulder and took a seat on the other side of her. 'Suba, this is Detective Chief Inspector Reece.'

Reece pulled a chair opposite both women and sat back to front on it, taking in the scene. The kitchen was plenty big enough, and almost a full square in shape. It was tidy too. 'Are you the one who mentioned the prowler to my colleague?' he asked Suba.

'No, that was me.' There were two other women standing near an aluminium sink and draining board, both wearing bed hair and pyjamas. The one called Lowri lifted her gaze from an area of linoleum flooring. 'Just something I said to one of the police constables outside.'

Reece used the back of his hand to wipe butter from his lips. 'Did Poppy get a description of the person who followed her?'

'No, but she insisted he was over there, next to the trees.' Lowri pointed no further than the kitchen wall. 'A man in a silver car.' She glanced at the housemate next to her. 'If we'd only believed her, then...' She didn't finish the sentence and broke down in floods of tears.

The other woman—Zoe—was strangling a bright-red tea towel one minute; using it to dry wine glasses the next. 'We weren't to know.'

'Have those been looked at by Forensics?' Reece asked the uniforms. He told Zoe to put the glassware down when neither officer could confirm either way.

'I'm sorry,' she said when she knocked the taller flute over. It hit the floor and broke into a scattering of small pieces.

'Leave it there,' Reece said when she reached for a pan and brush. 'We might still get lucky if there's anything to be found on it.'

'Did Poppy have a boyfriend?' Morgan asked. 'Only, we found evidence of recent sexual activity on the bedsheets upstairs.'

'There was Jordan. But they split up a few days back.'

Morgan penned the full name on a page in her pocketbook. 'Was there trouble between them?'

'He's a total pain in the arse,' Zoe said. 'Best thing Poppy ever did was to get shot of him.'

Lowri came away from the sink. 'You never gave him a proper chance.'

'And *you* gave him a lot more than that,' Zoe snapped. She turned her attention to the police officers and explained what she meant. 'Jordan's one of those possessive types. Always has to know what you're doing, where you're going, and who you're with.'

Lowri caught Reece's eye and mouthed: 'Not true.'

He spoke to Suba. 'What's *your* opinion of this Jordan fella?'

She pushed her empty coffee mug to one side. 'He and Harlan have been arguing a lot lately.' She shrugged when the other women gave her looks of warning. *'What?* It's true.'

'Who's Harlan?' Reece asked, glancing at each housemate in quick succession. There was no one present who might fit the name.

'Harlan Miller. He and I are medical students,' Suba said. 'He comes from Ohio, I think.' There was a nod to herself. 'Yeah, Ohio.'

Morgan finished scribbling. 'What made them argue?'

'Poppy, usually. Jordan had it in his head that there was something going on between her and Harlan.'

'Even accused her of sleeping with him a few days back,' Zoe said, side-stepping shards of broken glass. 'That's what had them break up in the end.'

'And had Poppy been sleeping with him?' Morgan asked.

Suba shifted her attention to the voices and activity coming from beyond the level of the ceiling. 'I guess your people upstairs will tell you soon enough.'

Reece went and helped himself to more coffee. 'Where will we find this Harlan Miller?'

'None of us have seen him since the night before last,' Suba said.

'Would that be usual behaviour for him?' Morgan's pocketbook looked set to receive another entry. 'Did he often stay elsewhere?' she asked before her first question got an answer.

'I don't remember him doing it previously,' Zoe said. The other women agreed.

Reece came back to the table, coffee mug in hand. 'Do you have any idea where he might have gone?'

All three shook their heads in unison. 'He's got no family over here,' Lowri said. 'Not that he's ever mentioned.'

'We'll need a recent photograph, if you have one.'

Lowri went to the door of the refrigerator and lifted a Volkswagen-Beetle-shaped magnet. 'Taken at Christmas,' she said, handing it over. 'You don't think he had anything to do with this, do you?'

The photograph was of a dark-haired man wearing an ill-fitting reindeer jumper. 'Unlikely,' Reece said, holding the photo at arms-length for Morgan to see. 'Remind you of someone?'

'We've fallen on our feet there, boss.'

'Which one of those rooms upstairs is Harlan's?' asked the DCI.

'The second door along the first landing.' Zoe followed him out of the kitchen. 'But it's Jordan you want to be talking to, not Harlan.'

Suba was on her feet. 'Don't you need a warrant for that sort of thing, Chief Inspector?'

'We won't be going in there,' Reece said. 'Not before our forensics team have taken this place apart.'

Chapter 23

Reece stood in front of the evidence board with a semi-circle of police officers and support staff watching and listening. Chief Superintendent Cable was at the front of the assembled group, wearing full regulation uniform minus the hat. 'Our stab-victim has a name at last.' Reece wrote it in red ink above the photograph of the man in the reindeer jumper. 'Harlan Miller: a twenty-three-year-old American studying medicine here in Cardiff.' He pinned a second photograph next to Miller's and wrote Poppy Jones's name alongside it.

Cable's eyes narrowed. 'Who is she?'

Reece quickly brought her fully up to speed with events. 'Needless to say, I'm treating their deaths as being somehow linked.'

Cable looked aghast. 'Why am I only just hearing about this? Two stabbings and—'

'It wasn't a stabbing in the girl's case.'

'What was it then?'

Reece shook his head and gave an honest answer. 'I don't know yet.'

'How can you not know?' Cable asked. 'Were there no injuries?'

'None that were obvious. We'll have to wait for the post-mortem to confirm the cause of death.'

'Should we put a round-the-clock guard on the house?' Morgan asked. 'In case all five occupants are being targeting for some reason.'

'That's a fair point,' Reece agreed. 'We'll need an ongoing uniform presence on the front and back doors, ma'am.'

Cable nodded. 'Okay. What else?'

'I want Jenkins back at work this week.'

'A conversation for another time and place,' Cable told him.

He moved on reluctantly. 'Give me a sec,' he said, putting his phone on speaker when it rang. 'Sioned, what did you find in Miller's room?'

The crime scene manager's voice sounded tinny through the small device. 'Not a lot, to be honest.' It was just as well she couldn't see the look of disappointment on Reece's face. 'We found one thing that might interest you, though. If the iPad images are anything to go by, then there was definitely something going on between Harlan Miller and Poppy Jones.'

'You've got photographs of the two of them together?'

'And video,' Williams said. 'I'm no prude, but...'

'Are we going to match that semen to Miller, do you think?'

'I'd imagine so.'

'Anything else?'

'Not as yet. I'll let you know if that changes.'

Reece expressed his thanks and hung up. 'That gives Jordan Patterson a motive for killing them both.' He sought out the criminal intelligence analyst. 'Any luck with the phone companies now we've got an ID and address for the victim?'

A frumpy-looking woman with spectacles, and hair that might have been parted with a hatchet, sprang to life with an enthusiastic nod. 'Miller's phone has been active several times already today.' She turned the laptop towards the DCI. 'Pinging the telecommunications mast here, and again, here.'

'Which means the other end of Mermaid Quay,' Reece said, squinting at the screen. 'Only a stone's throw from where we are now.'

The analyst agreed. 'But it looks like the user couldn't override the security PIN. There have been no calls or texts made from the device.'

'Good work. I want this person found and brought in,' Reece told his team. 'What's the door-to-door update for the Miller murder?'

Ginge read from his notes. 'Allensbank Road is a decent enough area, boss. People living there tend to be tucked up in their beds and fast asleep that late at night.'

'Lucky them.'

'There *was* a sighting of a car hanging about,' Ginge continued. 'By one of the locals letting her dog out for a wee. Something long and light in colour. Could have been grey. Might have been white.' He looked up apologetically. 'She's an old lady. That's the best she could do.'

'And the hospital CCTV?' Reece asked. 'Did that show anything matching the description?'

'Too much distance between the cameras and where Miller was found,' Ginge said. 'The pictures aren't great, but I did print this off.'

Morgan craned her neck to get a better view of the photocopy. 'That definitely fits the old lady's description of what she saw.'

'My best guess would be a Volvo 740,' Ginge said. 'Plenty big enough to transport a casualty in the boot.'

'You know your cars?' Reece asked.

'My dad owned a garage when I was in my early teens. He made me wash everything on the forecourt for pocket money. Boring as hell, but I got to memorise all the makes and models.'

'A Volvo 740 it is then,' Reece said. 'Let's get looking at the city's cameras and rule it out if it's innocent.'

Morgan's phone vibrated on the desk. She picked it up when Reece nodded. 'Uniform have found Jordan Patterson. He's kicking off, but on the way in.'

Chapter 24

Reece leaned against a one-way window in the wall of a small observation room. 'Take Ginge in there with you.' Jordan Patterson was sitting alone at a desk on the other side. His pose was horizontal, almost. His arms were folded across the front of a tight-fitting white T-shirt. His legs were stretched out under the table. Twice, he looked up and over at the window to blow them a kiss. 'You both happy with this?' Reece asked, taking a sip of hot coffee from a paper cup.

'Yep,' Morgan said, clutching a file to her chest. 'Come on then, Ginge, let's get this show on the road.'

Reece drew a chair away from the wall and positioned it in front of the glass. 'Any news on Jenkins's return?' he asked once they were alone.

Chief Superintendent Cable remained on her feet. 'I've spoken with the ACC—'

'And?'

'And he'll give your request the consideration it deserves.'

Reece twisted in the chair, spilling a small amount of coffee on his trousers. He stood and reached for a box of tissues on a nearby shelf. 'What's to think about?' he asked, rubbing furiously at a damp thigh. 'Jenkins is suspended; Ken Ward is dead; and Bean Pole in there is as wet as a fish's bathing costume.'

'Owain is an experienced police constable.' Cable waited for Reece to get rid of the tissue and settle in his chair. 'And might I remind you that it was you who okayed his secondment to the squad.'

Reece sighed deeply. 'Yes, but I thought Jenkins would be back by now.'

'ACC Harris will be making his decision first thing tomorrow morning.'

'That's good of him. I mean, there's no rush, is there?'

'Look, Brân. I know that you and—'

Reece turned away. 'Shush. They're about to start.'

Chapter 25

On the other side of the glass, Morgan and Ginge had taken their seats; Morgan running through the preliminaries while Patterson watched on with both hands tucked down the front of his jogging bottoms. Pressing a red button on the digital recording device (DIR), she waited for the long beeping sound to cease before calling out the date and time. 'Others present in the room are Detective Constable Ffion Morgan, and Detective Constable Owain Evans.'

Patterson sniggered and leaned towards Ginge. 'Are you sure you're old enough to be doing this?'

When Morgan finished, she took a photograph from an A4-sized envelope and slid it across the surface of the table. 'Do you recognise this woman?'

Patterson left it where it was and pressed his back against the upright of his seat. 'Yeah, that's Poppy.'

'Louder please. For the benefit of the recording.'

'It's Poppy. Poppy Jones.'

Morgan caught herself staring at the small port-wine stain birthmark on Patterson's right cheek. She did so only because her brother had one, and knew only too well how much it bugged him. 'She used to be a girlfriend of yours.'

'Still is.'

'That's not true.'

'She'll see sense soon enough.' Patterson looked away and sniffed. 'Always does. She can't resist me,' he said with a leery smile.

Morgan shook her head. 'Not this time, I'm afraid.'

Patterson kept the smile going. For his benefit or theirs, it wasn't clear. 'She needs her bit of rough, does Poppy. She'll be back.'

'Poppy Jones was found dead this morning.'

Patterson stared with increasing levels of disbelief. He shook his head. 'Nah. Nah. Nah. Ain't happening.' He was on his feet in a flash, all flailing arms and screaming obscenities. Ginge hit the alarm on the wall beside him, setting off a wailing siren. There was an almost-immediate sound of boots rushing along the corridor outside, before the door banged open against the wall.

'It's okay.' Morgan got up with her hand held in a STOP pose. 'Stand down,' she told them. 'We're all right here. Aren't we, Jordan?' She lowered herself slowly onto her chair. 'Jordan?'

Patterson sat and gripped his head. 'Poppy's dead?' He looked genuinely surprised and upset.

'Are you saying you didn't know?'

He looked right through the detective. 'Why would I?'

'Where were you last night?'

Patterson lowered his hands. 'What?'

'Last night. Where were you?'

'Playing snooker.'

'Where?'

'The Green Baize, on City Road.'

'That's Billy Creed's place,' Ginge said, making an entry in his pocketbook. 'Can anyone vouch for you being there?'

'Do they need to?'

Morgan folded her arms. 'Answer the question.'

'Both teams saw me. And Big Babs on the till.' Patterson's mood lightened suddenly. 'Babs did the after-match chip butties. Gave me a right bollocking for nicking one before she'd put them out on the table.'

'We'll need to check.'

'You do that.' Patterson reeled off a short list of names when asked.

Morgan slid a second photograph towards him. 'Why did you recently threaten to kill this man?'

'Slap,' Patterson corrected. 'I said I'd give him a slap, not kill him.'

'That's not what we heard.'

Patterson forced his head across the table. 'You heard wrong, then.'

Morgan didn't flinch. 'Give us your version of events.'

The crown jewels got another shakedown. 'Miller was always sniffing around Poppy. Wouldn't leave her alone. Even when she told him to.'

'How did that make you feel?'

The look on Patterson's face was worth a thousand words.

'You were jealous?'

'The fuck I was. Not of him, anyway.'

Morgan brought the photographs next to one another. 'You hated them both. Hated them for making a fool of you.'

'You killed Miller first,' Ginge said. 'Stabbed him to punish Poppy. Then it was her turn.'

Patterson's hands broke free from his joggers. 'You don't know shit.' He banged his fist against the tabletop. 'None of this has anything to do with me.'

'Where were you the night before last?'

Patterson collapsed onto the table with his head buried beneath his arms. 'Why are you keeping on?'

Morgan collected the photographs and put them to one side. 'Because you've got more motive than anyone else we know of right now.'

Patterson lifted his head and whispered: 'Motive?'

'When you found out they'd had sex together, it was more than you could bear.' She pointed at him accusingly. 'That's why you killed them. Make this easy on everyone and admit it.'

'Poppy wouldn't have. Not with him. No way.'

'We've forensic evidence suggesting she did. DNA checks are being run on it right now. Or was that *your* semen on the bedsheets?'

He gave no answer.

'I didn't think so. That's all the motive you needed right there.'

Patterson was on his feet again. Leaning on the table, glaring at her. 'You—'

She slapped Ginge's wrist when he reached for the alarm. 'Sit down, Jordan. I said park it!'

Patterson stayed where he was. 'I need a break.'

'You'll get one soon enough.' Morgan waited for him to settle. 'Do you see how this looks? Poppy Jones and Harlan Miller dead within twenty-four hours of one another, and the person with the strongest links to them both, is you.'

Chapter 26

Reece and Cable watched with interest from the other side of the glass. 'What do you make of him?' Cable asked. 'He sounded genuinely surprised when Ffion told him about the dead girl.'

Reece didn't turn around when he answered. 'He's been in and out of places like this often enough to put on a good show.'

'But do you think he did it?'

'What *I* think doesn't come into it.' Reece got up. 'The CPS will have to decide if there's sufficient evidence to get a conviction.'

'Unlikely, I'd imagine,' Cable said. 'No murder weapon, and what sounds to be a cast-iron alibi for both nights. Not to mention that we still don't know if the girl *was* murdered.'

'As if by magic,' Reece said, thumbing the screen of his phone. 'Cara Frost's trying to get hold of me. Must be something to do with Poppy Jones's post-mortem examination.'

Reece accelerated off the mini-roundabout. They were on their way to the hospital. He'd sent Ginge over to Billy Creed's snooker hall to check Patterson's alibi with the woman known as Big Babs. The Cardiff City football stadium went by on their right; the large dome of the *House of Sport* on the opposite side of the busy road.

'What did Cara tell you?' Morgan asked.

'Only that she didn't want to speak about it over the phone.'

'No clues?'

'None at all.'

'Curious.'

Reece pointed to the glovebox. 'Pass me that screwdriver. The short one with the black handle.' Someone beeped a horn behind them and got a sharp blast back in return for their protests. 'It's for the radio.'

She handed it to him. 'Jenks told me how you like to do this.'

'*Like* doesn't come into it,' Reece said, trying to keep his eyes on the road ahead. 'I've got no choice, have I?'

Morgan gave the vehicle's shabby interior a slow once-over. 'You can get some fabulous deals on new cars at the moment.'

'What's wrong with the one I've got?' He plunged the metal end of the screwdriver deep into a hole marked *channel select* and twisted it left and right until most of the hissing noise had disappeared. 'Do you like country music?' he asked, steering the car one handed.

'I'm more of a modern-day Taylor Swift girl.'

Reece handed back the screwdriver. 'Shame that, because country's all it wants to play today.'

Chapter 27

Ginge couldn't see for cigarette smoke. 'You do know this is illegal,' he said, waving a hand in front of his face.

The woman wore a tight vest-top, and judging by what was straining to get out of it, must have been Big Babs. 'Take it up with management. The office is over there.'

'It's you I came to see, not Mr Creed.'

'I don't know nothing about it,' Babs said, watching the office door on the other side of the room.

'About what?'

'Whatever it is you're here for.' She picked up a duster and spray can of polish and started rubbing at the wooden parts of the snooker tables.

Ginge followed, waving a photograph at her. 'Do you recognise this man?'

Babs balled the duster. 'I already told you. I know nothing.' She pointed towards the office. 'And if *he* gets sight of me talking to you, I'll be good for nothing.'

'Was this man in here earlier this week?' Ginge persisted.

Babs grabbed the photo. 'That's Jordan Patterson.' She handed it back. 'He's in here most nights.'

Ginge gave her the dates and times in question. 'You're sure about that?'

'Like I said. He—'

'Copper!' The voice was deep and came from the direction of the office. Big Babs was gone when Ginge next looked. The duster and polish likewise. Billy Creed came limping between the tables, flicking the polished cane out in front of him before planting it down again on the thin carpet. 'Thought I could smell pork crackling.' He stopped in front of Ginge and blew cigar smoke at him. 'Oink. Oink.' He turned to Jimmy Chin. 'What's this lanky string of piss doing here?'

'He must be lost,' Chin said. 'Couldn't be stupid enough to come in here on purpose.'

Creed leaned his full weight on the cane. 'I remember you,' he said, picking a speck of tobacco leaf off the tip of his tongue. 'You brought that blonde stripper to the Midnight Club. Turned up late for the Christmas curry. That was you, wasn't it?'

'I'm finished here,' Ginge said, preparing to leave.

Creed glanced at Jimmy Chin. 'Did you tell Copper he could go?'

Chin cracked his knuckles and went over to close the door. 'Not me.'

The gangster approached until he and the young detective were only inches apart. 'That means this conversation is only just getting started.'

Chapter 28

'It wasn't as obvious when I saw it back at the student house,' Dr Cara Frost said. 'It's not that obvious even now.' She didn't look up and leaned on a counter, leafing through a mound of paperwork. 'If I'm right, then this is one clever killer you've got yourselves.'

'That rules out Jordan Patterson,' Reece said, earning himself a smirk from Morgan.

'This is only a hunch at the moment, mind you,' Frost said, lowering the pen to give the detectives her full attention. 'Stay with me on this until I've finished.'

Poppy Jones lay naked on the extraction table. Her legs were extended. Her arms resting straight at her sides. Gravity had drawn her lifeblood to the lower levels of her body. A purple plimsoll line running full circle where skin touched metal. Her shoulder-length blonde hair had been combed away from a pretty face to reveal lips that looked stained by a full-bodied red wine. Beginning just above a folded white towel placed over her groin was a thick track of black stitching running up to the shoulders in a Y shape. The skin was puckered tight against the suture material.

Morgan sighed. 'Such a waste of a life. So young.'

'Fit as a fiddle too,' Frost said, tapping a porcelain-white thigh with the back of her hand. 'Not a thing wrong with her that I could find.' She circled the table and helped herself to a pair of gloves from a rack on the wall. 'And that's what got me thinking about something one of my old professors told us at university.' She pointed at a door to her left 'You'll have to come through to see properly.'

The smell was stronger on the other side of the glass. Hospital disinfectant fused with the stench of human decay.

Reece didn't notice. 'Show us what you've got,' he said, sidling up to the table and dead girl.

Frost took a pair of fine forceps and an even finer probe from a line-up of surgical instruments set out on a trolley. She used them to open up the track of Poppy's navel piercing. Then she leaned out of the way. 'See that?'

Reece moved in closer, his head bobbing side-to-side. 'What is it I'm looking for?'

'It's difficult to see,' Frost said, checking that the instruments hadn't moved and obscured the view. 'The piercing track itself is very well established. But this here alongside it.' She advanced the probe a little further. 'This is what I believe to be a more recent needle prick.'

'Recent, as in how long?' Reece asked.

'A day or so.'

He shifted his gaze. 'And by needle prick, you presumably mean an injection of some kind?'

'That's what I'm thinking, yes.'

'Could it be insulin?' Morgan asked from a position of not closer than five feet away. 'Was she diabetic?'

'Blood glucose levels were within the normal range,' Frost said, coming away from the table to drop her gloves into a bin. 'The only abnormal parameter was the amount of free potassium we found in the blood. And that lends more weight to my hunch.'

When the pathologist paused, Reece followed her into a side room and spoke to her back: 'Will you quit with the theatrics and just tell me what you think went on here?'

Chapter 29

They'd left the mortuary only a few minutes earlier, Reece leading the way as usual.

Morgan was hurrying behind him. Struggling to keep up. 'Isn't it too soon to be doing this?' she asked. 'Dr Frost reckons it's going to take at least another day for the full tox reports to come back.'

'There's no harm in us asking a few questions while we're here.' Reece stopped someone with a stethoscope draped round their neck. 'Where's the anaesthetic department?'

'Third floor. B-block. Lifts are just—'

Reece thanked the man and headed for the stairs.

'Really?' Morgan rounded her shoulders like a moping teenager. 'We're on Lower Ground. Why can't we take—'

'You don't want to go anywhere near the lifts in this place.' Reece spoke from painful experience. 'Not if you want to stay sane.'

They exited the stairwell on the third floor and turned left purely by chance. 'There it is,' Morgan said, out of breath but relieved to have survived the climb. 'The anaesthetic department.' There was an office door next to the sign, with the outline of a person dressed in white on the other side of a frosted glass window. Morgan knocked on the wood surround and waited.

'Yes.' The occupant was tall. Powerful looking. With a face that suggested he'd spent a lifetime perfecting a frown.

'I'm Detective Chief Inspector Reece.' He produced his warrant card. 'And this is Detective Constable Morgan.'

'Is there a problem?' the man asked. 'I'm Dr Richard Wellman, clinical director for anaesthetics.'

'We called in on the off-chance,' Reece said, pointing to the sign near the door. 'And this looked like the right place to be getting started.'

Wellman waited. 'Started on what?'

'Could we come in?' Reece asked with a quick glance up and down the busy corridor. 'It's not what I'd call private out here.'

'I'd normally insist you make an appointment with my secretary,' Wellman said. 'This is highly unusual, I'll have you know.'

'Two minutes and we'll be on our way,' Reece promised.

'At the very most,' Morgan reaffirmed.

The room was a tight fit for three people. 'I bet you've seen bigger prison cells?' Wellman said, keeping his bulk to the wall.

'I was expecting something a bit grander at your level,' Reece admitted. He took a fold of paper from his trouser pocket and held it close to the anaesthetist's face. 'How do you pronounce this word?'

Wellman adjusted his position. 'Suxamethonium Chloride. What of it, Chief Inspector?'

'Am I right in thinking you can paralyse a person with it? Even stop them breathing?'

'Temporarily, yes.' Wellman went and leaned against his desk. 'We use it to place a breathing tube in the windpipe prior to surgery. But I'd have to say its use is not as commonplace as it once was.'

Morgan made an entry in her pocketbook. 'So it wouldn't be available in these operating theatres?'

'Oh, it still has its uses,' Wellman said.

Reece took in the contents of the office. There was a desk, a chair, and a filing cabinet. A smaller room led off the back end of the main room. There were no photographs of a wife or children that he could see. And the place smelled. A cloying odour that hung in the air like a bad fart.

'It's the drains,' Wellman explained. 'Something to do with the plumbing for the ward above us. They've had the ceiling tiles down more times than I can remember.'

Reece turned his nose up at it. 'Is it always this bad?'

'It'll disappear for a few weeks and then raise its ugly head again when you're least expecting it.'

'Just the place for hiding a decomposing corpse if you ever needed to,' Morgan joked. 'No one would bat an eyelid.'

Wellman studied her before speaking to Reece. 'Could we please wrap this up now?'

Reece nodded. 'A couple more things and then we'll be out of your way. Where would this drug be kept?'

'In the fridges of each anaesthetic room.' Wellman sighed. 'Can I ask the reason for your visit and these questions?'

'Not at the moment,' Reece said. 'And would it be anaesthetists only who'd have access to the drug?'

'Not at all. Just about anybody working on the theatre suite could lay their hands on a box if they so wished.'

Chapter 30

Reece sat back and waited for Chief Superintendent Cable to react.

'I've never heard of such a thing,' she said, searching through her desk drawer until she found a bottle of aspirin. 'But it's still only a hunch of Cara's, you say?'

'Until the tox screens come back,' Reece admitted. 'But she seemed pretty confident we'd get a positive result.'

Cable swallowed the pills with two gulps of coffee. 'It all sounds like something from a spy movie.'

Reece stirred the contents of his mug with a pen and was happier with the taste when he next took a sip. 'The Novichok attack in

Salisbury was for real,' he said, returning the Biro to a pot on the desk. 'Who'd have thought that would ever happen on British soil?'

'Put the pen in the bin,' Cable said, watching him. She rested her paper cup on the desk. 'Tell me what you know so far. I'll brief ACC Harris once we're done.'

'Make sure you remind him about Jenkins, while you're at it.'

Cable looked up from her coffee and gave him a stern look. 'He's already said it's being dealt with.'

'Not quickly enough,' Reece replied, letting his temper get the better of him. 'Two youngsters are dead, and now this Hall woman is claiming Billy Creed's done her husband in.' He rose from his chair. 'I can't do it all myself, you know.'

'You don't go anywhere near Creed.' Cable pointed a finger in warning. 'His lawyers are already threatening to sue us for the part we played in him getting shot.'

'I got a collapsed lung and a shoulder full of shrapnel,' Reece said. 'What if I sue you as well?'

Cable almost choked on her coffee and put the mug down, spilling some. 'You got yourself shot. Wouldn't listen to a word you were told, as usual.'

'Would you have let me go to the club if I'd stuck about here and asked for your permission?' He watched her consider that. 'I thought not.'

Cable waited for the tension in the room to ease off. 'You almost got yourself killed. What you did that day bordered on recklessness.'

'I got Jenkins out alive. That wouldn't have happened if I'd waited for you or Harris to give the green light.'

'What were Cara Frost's exact words?' Cable asked. 'I need to brief the ACC.'

Reece stared at her, drumming his fingers on the surface of the desk.

'Okay,' she squawked in defeat. 'I'll remind him about Jenkins.'

'Good. Thank you.' Reece picked at the rolled lip of his paper cup while he spoke. 'When Cara was in training as a pathologist, she got one of those *let-your-hair-down* kind of lectures from her professor. You know the type: the case you're never going to come across in your career, but I'll tell you about it anyway.'

Cable nodded and let him continue.

'So this professor tells his students that Suxamethonium Chloride was once thought to be the perfect murder weapon. Pathologists don't routinely screen for it at post-mortem examinations, and the entry wound required to deliver it is no larger than a fine needle prick. There's no outward evidence of foul play. Not unless you really look for it.'

'That sounds just about perfect to me,' Cable said. 'I'm sensing a *but?'*

'Only a handful of documented cases exist—mostly in the United States—dating from the early sixties up to the mid-nineties, I think. Deaths involving otherwise fit and healthy individuals like Poppy Jones. But what was common to all these cases was the occupations of the spouse. They were anaesthetists, or intensive care nurses.

Even a friend of a veterinary surgeon in one case.' Reece lobbed his empty cup into a bin near the door. 'In each case, the police got lucky because of throwaway comments made by workmates or neighbours, leading them to test for the drug, and then secure a conviction. Frost remembers her professor saying—and it might have been from the newspapers, rather than something written in an official document—that there should be a push to screen for this drug if confronted with deaths in similar circumstances.'

'I'm guessing this isn't known in wider circles?' Cable said. 'Meaning not all pathologists would be alert to the possibility.'

'I'm hoping ours is a one-off,' Reece said. 'Can you imagine there being a serial killer loose in the city, injecting people with paralysing agents?'

Cable lifted the receiver off its cradle and hovered a finger over the keypad. 'If the tox report on Poppy Jones confirms Cara's suspicions, then everyone living in that student house becomes a suspect.'

Chapter 31

Richard Wellman listened to the late-evening news with a glass of his favourite Chateauneuf-du-Pape, and a rather good cheese board. He put Johannes Brahms on hold; but only for as long as it took the stupid woman on the television to update the principality on recent happenings.

There was nothing on there about the dead Poppy Jones. Not a mention of her, in fact. And the meddling Harlan Miller was already little more than a bad memory wrapped around greasy helpings of back-street fish and chips.

But that police detective might become something of a problem. Turning up at the hospital unannounced, asking questions.

Reece. Wasn't that his name? The man couldn't possibly know that Poppy's death was from anything other than natural causes. Wellman had been careful to incapacitate her with the Sevoflurane device. He'd breathed her down rapidly while holding her close so she couldn't injure herself by thrashing about. Once asleep, he'd taken her to her room and undressed her before choosing an injection site that no one was likely to notice.

Though convenient, the navel piercing had made him recoil with revulsion. Why was it that some women saw fit to spoil what was, in Poppy Jones's case, near-perfection?

Because they're whores. The very thought of it made him so angry he almost snapped the stem of his wineglass. *That's why you chose her. She was playing the field and had said so herself at work.*

What was it that counsellor had told him to do on such occasions of intense anger? He took a series of slow, measured breaths, reverse-counting until he was somewhere near calm again.

His mind drifted back to Poppy and her demise. He knew that pathologists didn't routinely screen for such metabolites, having had a conversation with one of them only recently. Not a colleague from Cardiff, obviously. That might have raised suspicion given current circumstances. Professional conferences had many benefits, and not all of them were for the greater good of the public.

He'd have to be more careful now that Reece was taking an interest. Lie low for a while. Wasn't that what they called it? Let things blow over and start again another time. Another place, even.

But the urge to kill again was becoming ever more intense. Fuelled in part by a plentiful supply of women who thought nothing of providing online running commentaries on their smutty indiscretions. *Breathe. Count.*

It was all he could think about for large parts of the day and night; his counselling sessions on Cathedral Road doing little to suppress it.

'What was that, Mother?' he shouted at the underside of the ceiling. 'You'd like more music and wine.' He got out of the chair and took the half-empty glass with him, turning up the volume on the old record player as he went past.

He could smell her from the bottom of the stairs, and held his breath before reaching the top.

He turned the brass knob of the bedroom door, pushed on it, and retched as he entered. 'Mother, you really are beginning to stink like a dead cat.' He went nearer the bed. Tentatively. Like a young child made to pay its last respects to a dead grandparent.

He held the glass above the rotting corpse's head and emptied its contents over the mottled face. 'Drink, whore.'

Chapter 32

Morgan tossed her bag onto the nearest desk and bounded towards Detective Sergeant Elan Jenkins with her arms held open. 'Look who's back.' She let go again and frowned. 'You *are* back, aren't you? Properly back, I mean?'

Jenkins ducked and dived. 'Bloody hell. Sort of. It's a bit complicated at the moment.'

Morgan perched on the edge of Jenkins's desk. She leaned forward and lowered her voice. 'The boss gave Cable some right earache after the outcome of the hearing. He said they were to bring you back or else.'

'So I've heard.' Jenkins was doing her best to resurrect a spiky fringe. She licked her fingers and pulled at it with some level of success. 'The whole thing has been a bit of a whirlwind, to be honest with you.'

'Better that way than to wait the best part of twelve months like most officers have to.'

'I'm not complaining,' Jenkins said, swinging on the back legs of her chair. 'Just knocked for six by the speed of it all.' She stifled a yawn. 'What have I missed lately? Any shenanigans with you know who?' She nodded in the direction of Reece's empty office.

'He's only just back to work himself. I'd say he was okay on the whole. One flashback I've been a witness to.' Morgan outlined the main case they were currently working. 'Looks like it could be a double murder. We're waiting on some tox screens before bringing the rest of the household in for questioning.' She paused, her face lighting up again. 'How are things with you and Cara, by the way? She seems very nice. Clever, too. I got talking to her during the post-mortem.' Morgan leaned again and placed a hand on Jenkins's shoulder. 'The two of you will have to come round to ours for a drink and nibbles sometime soon.'

Jenkins promised they would. 'Did Patterson say much at interview?'

'Mostly that he didn't do it. And if your Cara's right, then the girl's murder is well beyond his capabilities.'

'Can we stop calling her that?' Jenkins said. 'Plain Cara, will do fine.'

Morgan slid off the edge of the desk. 'Okay. No problem.'

'Everything's happening way too fast,' Jenkins explained. 'Especially after the Belle Gillighan fiasco.'

They watched the first of the troops wander in and fuel themselves with early morning coffee and stale croissants.

'The boss has called a briefing for a quarter past the hour,' Morgan said. 'He wants a quick round-up of everything we've got so far.'

Jenkins stared at the empty desk opposite. It had, until recently, belonged to their colleague, Ken Ward. 'That Ginge's now, I'm guessing?'

Morgan nodded. 'Ken had us all fooled.'

'Hook, line, and sinker.'

'You must have been terrified down there in that basement? I know I would have been.'

'Strangulation is no way to leave this world,' Jenkins said, putting a hand to the front of her neck. The scars had healed. The physical ones, at least.

'He was a bastard for what he did to you.'

'I've called him far worse,' Jenkins admitted.

'Have they arranged any counselling yet? You make sure they do.'

'Give them a chance. They're only just getting their heads around not sacking me.'

'You went way beyond the call of duty trying to sort out that shit-storm. They owe you big time for what you did there.'

Jenkins lowered her head. Her voice too. 'My actions contributed to the deaths of at least two people—let's not forget that—and I almost got the boss killed as well.'

'I got myself shot,' Reece said, entering the room from somewhere behind them. 'Me, not you.' He stopped in his office doorway. 'Is that cleared up now?'

Jenkins looked far from convinced. 'If you say so.'

'I do.' He closed the door, then opened it again not a moment later. 'Welcome back, by the way.'

Chapter 33

Reece arrived for the briefing ten minutes later than everyone else, apologising as he looked along the length of the table. 'Are we all here?' After checking the room for absentees, he gave the usual instructions regarding mobile devices and other unnecessary interruptions. 'It's confirmed,' he said with a single twitch of his head. 'Poppy Jones was killed by someone using the paralysing agent Suxamethonium Chloride.' It took him three attempts to pronounce the name, and even then, he found it tricky.

That got most people in the room shrugging. Few, if any of them, had a clue what he meant.

'There were high levels of something called choline in the victim's brain. Succinic acid in the tissue around the belly button. And the breakdown products of the drug itself in her urine.'

'Bloody hell,' Morgan said. 'Hats off to Cara Frost for finding it.'

'It was a good shout,' Reece agreed. 'Now we know: we've got ourselves two murders.'

'Connected?' Jenkins asked.

'We have to assume so. Unless we can prove otherwise.'

'What are you thinking?' Jenkins again. 'A revenge killing by a jealous boyfriend?'

'That would be the most obvious conclusion,' Reece said. 'Patterson's more than capable of stabbing someone—he's got previous for wounding with intent—but he'd need help to administer the drug.'

'And he's a cleaner at the hospital,' Morgan chipped in. 'If Dr Wellman is right, then he'd have no trouble at all getting his thieving hands on some of that drug.'

'Could one of the housemates be in on it with him?' Jenkins was reading from her briefing sheet. 'Says here they all have a medical background of one kind or another.'

'There's definitely two camps in that house.' Reece looked to Morgan for her opinion.

'I agree,' she said. 'Particularly where Lowri and Zoe are concerned.'

Chief Superintendent Cable wanted to know more.

'I got the impression Lowri was pro-Jordan, ma'am. And Zoe, pro-Harlan.'

Reece nodded. 'There was also a throwaway comment from Zoe that Lowri and Patterson have been intimate in the past.'

'So she might still hold a candle for him,' Cable said. 'And be only too happy to do away with the competition, as it were.'

Reece had already considered that angle. It made the most sense. The pair had motive, means, and opportunity. People had spent lifetimes behind bars on less evidence.

'And the Indian girl.' Cable again. 'Isn't she also a medical student?'

'She's the quietest of the bunch.' Reece gave his head a good scratch. 'I'd be surprised if she had anything to do with this.'

Cable studied him over the upper rims of her glasses. 'You know what they say about the quiet ones?'

'I do, but not this time, ma'am. Not in my opinion.'

'How does this *Suxa-whatever-it-is* affect a person?' Jenkins asked. 'And how does the killer get the victim to keep still long enough to inject it so precisely?'

Several others at the table were asking the same question.

Reece leaned on his elbows. 'Ordinarily, it's injected into a vein before surgery, and about a minute or so later, the recipient starts twitching all over.' He checked with Morgan. 'What did Cara call the medical term for it?'

Morgan referred to her pocketbook and pronounced the word deliberately. 'Fasciculations.'

Reece nodded. 'After those, you're paralysed for somewhere up to ten minutes. Even the muscles used for breathing come to a complete standstill.'

'Christ,' somebody said. 'I'm not putting my name down for surgery any time soon. Paralysed. I never knew that.'

'You're given an anaesthetic beforehand,' another pointed out. 'And asleep by the time it happens. I've had plenty for my knee and can't remember a thing.'

'But getting the drug into her in the first place,' Jenkins said. 'How did the killer manage that when there were no injuries suggesting a physical struggle?'

'I don't know,' Reece admitted. 'Suggestions anyone?' Ginge's hand went up like a kid's in a schoolroom. 'Just shout it out,' Reece told him.

Chapter 34

'Maybe it was like they do it in the movies,' Ginge suggested. 'Hold a hanky soaked with chloroform over the victim's nose until they go unconscious?' He put a cupped hand to his face in an unnecessary demonstration of what he meant.

Morgan nodded. 'If you can steal this stuff so easily, then chloroform isn't at all far-fetched.'

'Do they even use that anymore?' Jenkins asked.

'Find out,' Reece told her.

'Let's hope Ginge is right and the poor girl was asleep the whole time,' Cable said.

'Any evidence of sexual assault?' Jenkins asked.

Reece shook his head. 'Thankfully not.'

'That could lend more weight to one of the girls being involved. This Lowri is looking more and more like a person of interest, if you ask me.'

'Agreed.' Reece sat back and checked his watch. 'Let's go round the table and see what else we've got.'

'You know about Harlan Miller's phone,' a uniform said. 'A homeless guy at the docks says he found it in the cemetery on Allensbank Road.'

'What was he doing there?' Reece asked.

'Buying a fix.'

'In a cemetery?'

'Unlikely to get robbed by the locals,' someone said to stifled laughter all round.

Reece allowed himself the briefest of grins. 'Did he see anything?'

'High as a kite and good for nothing, boss. We left him to sleep it off in the cells overnight.'

Reece got Morgan's attention. 'Once we're done here, you and Ginge go find out what he knows.'

'Jenkins can do that,' Cable said.

Reece shook his head. 'I want her to talk to the housemates. She might get more out of them than I did. Especially from Lowri.'

Cable stared at him. 'ACC Harris's orders are for her to concentrate on the Harlan Miller case, and nothing else for now.'

'But—' Reece protested.

'It's the *nothing else for now* bit that makes it quite clear, don't you think?' Cable was up on her feet and preparing to leave. 'While I remember, the boy's parents are arriving later this afternoon. I want you to be around for that.'

Reece pulled a face. 'I'm going to be busy here. Why can't you do it?'

'I'll be there too. As will ACC Harris.'

'You're kidding me?'

'They've got clout, this lot,' Cable said. 'The father used to be a—'

'I knew *it!*' Reece slammed his hand against the desk. Most in the room lowered their heads, not wanting to get involved. Several watched with one eye open. 'And Poppy Jones was only a nurse. Is that it?'

The chief super came back to the table, red-faced. 'That's not what I meant, and you know it.'

'And the CCTV guy,' Reece continued, unable to stop himself now he'd started. 'What about that poor bastard? I doubt his family has any clout with the pen-pushers up at headquarters?'

'Just remember who you're speaking to, Chief Inspector. And you'll quit with the Billy Creed angle, if you know what's good for you.'

Reece got up and followed her out of the room. 'Creed tried the scare tactics on Ginge yesterday. Didn't like us asking questions.'

Cable's eyeballs bulged in their sockets. 'You went round there?'

'No. Ginge did.'

'But you must have sent him?'

Reece shrugged. 'No one said I couldn't. It's me you've slapped the ban on. Not members of my team.'

Cable clenched her fists, and for a moment, looked like she might swing for him. 'It's not me who's stopping you. It's the lawyers, for Christ's sake.'

'I was following up on a lead. Checking Jordan Patterson's alibi for the Miller murder. You heard him say he was playing snooker that night.'

Cable's fists relaxed. 'Just as long as we understand one another.'

Ginge appeared in the doorway. 'Boss. I've been waiting for the staff rotas to come across from the hospital. They had to get Human Resources approval before they'd—'

'Just give me the bloody punchline.'

'Sorry, boss. When Lowri Hughes told us she's a nurse, she neglected to mention her speciality being anaesthetics. And there's something else you should know.' The newbie looked pleased with himself. 'The night Poppy Jones died; Lowri rang in sick for work.'

Reece slapped him on the back. 'What are you waiting for? Get a car round there and bring her in for questioning.'

Chapter 35

Reece decided last minute to join Morgan in the interview room while waiting for the arrival of the Americans.

'Nobody asked which department I worked in,' Lowri said. She held a paper tissue in her hands and was busy tearing the thing to shreds. 'How was I supposed to know it was important?'

Morgan used a broken-ended Biro to doodle on a pad of yellow paper and didn't look up when she spoke. 'Any of the others in the house work in areas where anaesthetic drugs might be stored?'

Lowri tried to catch the detective's eye. When she failed, she set about rolling torn bits of tissue into compact balls, lining them up across the table in neat rows. 'Zoe's a physiotherapist. They rotate every few months, but lately she's been doing stroke-rehab or something similar. You'd have to check with her to be sure.'

'And Suba?'

'She was on a cardiology block last time we spoke.' Lowri fell silent and began a third line of paper balls. 'Harlan was on an anaesthetic placement. So if you're asking who else, apart from me, had access to that type of drug, then look no further than him.'

Reece shifted in his seat, his shoulder reminding him that it had only recently come off second best in a fight with a stray bullet. He gave it a gentle rub. 'You're saying he was recently on the operating theatre suite?'

Lowri took one of the paper balls and unravelled it. 'Why are you asking me this?'

Morgan stopped doodling. 'What do you know about Suxamethonium Chloride?'

'Why all the questions about work and drugs?'

'Answer.' Reece's voice was calm but firm in its tone.

'It's used to intubate patients—place breathing tubes—whenever we need to do it in a hurry.'

Morgan lay the Biro on the notepad and made no attempt to stop it when it rolled towards her. 'Have you ever taken some home with you?'

Lowri's jaw dropped open. 'You're freaking me out now.'

'Did Jordan ever ask you to get him some?'

'What?' Lowri bumped against the table, knocking several paper balls and Morgan's pen to the floor.

'Where were you when Poppy Jones died?' Reece asked.

Lowri was visibly shaking. 'I already told the officer back at the house – we were all at work.'

'You included?'

'Yes.'

Morgan stared. 'Let's try that again, shall we?'

'What?'

'Where were you when Poppy Jones died?'

'Work.' Lowri looked towards the greyed-out window in the far wall. 'I was at work.'

Reece turned his file to face her. It was open to a page sent over from the hospital. 'This rota sheet says otherwise.'

Chapter 36

The homeless man's name was Charles Rash. He was fifty-two, but looked older than dirt. 'They calls me Itchy,' he said with a broad Cardiff accent and toothless grin. 'Itchy rash. Get it?'

Jenkins did and considered it wholly appropriate for a man who hadn't stopped scratching since he'd entered the interview room more than ten minutes earlier.

'It's a German surname. On my father's side.' Itchy set his bloodshot eyes on Ginge. 'That's right, sonny, my grandfather was a Kraut.' He stood up suddenly and saluted. 'But I was in the British Army: C Company, 1st Battalion of the Staffordshire Regiment.' Saluting for a second time, he stamped a foot. 'Saw action in the Gulf.' He fell quiet then. Looked to be deep in thought and lowered himself onto his chair. There were tears in his eyes. 'Not all of us came home,' he said with a faltering voice.

Jenkins gave him time. Found a tissue and offered it.

'I know you're both thinking I don't look like a soldier. But looks can be deceiving,' he said, brandishing a pair of fists, southpaw fashion. 'Regimental boxing champion, I was. And fully trained in hand-to-hand combat.'

Jenkins had no idea how true that might be. Unlikely, was her best guess. 'How come you're living on the streets now?'

Itchy looked sad again. 'Damn politicians send us off to war and sell our jobs while we're away. Snakes – the lot of them.'

'What was it you did when you left the military?' Ginge asked.

'I was a steelworker in Port Talbot.'

'Hard job that.'

'It was good honest graft. I loved every minute of it.'

'But they let you go?'

'Last in, first out.' Itchy took a sharp intake of breath. 'Job, house, and wife. Lost them in that order,' he said. 'Fourteen months start to finish.'

Jenkins shook her head. 'Where do you stay now?'

'Under one of the container units down the docks.' Itchy forced a smile. 'It's not as bad as it sounds. Keeps the rain off, anyways. But a bit cold in the winter.'

Jenkins looked away, worried she might cry if their eyes met for longer than a few seconds. When she'd composed herself, she said: 'I'm not having that. Once we're done here, I'll be making some phone calls to the Veteran's Welfare Service to see what they can offer you.'

'You'd do that for me?'

'You bet I will.'

Itchy puffed his chest and grinned at Ginge. 'Don't you be letting this one get away. She'd make a great wife.'

Chapter 37

Once she'd stopped laughing, Jenkins pressed the red [Rec] button on the DIR device and waited for the long beep to silence itself. 'Okay Mr Rash, let's make a start on why we're here.'

'Itchy,' he corrected, and held the paper cup out in front of him. 'Can I get another one of these before we do? And more sugar this time.'

Once the coffee arrived, Jenkins continued. 'What if we call you Charles? That's much nicer, don't you think?'

'Charlie's better.'

'Charlie it is, then.'

'I'm gasping for a smoke.' Itchy hunched his shoulders. 'Any chance of a couple of those as well?'

'Not allowed, I'm afraid.'

'Who'll know? There's only the three of us in here.' He winked and tapped his pimpled blue nose. 'I won't tell if you don't.'

Jenkins pointed to the camera overhead. Then at the window in the far wall. 'You wouldn't want me and Owain here to get into trouble with our boss, would you?'

'Suppose not. You've been good to me so far.'

Jenkins put her elbows on the edge of the table and rested her chin on closed hands. 'I want to ask about the phone you were found with.'

'It's mine.' The claim was so confident, it was almost believable.

'We know it's registered to someone else,' Jenkins said. 'A murder victim.'

'I found it in the graveyard next to the hospital.' The explanation was delivered faster than the previous ownership comment.

'That's better.'

'Can I keep it?' Itchy asked. 'They won't be needing it now they're dead, will they?'

'No can do, Charlie. Tell us what you saw that night.'

'I went to buy me a fix.' Itchy scratched his side like a flea-ridden dog and looked suddenly worried. 'You're not going to nick me for that, are you?'

'On what evidence?' Jenkins asked.

Itchy relaxed enough to shift his attention to the opposite armpit. 'Minding my own business was all I was doing. I weren't there damaging nothing.'

'Did you see or hear anything odd?'

'*Felt*, more like.' Itchy put a finger to a nick in the skin on his forehead. 'Landed right there, it did.'

'The phone?'

'Aye. Heavy bugger it was too.'

'Did you see who threw it?'

'Course I did. He scared the shit out of me, hanging on those railings, moaning like a zombie. Next thing I knew, he was down on the floor mumbling away to himself.'

'What did he say, Charlie? Did he give you a name?'

'Kept repeating the word, *doctor*. Nothing else. Just that.'

'Why didn't you call for an ambulance?'

Itchy looked everywhere except straight ahead. 'I've been on the streets long enough to know you don't get involved in such things. Besides, he was a goner. I could tell as soon as I set eyes on him. Too much blood.'

'You took the phone and ran?' Ginge said.

Itchy folded his arms. 'I'm not proud of it, son.'

'Did you see anybody else?' Jenkins asked. 'Anyone at all?'

Itchy pointed to his right. 'Just a car driving in *that* direction.'

Ginge got his bearings. 'You mean away from the Maindy Barracks?'

'Aye, but I don't know the name of the road.'

Jenkins flipped a page in her pocketbook. 'I don't suppose you got a look at the number plate?'

LIAM HANSON

Another scratch. This time somewhere south of the waistline.
'Nope. But I knows it was a silver Volvo.'

Chapter 38

Lowri stared into another handful of wet tissues. 'I needed the money. How else was I supposed to keep my car on the road?'

Reece got more comfortable in his chair. 'What is it you drive?'

'A Volkswagen Polo.'

'Colour?'

'Navy blue. You're not going to tell them at the hospital, are you?'

'They're the least of your worries,' Reece said.

'But I've seen them strike nurses off the register for doing what I did.'

'And what *did* you do?' Morgan asked.

'Phoned a sickie, then worked the night shift for an agency somewhere else.' Lowri dabbed her nose and sniffed. 'I'm not the only one who does it. Loads of nurses do. It's the only way for most of us to make ends meet.'

'Let's get this straight, so I understand,' Reece said. 'You were supposed to work the night—'

'Day shift,' Lowri corrected. 'That way, you're fresh enough to do the night.'

'And you get paid for both shifts, presumably? Sick leave from your employer, and enhanced rates from the agency?'

'My car failed its MOT, Friday of last week.' Lowri looked to the ceiling and threw her head back in resignation. 'One hundred and sixty quid to fix the brakes. Another fifty or so to get the thing retested.' She closed her eyes. 'Where am I supposed to find that sort of money halfway through the month?'

'You moonlighted.'

'The agency shift paid almost exactly what I needed. It was a no-brainer.'

'Couldn't anyone in the house help you out until payday?'

'There's five of us living there for good reason,' Lowri said, blowing her nose. 'We're all young and broke. Except for Harlan, that is. His parents are worth a fortune.'

'So why not ask him?'

'If it had been Poppy needing help, then yeah, I'm sure he'd have been only too keen.'

'But not you?'

'He and I didn't have the same type of relationship, if you catch my drift?'

'The two of you didn't get on?'

'He wasn't my type. There was something about him I didn't like.'

'Unlike Jordan.' Morgan had her pen and was doodling again. She'd drawn a syringe and needle, complete with a tiny bleb of fluid at the needle's tip. 'I'm told he's more your thing?'

Lowri scowled. 'Let me guess. You've been talking to Zoe.'

Chapter 39

Reece counted eight people present, including himself. Cooper and Vera Miller were the dead man's parents. Cable and Harris, he already knew. He vaguely recognised the pair of family liaison officers—FLOs—who went everywhere together like conjoined twins. And then there was a suited-and-booted man sitting in front of a file containing paperwork. A lawyer was Reece's best guess. Deputy Chief of Mission at the American Embassy, he was told when he asked.

Reece helped himself to coffee before joining them at an over-polished table. 'Condolences for your loss,' he said, taking a seat.

Vera Miller didn't wait for him to get comfortable. 'What are you doing to find our son's killer?' The accent was Midland American English. A couple of hours south of Lake Erie.

Reece put his cup to rest on a sparkling glass coaster and thought it nice that the Assistant Chief Constable had made such an effort in welcoming the oversees guests. Perhaps there'd be a Welsh choir laid on in the foyer downstairs. A visit to the local Heritage Park thrown in for good measure. 'It's not easy when something like this happens in another country.'

'And what would *you* know of such things?' Vera Miller asked.

There was no reason not to tell her, Reece decided. 'My wife was murdered in Rome just over eighteen months ago. On our honeymoon. Stabbed and left to die on the road like your son.' He ignored Harris's fiery glare. 'That makes me the only person in this room who knows exactly what you and your husband are going through.'

Cooper Miller squeezed his wife's forearm. 'Condolences then to you also, Chief Inspector.'

'The Italians are no closer to catching Anwen's killer than they were on the day she died,' Reece said. 'No arrests. No leads. Nothing at all.'

'And that's supposed to make us feel better?'

Harris shifted in his chair, preparing to say something.

'Not everyone likes me,' Reece said before the ACC could spout his usual drivel. 'Some might say I'm unconventional in my approach to policing.' When he checked, Cable was whispering to herself, possibly uttering a prayer. 'I'll catch your son's killer. You have my word on that.' He finished the dregs of his coffee and got up. 'All I'll ask is that you leave me and my team to do our jobs unhindered.'

Chapter 40

Reece sat alone at the table in the press room, watching journalists circle like vultures eyeing up roadkill. Their crews were busy working through a battery of lighting measurements and sound checks before things got going. There were several television cameras, and miles of cabling running in all directions.

A few of the reporters stood preening themselves in anything that offered a half-decent reflection. Rehearsing scripts and anchor-lines while they were at it. Reece wondered how they could do that without having any clue as to what the police were about to say. He did nothing to correct them.

There were brightly coloured microphones set out along the table in front of him. Each belonging to one of several news channels in attendance. It looked to him more like the prep for a world sporting event than it did a call for potential witnesses to a particularly violent crime.

He unscrewed the lid from a bottle of sparkling water and checked the folded name-cards set out either side of his own. The ACC was to sit on his right. Sod that for a game of soldiers. He leaned over and moved Harris up two places. He left Cable where she was to his immediate left. Suited-and-Booted was already placed at the far end of the table. There was no reason to change that.

Chief Superintendent Cable waved from a doorway, out of sight of most people in the room. She was calling for him to join the rest of them outside. He turned his chair away from her and took another swig of water.

When at last they got started, Cable did the housekeeping and introductions. Reece was to outline what was known of Harlan Miller's murder and appeal to the listening public for information. Cooper Miller would then read a tribute to his son. There would be no questions taken on this occasion.

'Someone must have seen or heard something,' Reece said, finishing his bit. 'Or maybe you know of somebody in the area who drives a silver Volvo car? We're asking that you—'

'Ten-thousand pounds!' someone shouted from his left. 'Help us secure a conviction against our son's killer and the money is yours in cash.' It was Cooper Miller. Suited-and-Booted was egging him on.

Reece leaned out of line and shook his head enough for both men to notice. 'Stop that.'

Miller looked for the nearest active television camera, reached into his jacket pocket, and tossed five white envelopes onto the desk in front of him. 'There's two-thousand pounds in each,' he said, tapping the nearest. 'And plenty more where that came from.'

'Make him put the money away,' Reece told Cable. 'We didn't agree to this.'

Cable whispered something to the American, who responded by raising an envelope to the camera. 'Ten thousand pounds. All yours for information leading to an arrest and conviction.'

Chapter 41

'What the hell do you think you were doing out there?' Reece refused to take a seat and was prowling all four walls of the meeting room. 'We'll have switchboard inundated with nothing but crank callers looking to win a jackpot.' He glared at Cooper Miller. 'I told you to leave things to me. It's not a Saturday night game show we're playing.' He shifted his attention to Suited-and-Booted. 'Does this have anything to do with you?'

The man squared up to him. 'Where I come from, Detective—'

'You can do what the hell you want,' Reece said, interrupting. 'But you're not at home now—you're in my city—where I know best.'

'Says you.' The man snorted before looking away.

'This kind of approach doesn't work,' Reece told Cooper Miller. He made an effort to calm himself. The man had just lost a son, after all. 'People who genuinely want to help, will. Those who are purely after the money will make up any old bullshit in the hope they'll get lucky.' He sighed. 'But we're obligated to follow up those leads, knowing fully well that we're wasting our time and resources.'

Miller stopped arguing and hugged a wife who was in floods of tears and unable to speak.

Suited-and-Booted—or Logan Johnson Jr III, to use a name that on first hearing it, left Reece wondering if the man was named after an aircraft carrier—was on his feet again. This time, rounding the table to comfort the grieving parents. 'What lines of enquiry are you following?' His question was directed at ACC Harris and not Reece.

Reece listened to Harris flounder. When he could take no more of the man's babbling, he said: 'There's reason to believe your son's death is connected to that of a young woman he shared a house with.'

Cooper Miller straightened. 'You've got two murders on your hands?'

Reece nodded. 'That's right.'

'And no suspects to date?'

Reece shook his head.

Miller raised both arms in the air. 'Well, Jesus *H.* Christ.'

Reece stormed through the incident room like he was looking for someone to punch. 'Give me good news, someone.' He slammed the door to his office and dropped into the squeaky swivel-chair. 'Logan Johnson Jr III. For fuck's sake,' he muttered to himself.

There was a knock at the door, Ginge loitering on the other side of it, checking the area behind him repeatedly.

'What?' Reece shouted through the glass. 'Open the bloody thing,' he said, pointing.

'It's about the CPS, boss.'

Reece put a pair of clenched fists on the desk in front of him. 'I only want good news, remember?'

Ginge looked as though he might go away and leave it until there were more people around.

'Tell me.'

The newbie cleared his throat. 'The CPS, boss.'

Reece's fists tightened. 'We've done that bit already.'

Ginge edged his way inside the office and checked over his shoulder twice more before coming to a full stop.

'They won't let us charge him, will they?' Reece said, picking up on the telltale signs.

Ginge looked relieved he hadn't needed to speak the words himself. 'No, boss.'

In truth, the news didn't overly upset Reece. Jordan Patterson might still turn out to be their killer—aided by Lowri, the anaesthetic nurse—but the detective was already thinking he should be looking elsewhere.

'What shall I do with them both?' Ginge asked.

'Go find Ffion,' Reece said. 'Have her show you how to get them out of here.'

Chapter 42

Reece hesitated outside the Cathedral Road offices of Dr Miranda Beven. It was late afternoon and large spots of rain were pebble-dashing the pavement a shade of battleship grey. He leaned beneath the overhang of the cast-iron guttering, sheltering while waiting for the click of the door and an invitation to enter. When he reached for the bell-press a second time, the door opened without warning. 'Fancy seeing you here,' he said, stepping aside to let Dr Richard Wellman exit.

Wellman replied with little more than a cursory nod and hurried through the small roadside garden without so much as a backward glance.

'Doctor, one minute please.' Reece followed him down the path, ignoring the onslaught of a heavier shower. 'Harlan Miller. Does his name mean anything to you?'

Wellman slowed, but didn't fully stop. 'Should it?'

Reece caught up and walked alongside. 'He was a medical student on an anaesthetic placement. That would put him in your department, wouldn't it?'

'Together with a hundred others during the course of any academic year.' Wellman raised his hands in defeat. 'I can't be expected to remember them all.' He sped up again and was soon through the gate.

Reece returned to the front door and entered a square hallway, shaking himself like a wet mongrel.

The office door at the top of the carpeted stairs was ajar. He knocked and went through when invited. 'I'm a touch early,' he said, waiting on a large rug that marked the centre of the room.

'Some might say late. Or absent,' Beven replied without looking at him. 'For the sessions you failed to attend,' she added for clarity.

'Snow.' Reece got rid of his coat and helped himself to a chair. Getting comfortable, he straightened the sleeves of his suit jacket. 'Brecon gets a lot of it.' He nodded. 'Always around this time of year.'

Beven crossed the room and handed him a coffee. 'And there's me thinking you were avoiding me.'

'Snow. Definitely.'

She took a seat opposite and waited for him to return his spoon to the saucer. 'Never mind. You're here now.'

Reece turned side-on to the door. 'The man who just left: is he one of your clients?'

'You know I can't possibly tell you that.'

'I didn't ask why he was here.'

'My lips are sealed,' Beven said, drawing an imaginary zipper across her mouth.

'He could have been seeing his accountant in the office next door, I suppose?'

'Nice try. I'm saying nothing, Chief Inspector.'

Reece leaned to place his cup and saucer on a low table that was equidistant between both their armchairs. 'You've had your hair done.'

'Chief Inspector.'

He winked. 'It was a compliment.'

'We're still doing this,' she told him.

He checked his watch and let out a loud sigh. 'Get on with it, then. I can't stay long.'

'What went through your mind when you first entered the basement of the Midnight Club?' Beven asked.

The memory made Reece squirm in his chair. He caught himself rubbing his shoulder and stopped when he realised what he was doing. 'I didn't know who or what I'd find there.'

'What were you most in fear of finding?'

'Casualties, obviously.'

'DS Jenkins, in particular?'

'Me not being at work at the time meant she'd taken up most of the slack in the department.'

'But there was another senior officer available to her.' Beven read from an open file on her lap. 'A DI Adams.'

'A complete dipstick. And the main reason I told Elan she should go it alone.'

'How would you have felt had that advice resulted in more serious injuries to DS Jenkins?'

'Do I have to answer that?'

Beven told him he didn't. 'What *did* you find in the basement?'

'Denny Cartwright was already dead. Shot in the chest by Belle Gillighan. She'd caught him throttling Jenkins and took him out straight away.'

'And how was it meeting Belle again after all these years?'

Reece gave the question due consideration before answering. 'I don't know. There wasn't time for a catch up, if that's what you mean?'

'Did you still feel guilty for failing to convict her attacker all those years ago?'

'She was pointing a gun at me. All I could think about was what might happen next.'

'But you knew Belle wanted closure. That she was there to serve her own form of justice.'

'Believe me, there's nothing I wanted more than to watch her blow that bastard's brains all over the back wall.'

'And yet you threw yourself in front of him. Took the bullet and saved the life of the man you despise.'

Reece sat quietly staring into space.

'You knew exactly what you were doing,' Beven said. 'And it wasn't for Billy Creed's benefit.'

Reece clawed at the leather arms of the chair. 'I don't know what it is you're suggesting?'

'I think you do, Chief Inspector. You saw a quick way out of this hell you're in and took it.'

Chapter 43

Richard Wellman pressed himself against the damp wall of the local park, hidden the whole time by the rear section of a concrete bus shelter. The recent rain shower had done nothing to wash away the fusion of human and cat pee. The wind lifted an empty crisp packet from an overfilled bin and carried it down an otherwise deserted street.

The wet pavement glowed orange under the light thrown by the overhead street lamp. Rain turned to drizzle, suspended in the night air like strands of silver thread.

A car went past. Just the one at such a late hour, its red taillights following the curve of the road before disappearing from sight. With the car gone, all was deathly quiet again. There wasn't a soul to disturb him, except for the tabby cat pacing high on the wall above. He tossed a small stone at it. Another when the first one missed by a fair distance.

The stage was set. The leading lady unwittingly approaching what was soon to be her worst nightmare. She didn't see him when she went by. Nor did she hear the hushed release of excitement from his lips.

He let her get a good ten to fifteen metres ahead before stepping out of the shadows to follow in the same direction, the tools of his trade hanging from his shoulder in a small canvass rucksack.

He caught a waft of cheap perfume on the night air and turned his nose up at it. This particular victim didn't fit the usual profile. Not in a million years could she compete with the likes of Poppy Jones. Or Smiler, the student nurse. But she was on the list nonetheless, and for reasons of her own doing.

The woman turned into a narrow street flanked on both sides by parked cars and rubbish bins. Wellman ducked when she stole a brief look over her shoulder, losing his footing on a broken slab of kerbstone. He swung an arm, pirouetting in a violent attempt to stay upright, a wayward fist catching the wing mirror of a parked van.

He was thankful the impact hadn't set off the vehicle's anti-theft alarm. Licking his bleeding knuckles, he reached into his jacket pocket with the other hand and slid on a pair of surgical gloves.

He wouldn't be leaving DNA at the crime scene. Wouldn't be ruining things before he'd properly got started. He'd read extensively on the subject. Knew exactly what CSIs looked for, and how they found it.

The woman turned her head towards him with a swish of black-dyed hair, self-consciously pulling at the hem of her coat. He could hear her breathing heavily with the effort required to increase the shortening distance between them. That's what older women did when pushed hard. Panted like knackered dogs on their last legs. Such a stark contrast to his first two victims.

Poppy had such beauty in life. He'd lain with the young midwife when it came time for her to leave this world. Stared into her eyes so she knew she wasn't alone at the end. She'd stared back, and had she been able, would have begged and screamed for more of his air. He'd savoured the silence as she slipped away, the pulse in her swan-like neck shifting from racing to absent in only a few short minutes.

Coco the Clown tottered ahead of him on heels that were too tall. Wearing a dress and coat that were far too short. And the makeup. The *fucking* makeup!

He'd caught her talking about him again that day. She was the reason Smiler hadn't returned after her lunch break. Coco must have told them to remove the girl for her own safety. That meant other people knew. Everyone was at it. Spreading gossip like wildfire.

Coco stopped on a doorstep three or four houses away from where he was, rummaging frantically through a gold-coloured handbag held close to the soft swell of her belly. He knew there was no point in her knocking on the door. She'd earlier informed the entire operating theatre team that her husband was working abroad.

He was a long-distance lorry driver and wouldn't be home until the next day. The couple had no children. The opportunity had presented itself thus.

Coco was panicking. Looking up. Looking down. Not looking at Wellman as she fumbled with the key. He could tell she was unable to steady her hand anywhere near enough to unlock the door.

'Sandra.' He chose not to use her pet name, believing she might consider that rude. 'Is everything all right?'

'Dr Wellman.' The woman raised her head and peered into the darkness, her facial features looking as though they'd been painted onto a grotesque death mask. Apt under the current circumstances. 'Hell's bells. I thought that prowler-fella was following me.' She laughed almost hysterically once she got going and cleared a smoker's throat with a series of hearty coughs.

'Just me, I'm afraid,' Wellman said, drawn to smudges of mascara she'd somehow wiped like war paint across both cheeks. A nervous silence hung in the air after that. Followed by the offer of a hot drink. 'I suppose a coffee would warm me up while I wait for my taxi,' he said, not wanting to miss a gifted opportunity.

This was turning out to be far simpler than he could ever have imagined.

Chapter 44

The key slid easily into the lock; the door opening to suggest a home-made curry had been on the menu earlier that evening. 'You'll have to excuse the mess,' Coco said, leading the way inside. 'I'm a very untidy person.'

That didn't surprise him at all. 'Our lives are so busy these days.'

'You're telling me.' She tossed her wet coat over the back of the sofa. When it slid to the floor, she left it where it was and went through to a kitchen that looked as though a school cookery class had only just finished in there. Pots, pans, and jars of ingredients covered most of the horizontal surfaces. 'Work, cook, clean. It never stops,' she said, making space for two mugs and a carton of milk. 'I bet you've got yourself a nice young 'un to do it for you, eh?'

Wellman's eyes narrowed, his gloved hands forming tight fists in his pockets. *What is she suggesting?* He laughed awkwardly in an attempt to lighten an atmosphere that was on the verge of turning as sour as the milk smelled. 'No such luxury, I'm afraid.'

'And Mrs Wellman? A kept woman, I bet?'

She's trying to trick you. 'I'm not married, and never have been.'

Coco reached to squeeze his biceps. 'A big strong man like you would have had plenty of opportunities, I'll bet?'

He reeled at the smell of cigarettes and alcohol on her breath, and punched her square in the face. The ferocity of the blow lifted her clean off her feet. She stumbled backwards with her arms flailing behind her as she sought something of substance to grab hold of. They glanced against the side of a chair, doing nothing to cushion her fall onto the tiled floor. Her left hand folded beneath the weight of her body, a loud snapping sound confirming a broken wrist.

This wasn't supposed to happen. The woman had an obvious depressed fracture of the cheekbone and a hand that stuck out of her arm like the bottom end of a golf club. He threw his rucksack against the door of a kitchen cabinet. Then set about kicking it around the kitchen. There was a knife on the worktop. Discarded layers of onion and mushrooms piled alongside it.

Dropping on top of her, he straddled her chest while sorting through the contents of his bag. The bottle was broken – Sevoflurane seeping through the material, filling the kitchen with a sweet and solvently smell. Hooking the collar of his jumper over his nose, he took the pre-filled syringe of Suxamethonium Chloride and jabbed it straight into Coco's shoulder. She stirred. Tried to sit up, but couldn't under the pressure of his weight.

He watched the second hand make its way around the face of a plastic clock, counting minutes that went by woefully slowly. 'Shut up,' he said when she tried to speak, and forced the pungent bag against her face. She began to fasciculate – the telltale sign that the drug had locked on to the correct neuro-muscular receptors. 'Do you know what I call you?' he asked, hovering over her.

She didn't answer.

Couldn't answer.

All opportunities to make the woman's death look innocent were now gone. He twisted and reached for the knife on the counter. 'That disgusting make-up,' he said, using the sharp blade to spread mascara across her fractured cheek. He ran the pointed tip of it over her nose, lips, chin, then throat. He tore open her blouse and slid the cutting edge beneath the shoulder strap of her bra. 'It makes you look like the whore you are.'

Chapter 45

It was a little after 4am, and Reece had given up all hope of sleep. Wandering the dark living room downstairs, he tried to make sense of the current case under investigation. The two murders were in some way linked. They had to be. Even though the methods used to kill Harlan Miller and Poppy Jones were very much different.

He pulled a sweatshirt over his head and went through to the kitchen to flick the manual override switch for the central heating system. The house would be toasty-warm by the time he got back for a well-earned shower.

Had Lowri and Jordan Patterson acted together? Jordan stabbing Miller. Lowri injecting Poppy with the paralysing agent. It was an idea that could still go somewhere and he hadn't yet fully discounted it.

He pulled the front door closed and dragged a woollen hat over his ears. Then started the timer on his sports watch. The first few breaths of cold air penetrated his airways like icy fingers poking deep into his lungs. His teeth ached when he mouth-breathed. He closed it and used his nose instead, settling into his rhythm, moving with a graceful motion that belied his fifty-something years.

On the roads, hills, and mountains was a peace he experienced nowhere else. He loved it there. Glancing left, he crossed the wide expanse of highway, speeding up as the first of the early morning commuters rounded the bend some twenty or so metres away.

Had he really tried to get himself killed at the Midnight Club? That's what the shrink had him close to admitting in a moment of weakness. She'd pushed him into a corner until he was on the verge of saying almost anything just to be let out of her office. He'd been trying to preserve life when he threw himself in front of the bullet meant for Billy Creed.

That's what he'd told himself.

Dr Beven had tried putting words in his mouth. Was probably in cahoots with the chief super and ACC Harris. Deciding it was far too early in the morning to be delving into the darkness of his messed-up mind, he went back to thinking about the case.

Dr Richard Wellman: something didn't sit right there. Reece had learned early in his career how to read people. How to push, prod, and test them – observing their reaction to the pressure he put them under.

Emotionless was the adjective that sprang to mind when picturing Wellman. And a man of few words, certainly.

Reece squeezed through a narrow gap in the rusted railings, setting off across a frost-covered field that crunched underfoot. Even in the weak dawn lighting, he could make out the imposing silhouette of Llandaff Cathedral rising high above the surrounding oaks.

Built in the twelfth century, on the site of an earlier church, the cathedral had been extensively damaged during Owain Glyndwr's rebellion. Again, when Parliamentarian troops had overrun it during the English Civil War. Then, in circa 1703, the devastating effects of an extratropical cyclone had almost resulted in the building being taken down and abandoned.

Positioning himself on the dead-ball line of the rugby field, Reece did ten sprints to the twenty-two metre markings, with a slow jog back on each length. He bent at the waist when done, breathing heavily, listening to the traffic get busier on the adjacent road.

After two full circuits of the field's outer perimeter, he was on his way home, thoughts of Dr Richard Wellman still niggling him.

Chapter 46

Reece had wondered what his first visit to the Midnight Club—post shooting—would be like. As he pulled up in the alleyway behind it, he found himself struggling to recollect events with any clarity. He vaguely remembered standing outside, talking to the Polish cleaner, when the first shot sounded from somewhere deep within the building. He'd gone running in unarmed with Ffion Morgan calling for him to wait until backup arrived.

Had there been a second shot? He couldn't remember, but knew he'd followed the sounds of voices coming from the basement.

The scene when he got there had shocked him. He didn't mind admitting it. Denny Cartwright was lying dead against the bars of a cage used to parade half-naked women. Jenkins was hunched on all fours in front of the big-man, red welts on her neck and gasping for breath.

Belle Gillighan was standing somewhere off to one side of everyone, waving a handgun and shouting at anything that moved.

Reece pressed the buzzer next to the security camera. It had been fixed since his previous visit. He held it down for a full ten seconds.

'Copper's making a noise,' Creed said through the intercom.

'Open the door, Billy.'

'Copper shouldn't be here.'

Reece pressed again. Three sharp bursts.

'My lawyer's drawing up papers to have you directing traffic.'

'If I come back, it'll be with a warrant,' Reece promised. The door clicked open a moment later. He remembered the smell of cheap booze and disinfectant. There had been a blonde woman lying flat on her back on the day of the shooting. Near the bar. Mumbling incoherently. Strange how he'd forgotten her until now. She'd been the one to send him down to the basement. He couldn't remember her name. Someone outside would have taken it for the record.

There was a metal staircase directly ahead of him, rising from behind the DJ's station, up to a mezzanine level and Billy Creed's office. Standing at the top of the stairs was a man who dwarfed him. A man whose lower jaw looked like it might have been fashioned from the same steelwork as the surroundings. 'Step aside,' Reece said. Jimmy Chin shifted not more than an inch. Definitely not enough for the detective to get past. 'I said move.'

'Or what?'

'Chill, Jimmy.' Creed's voice came from somewhere within the office. 'Let Copper in. He's come to entertain us.'

Chin retreated another half-step only, both men practising their *I'm the bigger dog* stare as Reece pushed through.

The room smelled of cigar smoke and patchouli oil. Creed was lounging on a leather sofa opposite the door, his leg stretched out in front of him on a low stool. There was no one else there. 'Take a pew,' he said, offering a chair near the door.

Reece glanced over his shoulder.

Creed grinned. 'Jimmy won't hurt you. He's on a short leash today.'

Chin howled like a wolf, turning in circles, panting loudly.

'And that's the best replacement you could find for Denny Cartwright?' Reece jerked his head in the general direction of the stairs. 'You've been dragging the bottom of the pond this time, Billy.'

Creed's grin slipped away slowly. 'Don't underestimate him, Copper. Jimmy comes with a public health warning.'

'So does the pox,' Reece said, making sure Chin caught his every word. 'I see the security cameras are up and running again.' Creed's eyes narrowed a fraction. Others might not have noticed. Reece did. 'Who did you use this time? Couldn't have been the same bloke.' The eyes again. Guilty as sin.

'Denny took care of it.' Creed shrugged. 'Shame he's no longer with us. He'd have loved to help you.'

'You'll have bank statements and receipts for the work?'

'All done with cash from the safe.'

'Convenient.'

'It's the way I works,' the gangster said in local dialect. 'Why'd you come here today?' He patted the sofa all around him and dry-smoked a thick Cuban when he found it.

'Pete Hall.'

'We playing name-games now?' Creed caught Chin's attention. 'You next, Jimmy. Give us a name.'

'Idris Roberts.'

Reece tensed at the mention of his father-in-law.

'Does it still count if they're dead?' Chin asked with a smirk.

Creed struck a match and held it to the air, its orange flame dancing wildly in the draft coming from the open doorway. 'My turn. Let's do boy-girl.'

There was the sound of a scooter passing in the alleyway outside. Reece pulled at his collar. *You utter her name and I'll kill you both.* Swallowing hard, he fought to control his breathing. Creed was speaking, but he couldn't make out what was being said. He shook his head and blinked. Took a deep breath and rebooted his brain. He was in Billy Creed's office, covered in sweat, and wasn't sure how he'd got there. 'What did you say?'

'Gabby Logan.' Creed let out a throaty chuckle. 'Bet you've given her some thought – what with you being single all this time.'

'Pete Hall fixed your security system.' Reece said.

'Fucked it up, more like.' Creed peered through a cloud of clearing smoke. 'It worked better *before* that useless tosser got his paws on it.'

'Is that why you killed him?'

'Copper's poking his nose where it don't belong.'

'You look nervous, Billy. You got something to hide?'

'Copper knows nothing.'

Reece had the measure of the gangster. He stood and loomed over him. 'That's where you're wrong, Billy. Copper's going to put you away.'

Chapter 47

Creed was left to his nagging thoughts and a thrice-daily physiotherapy session for a ruined knee. He walked in straight lines along the dance floor, stopping to turn at either end of the room. He leaned on the cane and caught his breath. 'I wants the old lock-up in the docks cleared out,' he told Kyle Cartwright and his dreadlocked sidekick, Albino Ron. 'Make sure you torch the van some place out of the way.'

Denny's younger brother waited for Creed to stop grimacing. 'Expecting trouble?'

'Tying up loose ends. Copper's been sniffing about again. Can't help himself.' Creed pushed a finger beneath the Velcro strap of the knee brace when it bit into his skin. 'Give the place a good once-over before you're done. I wants nothing of ours left there.'

'Whatever you say, Billy.'

Creed shifted his weight and bit down on his lip, not yet satisfied with the position of the knee brace. 'There'll be someone along to collect the keys to the place in the morning. A posh ponce with a wad of cash. Make sure one of you is there to meet him.'

'You want him fucked up?' Cartwright asked.

Creed wrapped an arm around the younger man's shoulders, pulling him close. 'Just take his money, give him the keys, and let him go.'

Cartwright's cogs turned slowly, and even then, he didn't get it. 'You sure?'

Creed stepped away and gave him a playful slap across the back of the head. 'I'm tying up loose ends, Kyle. Just tying up loose ends.'

Chapter 48

Reece was driving through the narrow lane at the rear of the building when Jenkins called. He braked to a full stop and put the car in neutral gear.

'There's another dead nurse,' she told him. 'Killed at home last night.'

'As young as Poppy Jones?'

'Older this time.'

'And the MO?'

'Different.'

'How did she die?' he asked, when Jenkins was slow to elaborate.

'There's some facial trauma and signs of a struggle. But again, no obvious cause of death.'

Reece checked his watch. 'Give me the address. I'll be—'

'There's something else, boss. This woman has the word *WHORE* carved into the skin of her chest.'

Chapter 49

There was a white van, two patrol cars, and an ambulance waiting outside a row of terraced houses when Reece arrived. He parked on the opposite side of the road and took a full briefing from Jenkins while donning the usual protective gear on the doorstep. 'Is the pathologist here yet?'

'On her way,' Jenkins said, leading him inside. 'Where have you been? It took me ages to get hold of you.'

'Billy Creed's. Don't look at me like that. I promised Pete Hall's wife I'd ask some questions.'

'And you promised the chief super you wouldn't.'

'Did I?' He shrugged. 'Must be one of those amnesia things the shrink keeps going on about.'

Jenkins had her arms folded. 'You *did* go back for a second session, then? And there's me thinking they'd have to drag you, kicking and screaming.'

'Who says they didn't?'

She followed him down the short hallway. 'You can't really believe that Creed killed the man just because the security system failed?'

'Creed lost Denny Cartwright and a knee in that shooting.' Reece came to a halt in the living room, twisting and turning to take in the full scene. 'He's killed people for a lot less than that.'

'I suppose.'

'Who's in the kitchen?' Reece stuck his head through the doorway to see for himself. 'Sioned, how are you doing?'

'Good. And you?' The crime scene manager stopped brushing the handles of two full mugs. 'Looks like the victim knew her attacker. Even made them a coffee.'

'Who found her?' Reece cast an eye over the dead body. Sandra Cole lay face up and in a somewhat awkward pose on the kitchen floor. Her legs were bent at the knees. Her body drawn slightly over to her left, causing the hip on the opposite side to be raised by an inch or so off the floor tiles. He stared at the smudged make-up. The broken wrist. Then the chest carving. The blade had ripped through the skin, rather than slice its way, tearing a nipple and leaving ragged edges of raw flesh in its wake.

'The husband.' Jenkins said. 'Got back from Toulouse this morning to find her like this.'

'France. What was he doing there?'

'Picking up aircraft parts. It's his job.'

Reece couldn't see the man. 'Where is he?'

Jenkins moved for someone to get past. 'A few doors along the street with a neighbour. There's a uniform with him.'

'Someone's checking his alibi?'

'All done,' Jenkins said. 'His paperwork is dated and stamped for the journey back to the UK.'

Reece went further into the kitchen, noting the mess. 'No evidence of a break-in then?'

Sioned Williams shook her head. 'This one has all the signs of our victim letting her attacker in before the assault began.'

'That makes it unlikely to be our prowler,' one of the other CSIs said, coming in on the tail end of the conversation.

'Why do you say that?' Jenkins asked. 'Maybe he's moved up a notch.' She glanced at Reece. 'It's what they do, isn't it? Start with stalking or pinching knickers off clotheslines. Next, they'll enter a property and have a look around when the owner is out. Take a personal trophy. And if they're not caught, it's only a matter of time before they make physical contact – with escalating levels of violence.'

'True,' Reece said. 'But it's also sexually motivated in most instances. Poppy wasn't interfered with. We know that for sure.'

Williams looked up from what she was doing. 'And apart from the blouse and bra being torn open, this woman's clothing is intact.'

'Sex isn't his primary motivation,' Jenkins said. 'He's not ready for that sort of thing yet.'

Reece didn't like the sound of that. *'Yet?'*

Jenkins got out of someone else's way. 'I don't think he'll be able to help himself once he's more established.'

'You sound like an expert on the subject.' They all turned when Cara Frost entered the kitchen.

Reece saw her wink at his DS. 'I want you to run the same tox screens you did on Poppy Jones,' he said, before the pathologist had a chance to get anything of a handover.

'Are you sure about that?' Frost tilted her head to read the engraving on Sandra Cole's chest. 'First appearances suggest a different killer.'

'I want them run regardless,' Reece said, and proceeded to tell Frost what they knew so far.

'I'll get it done once we have her back at the mortuary. Did that knife do this?' Frost pointed to one that was bagged and labelled on the kitchen counter.

Williams handed it to her. 'There's skin and fat tissue on the serrated edge. And plenty of fingerprints on the handle.'

CHAPTER 50

Reece found the victim's husband warming himself in front of a gas fire. The man looked tired, unshaven, and traumatised by events he neither understood or had any control over. 'I'm DCI Reece.' The tone was gentle and delivered by someone who knew first-hand what it was like to lose a spouse under similar circumstances. 'I'm very sorry for your loss, Mr Cole.' The man burst into tears almost immediately and searched for somewhere to sit. Reece took his elbow and walked him to the empty sofa.

A middle-aged woman appeared in the kitchen doorway carrying a tray of steaming mugs. 'Oh,' she said. 'Now there's two more of you.'

Jenkins told her that she and Reece were fine. 'Do you live here?'

The woman lowered the tray onto a glass table and nodded. 'I've been friends with Ian and Sandra for years.' She took a mug over to the man on the sofa, hovered there a while when he made no attempt to relieve her of it, and took it away again, shaking her head at the detectives.

'Had your wife mentioned anything recently about being followed home from work?' Reece asked.

Ian Cole lifted his head and wiped the back of a hand across his nose with a loud sniff. 'I saw what was carved on Sandra's chest. What kind of monster would do that to a person?'

'Had she been followed?' Reece pushed.

'Not that I'm aware. Did she say anything to you?' Cole asked the neighbour.

The woman couldn't remember such a thing coming up in conversation.

Reece lowered himself into an armchair and rested both hands on his knees. 'Can you think of anyone who might have wanted to harm your wife? Someone at work, especially?'

Ian Cole's face crumpled. 'You think somebody from the hospital could have done that to her?'

'It's only one line of enquiry,' Reece admitted.

'It's not true, you know – that rubbish on my wife's chest. Not true at all.'

Reece had no way to be sure, but knew the man had suffered enough. He kept it simple and nodded.

'What happens now?'

'We'll need to confirm the cause of death with a post-mortem examination.'

'Cut her open?' Ian Cole balled his fists. 'After everything she's been through?'

'It'll help us catch the killer,' Jenkins said.

Cole looked. 'When can I bury her?'

'Things are more complicated in a murder investigation. We'll do all we can to get Sandra back to you as soon as possible.'

Chapter 51

They'd stopped for pizza on the way back to the station, Reece wanting to organise his thoughts before letting the team escape home for the evening. 'I'll have anything except the one with pineapple,' he said, tossing his jacket onto the desk in his office. 'Which one of you heathens ordered it anyway?' he asked, cocking his nose up at the unopened box.

No one admitted responsibility for such a dirty deed.

Jenkins was having a hard time working her way through the contents of the boxes with nothing sharper than a plastic knife. 'Does anyone mind if I use my fingers to tear them apart? We'll be here all night otherwise.'

'Fine by me,' Reece said, loosening his tie. 'Just make sure I don't get pineapple on mine.'

Jenkins stopped what she was doing and pointed the knife in warning. 'I heard you the first twenty times.'

Ginge was loitering like a family dog waiting for table scraps. 'I don't mind what I have. I'm starving.'

'Give *him* the pineapple,' Reece called from the other side of the room.

'He's messing with you,' Jenkins said in response to the newbie's reaction. 'Help yourself to whatever you want.'

Ginge did, and lots of it. 'Thanks for this, boss. Are you sure you don't want us to chip in?'

Reece waved from the other side of the room and let his team tuck in first.

Ginge poked his tongue out and arched his head backwards as the pizza slice bent towards him. He used a finger to support the end of it. 'This is stonking.'

'*Look!*' Reece said once the feeding-frenzy had finished and everyone moved out of the way. 'Bloody pineapple is all that's left.'

'Pick the bits off,' Jenkins told him. 'The other stuff is ham.'

Ginge offered a half-eaten slice of meat feast.

Reece circled the table. 'Any garlic bread left?'

The newbie searched through the boxes. 'Just the crusts, by the looks of things.' He laughed. 'You should have got stuck in like the rest of —' He left it there when he saw the look on the DCI's face.

Reece piled bits of pineapple on the tabletop and searched for somewhere to wipe his fingers. 'Anything new to report while we were out?'

'Got another sighting of the silver Volvo on the night Harlan Miller was killed,' Ginge told him. 'A guy walking his dog. He wouldn't leave his name and wasn't interested in the money.'

'Did he get the number plate?'

'Part of it.' Ginge used a paper-clip as an improvised toothpick. 'And only because it reminded him of his late wife, Molly. M followed by some numbers he couldn't recall. OLL was the last bit.' Ginge went over to his desk and came back with a notepad. 'I did some digging around with the DVLA and the best match we could come up with was this lady.' He read the name directly off the page: 'Molly Gantry.' Ginge closed the pad. 'She's local and appears on the voting roll. I tried ringing her but got no answer.'

'I want you and Ffion to go over there first thing in the morning,' Reece said. 'See what this Gantry woman has to say for herself. And find out if anyone else has access to that car – like a neighbour or other family member.'

'I haven't seen Ffion all afternoon,' Ginge replied. 'I assumed she was with the two of you.'

Reece frowned at Jenkins. 'Do you know where she is?'

'Shall I give her a ring?'

'It can wait until we're finished here,' he said.

Jenkins lowered her phone without dialling. 'She wasn't herself this morning, come to think of it. You know what she's like most days—doesn't come up for air—but today, I could barely get a word out of her.'

'She snapped at *me* once or twice,' Ginge said. 'I thought it must have been her time of the month.'

'Oi!' Jenkins threw a short length of pizza crust at him. 'Cut it out.'

Chapter 52

"I'VE GOT BREAST CANCER." Those were not the words Jenkins expected to hear when she called Morgan after the briefing. *"I had myself a bit of a meltdown and couldn't talk to Ginge about it."*

That wasn't the type of conversation you had on the phone. Not with a friend. Not with anyone. So she went straight round there on the way home to find out more.

They'd hugged and cried on the doorstep. Again, when they moved silently through to the living room. Josh was there too—Morgan's boyfriend—on the sofa opposite the television, red-eyed and puffy-faced. He said hello, but little more than that.

'What happened?' Jenkins asked. 'How do you know?'

Morgan joined Josh and squeezed his hand. 'I found a lump just over a week ago. At first, I thought it was related to my cycle and decided to keep an eye on it.'

Not wanting to sit any great distance from the couple, Jenkins rested on her knees in front of the sofa.

'I checked it every day. A dozen or more times.' Morgan made a poor attempt at a laugh. 'But it was still there, and didn't feel like any of the usual lumps or tenderness you might get during the month.'

'That's when I made her go and see about it,' Josh said. 'It's what they tell you to do, isn't it? Don't delay with these things.'

'Absolutely.' Jenkins took Morgan's hand in hers and found herself tapping it gently. She stopped, but didn't let go. 'You went to see a doctor?'

'I made a private appointment for lunchtime today.' Morgan looked suddenly embarrassed. 'We're lucky Josh's job pays well.'

'Don't apologise,' Jenkins said. 'It's the way I'd go, if I had the money.'

Morgan nodded. 'Get down there, I thought. In and out and then back to work in time to help Ginge sort through all those calls we've been getting.' She started crying again and took a while to compose herself. 'But I could tell the second the doctor put her hand on it. The look on her face. The way she went back to it and examined it again and again. I knew, Jenks. I knew.'

Jenkins willed herself to be strong. 'But they can't know for sure. Not without more tests, surely?'

'They've already taken bloods and booked me in for some scans and a biopsy.'

'When?'

'Tomorrow.' Morgan leaned forward on the sofa. 'Will you speak to the boss? I don't think I can.'

'Of course I will,' Jenkins said. 'Look, there's every chance the results of this will come back as an all-clear.'

Morgan cleared her nose in a paper hanky. 'My mother died of breast cancer when she was thirty-seven. I'm thirty-two. Too young to die.' She collapsed into Josh's arms.

Jenkins willed herself not to break down and sob, if only until she got out of the house and back to her car.

Chapter 53

Kyle Cartwright drove the van away from the lock-up in the Cardiff Docklands, turning on the roundabout to head north up Rover Way. Albino Ron was lounging in the passenger seat, watching porn on a mobile phone.

The usual suspects were out and about. All hoodies and baggy trousers. Some loitered on street corners. Others raced along the pavements on stolen shopping trolleys. More still wheel-spun cars that popped-and-banged from their oversized exhausts.

One onlooker threw a can of something into the middle of the road; a spray of white foam turning circles on the broken tarmac when the van's front wheel hit it.

None of it was anything out of the ordinary for Cartwright. This was home. He'd grown up here on a diet of fights, cider, and anything he could get his hands on for free. His big brother had been his only father figure, teaching him all he needed to survive in a dog-eat-dog environment. He thumped the horn, giving the onlookers a loud salute as he went racing by. Someone shouted his name. Others gestured *wanker*. All laughed hysterically. Including him.

It started raining just then. Slamming against the windscreen. Drumming on the panelled roof of the van. Cartwright took his foot off the accelerator, not only because he could no longer see where he was going, but mostly because he'd been struck by a thought. 'How the fuck do we get home after torching this thing?' He pulled over on the side of the road and twisted in his seat.

'Taxi,' Ron said, mesmerised by whatever was happening on his phone screen.

'You paying?' Cartwright asked over the sounds of deep-throated moaning. 'Put that thing away,' he said, knocking the handset out of Ron's hands and into the dark wheel-well.

'Shit, man. It was just coming to the best bit.' Ron pointed between his feet. 'You should see the way that bird—'

'Leave it!' Cartwright wound the window down and stuck his arm outside. 'We're going to get fucking soaked.'

Ron reached for his phone, his dirty-white dreads hanging like tentacles between his knees. The woman wasn't getting any quieter down there. 'I was only getting it to call Jimmy,' he said when

Cartwright looked set to punch him. 'He can send someone to pick us up.'

'Tell him we'll be waiting on that bit of waste ground behind the Water Works.' Cartwright sat back and listened to what little he could hear of the conversation. At least the on-screen blonde had been given some down time. The poor woman must have been knackered. 'What did he say?'

'He's sending one of Billy's cabs. An unmarked one. And it won't be coming anywhere near this place, so we'll have to leg it back down to the roundabout and wait when we're done.'

'Fucking hell.'

They went along the coastal road, passing industrial buildings that looked more suited to the set of a George Orwell movie. They were tall. Sprawling. Most having long lengths of ducting reaching across the wide expanses of concrete yard.

Cartwright turned the headlights off, slowing to what was little more than a crawl. There were no buildings further out, only chain-link fences and the sound of the sea breaking against the rocks. He drove the van onto an uneven area of waste ground. It leaned left, then right, shaking and banging.

Albino Ron got out and cut a new hole in the fence that was only just big enough to get the van through. No bother – fresh scratches in the paintwork wouldn't be an issue.

Cartwright put the window down and stared into the darkness. 'This is as good a place as any,' he said, opening the van door. He went round the back to empty the contents of a full jerrycan over the floor of the vehicle. Used a second can on the front seats and steering wheel. The door handles got a dousing of their own. He lit the lot with a single match. The heat was face-drying hot; the surrounding area lighting up like a bomb had gone off.

'Oi, you pair.' The call came from behind them and belonged to one of two men waving torch beams in their direction. 'Stay where you are.'

'Scarper!' Cartwright shouted, as one security guard ordered the other to get an extinguisher from the boot of their car.

Chapter 54

Dr Richard Wellman had followed the televised press briefings and local newspaper articles; reports of a silver Volvo in the area giving him a useful heads-up on what leads the police were now following.

And had it been sheer coincidence, or because of divine intervention, that he'd come across the advert for the lock-up when he'd needed one most? As a devout Christian, he'd settled on the second of the two possibilities. Using the mobile telephone number supplied with the advert, he'd spoken with a particularly unsavoury character. The man asked no questions regarding his plans for the place. Would deal in cash only. And insisted on there being no paperwork to exchange between them. Perfect. For a modest sum of money, and little effort on Wellman's part, the hiding place had become his own.

And that hadn't been his luckiest break of all. A card in the window of the local post office had, a few weeks earlier, trumped the newspaper advertisement by some distance.

He'd gone to buy a car—something roomy enough to transport victims should he need to—and came across his biological mother in the process. He knew who she was the moment she flashed a disingenuous smile with such well-practised ease. The way she made small talk and led him on for the purpose of getting what she wanted. Mother hadn't changed her ways, and never would.

How different things might have been had she opened her arms and hugged him. Taken him inside her home and apologised for tearing their young family apart all those years ago.

When he'd entered the Gantry woman's house—Mother's house—he'd told her who he was almost immediately. Couldn't help but blurt it out.

She hadn't listened, and turned him away again, unwilling to fulfil her maternal responsibilities even after the passing of so much time.

He cried. Wept in her presence and laid himself bare. He begged. Apologised. But for what, he didn't know.

His pleas fell on deaf ears. Still she refused to accept him as her own, insisting he was mistaken, despite having every opportunity to end the cruel charade and tell the truth.

Even when he closed his hands around the wrinkled skin of her neck and squeezed, the whore refused to repent.

He'd cleaned the house once the deed was done. Got rid of all traces of himself, claiming the Volvo for his own use. When he met one of the neighbours at the bottom of the drive, he'd told the man he'd been working abroad. That he'd already taken Mother to stay with him for what would be a few months at the very least.

The man had wished him well. Said he rarely, if ever, saw her and asked if they wanted the mail forwarded to any particular address. Wellman declined, saying he'd be back from time-to-time to make sure the place was okay.

It was just before dawn when he squeezed the Volvo down a narrow lane in the docks area of the city in search of the lock-up. So far, so good. No blue lights or loud sirens on his tail. If they'd spotted the car on their ANPR system—Automatic Number Plate Recognition—there was no evidence of it as yet. And once the vehicle was stored under cover, it would stay that way for the foreseeable future.

A man stepped out in front of him, his eyes shining in the light thrown by the Volvo's headlamps. He braked hard, and despite the slow speed, lurched forward in his seat. There was a second man standing behind the vehicle, his face hidden behind a curtain of dreadlocks. The muscular man in front tapped on the bonnet, his cue for Wellman to kill the engine and get out. There were no handshakes or pleasantries exchanged between them. They were there to do business, neither party having any interest in the other's intentions beyond that.

'It's all there,' Wellman said, handing over a supermarket carrier bag folded in two. Kyle Cartwright counted the money, regardless. The two men smelled of smoke and accelerant. Wellman knew better than to ask.

'I don't fancy your chances of getting out of here alive,' Cartwright said, tucking the bag of money down the front of his jeans. Dreadlocks took a step closer.

Wellman's hand hovered next to his jacket pocket. He had one pre-made syringe and decided its contents were destined for the more powerful looking of the two should things get out of hand. 'I've given you the money.'

'Not us.' Cartwright laughed and turned away. 'Even the rats avoid this place.'

'I'll take my chances,' Wellman said. He'd chosen well.

Chapter 55

Reece had Ginge attend Sandra Cole's post-mortem while he and Jenkins paid the owner of the silver Volvo a visit. Jenkins said she needed to talk, and this way, they could do both at the same time.

She stared out of the side window of the car, concluding what she could remember of the previous evening's conversation. 'That's why Ffion went AWOL yesterday afternoon.'

Reece pulled away from the traffic lights. 'Is there anything I can do to help? I know a couple of people who wouldn't mind me calling them.'

'She's gone private,' Jenkins said. 'Most of what needs to be done at this stage should be over by the end of today.'

Reece's focus of attention was a trio of cyclists using the full width of their side of the road. 'If she needs it, I've got money put away.'

Jenkins patted his knee. 'Josh has it sorted.'

Reece tried to get past the cyclists for the umpteenth time. 'Get over, you fucking idiots!' he shouted in Jenkins's right ear.

'Boss.'

He accelerated. 'They're doing it to piss me off.'

'Don't go round them,' she said, screwing both eyes closed. She gripped the dashboard and turned her head away. 'There isn't enough *roooom!'*

Reece accelerated harder, swapping vulgar hand-gestures as he sped past them. 'And you, pal!'

Jenkins sank into her seat, shaken and embarrassed all at once. 'I can't believe you did that.'

'Twats, the lot of them,' Reece said, risking a peek in her direction. 'Name me a man worth his salt who goes about parading his ball-bag in pink Lycra. Go on. Name one?'

Jenkins held onto the urge to laugh for as long as she could before folding in two at the waist.

'It's not funny. They should make dressing up like that illegal. It scares kids and old women.' He double-took. 'What's wrong now?'

'You. Just you.'

For a while, there was nothing but silence between them. Reece craned his neck as they went past the castle. The Griffin was there, high above one of the castellated towers, watching over the people of Cardiff from its vantage point. A right turn at the next junction took them past the museum, then the Redwood Building that belonged to the university's School of Pharmacology.

Jenkins was first to speak. 'It's that breast cancer gene you hear about in the press. Most of the women on Ffion's mother's side went on to have mastectomies.' She paused, composing herself. 'Imagine waiting for the day you've always dreaded, but know is coming.'

'I wouldn't want to know.'

'Not even if there was something you could do about it?'

Reece couldn't fully comprehend how awful it must be. 'Those women are far braver than me, that's for sure.'

They were now clear of the city and en route to one of its more affluent suburbs. 'Nice houses,' Jenkins said, watching double-fronted, detached properties go by on both sides of the road. 'You could play tennis on that lawn.'

Reece slowed. 'I bet this lot keep the local golf and bridge clubs going.'

'This is it,' she said, tapping him with the back of a hand. 'That one there with the gravel drive.'

'You sure?'

'That's what it said on the post next to the hedge.'

He stopped and reversed a short distance. 'You're right. Come on, we'll walk up and have a nosey on the way.'

Jenkins got out and followed. 'How are we going to play this?' she asked, breaking into a trot to keep up.

'We knock on the front door and ask whoever answers if they drive a silver Volvo.'

'Simple as that?'

'Why would you want to make it any more difficult than it needs to be?'

Chapter 56

When they reached the brow of the rising drive, they were confronted with a garage on one side and the house just ahead. The property itself wasn't as large as the others in the area and looked tired. There was a green mould growing on its walls, where sunlight was unable to penetrate the encroaching treeline.

'It could do with a lick of paint,' Reece said, knocking on the door. 'Looks like no one's done anything to it for years.' After knocking a second time, he went to one of two front windows, put his hand against the glass and peered inside. 'I can't see anyone.' He passed behind Jenkins to get to the window on the other side.

'Don't be smashing it like you did mine,' she warned.

'That was Ffion's idea.'

'I've still got scratches on my wood floor.'

Reece came to a halt and sighed. 'Do you want me to buy you a new one? Is that what you're after?'

'No. I'm just saying.'

'Shut up about it then.' Before they got round the back of the property, he did a detour over to the garage. When he twisted and pulled at the rusting handle, the door lifted up-and-over with a high-pitched squeal.

'You really shouldn't be doing that. There's no reason for us to be going in there without a warrant.'

'Who's going to know?' Reece went inside. There wasn't much to be found: mostly piles of old stick drying for a night on the log burner.

Jenkins nodded at a man marching up the drive towards them. '*He* might.'

'Can I help you?' the man shouted. His pace slowed, as though he were suddenly unnerved by what he might have got himself into.

Reece held up his ID and pointed towards the house. 'Do you live here, sir?'

The man indicated a neighbouring property. 'Over there,' he said, looking decidedly more confident now he knew they were police officers. 'This is Mrs Gantry's house.'

'She's not in,' Reece said, closing the garage door. 'And the car's gone.' There were tyre tracks in the damp soil beneath his shoes.

The neighbour wrung warmth into his hands, a green woollen tank-top with matching check shirt not nearly enough to keep out the chills of the March morning. 'Her son took it a couple of weeks ago. He's home from working abroad. Came for Mrs Gantry first. The car a few days after that.'

'Did he leave a name, or forwarding address?' Jenkins asked.

'I'm afraid not. He was very much like his mother. Not one to stop and chat.'

'What about a description?' Reece asked. 'You must have got a good look at him?'

'Not really. He never got out of the car and the window was down only an inch or so. What with the trees blocking out most of the light...' The man shrugged. 'Sorry, I can't tell you any more than that.'

'But you saw the car?' Jenkins asked.

'An old Volvo estate.'

'Colour?'

'Silver.' The neighbour looked suddenly worried. 'Nothing's happened to Mrs Gantry, has it?'

'Was she in the habit of going out late at night?' Reece asked.

The man shook his head. 'Very much the opposite. She rarely went out at all.'

Reece stopped next to Ginge's desk. 'What did you find out at the post-mortem?'

The newbie handed him a copy of the interim report. 'Sandra Cole had enough coronary artery disease to kill her within the next five years. But her urine tested positive for the breakdown products of that paralysing drug. Says so on the last page.'

Reece skipped to it and read for himself. Why had the killer acted so differently on this occasion? It had to be the same man. There couldn't be two people out there using Suxamethonium Chloride as a weapon of choice. Not a chance.

'Any luck with the car?' Ginge asked. 'Were you aware that an ANPR camera picked it up last night?'

Reece was walking away. He spun and came back. 'Where?'

Ginge gave him an overview of the route taken by the silver Volvo. 'And then it vanished. Disappeared into thin air.'

'But it *was* heading towards the docks when we could track its movements?'

'Looks that way. I've already asked a couple of the patrols to swing by the area on their way back to the station.'

'Good.' Reece dropped the report onto the desk. 'I'm told you know your way around a database or two?'

Ginge nodded. 'Boss.'

'Right then. See what you can dig up on Molly Gantry's son while I'm with the chief super.'

Chapter 57

'Jenkins will lead things while I'm away for the weekend,' Reece said, scratching his chin. 'I'll be in Brecon watching the Wales–England game at my local. There's no way I'm missing that one.'

Chief Superintendent Cable removed her spectacles and lay them open on the desk in front of her. 'DS Jenkins is meant to be concentrating on the Harlan Miller case. Did you not listen to anything ACC Harris, or I have had to say?'

'I heard, but I still don't see why Miller should get any more time spent on him than Poppy Jones or Sandra Cole.'

Cable leaned her elbows on the desk and massaged her temples. 'The Americans are threatening to ask for another police force to come in and investigate their son's murder.'

Reece waved a dismissive hand at her. 'They've got no chance.'

Cable hunted through the drawers of her desk, opening each one in the order of top to bottom. 'Money is what they have. And with that comes influence.'

'I don't give a shit who they've got in their pockets.' Reece tapped his chest with a finger. 'I, for one, won't be dancing to their tune.'

Cable put a bottle of aspirin next to her spectacles and thumbed at the lid. 'I'm not getting into another fight with you. Not today.'

'Who's fighting? I'm telling it like it is.'

Cable closed the drawer with a firmer shove than was absolutely necessary. 'What can I tell them?'

'Do you really want to know?'

'Reece. Please.'

His attention was drawn to a scene outside the window. There were a pair of seagulls dancing on the wind. For some strange reason, they reminded him of his wedding day, and Anwen's *father-daughter* dance with Idris. Snapping out of it, he said: 'You can tell them all three cases are related.'

Cable groaned and sank further into her seat. 'Don't you think you might be clutching at straws?' She counted the points off on her fingers: 'Miller was stabbed in the chest. Poppy Jones killed by what appears to be very sophisticated methods. And poor Sandra Cole was viciously assaulted. I'll be frank and admit to not following your logic.'

Reece screwed his eyes shut. 'Sandra Cole tested positive for that paralysing drug in her urine, linking her death directly to that of Poppy Jones.' He gave Cable a moment to catch up. 'And as we've already said at the briefings, the chances of the first two murders not being linked are next to zero.'

'And you remain satisfied that none of this has anything to do with the ex-boyfriend?' Cable sifted through her paperwork, looking for the name.

'I'm not ruling Jordan Patterson out of the stabbing just yet,' Reece said. 'But the injections are way beyond his capabilities, even with help from one of the others in the house.'

'What else can I tell Miller's parents?' Cable gave him a look of warning.

'We're following fresh leads on the Volvo, now we know who it belongs to. I've got Ginge tracking down the son of the owner.'

Cable broke into what might have been her first smile of the day. 'Why didn't you mention this earlier?'

'You know now,' Reece said, getting to his feet.

'Sit down, Brân.'

He didn't like the sound of that and pointed to the office door. 'I was just going to—'

'Sit.'

'Will this take long?' he asked, reluctantly accepting the seat.

'I've been speaking to Dr Beven about your counselling sessions.'

Reece had been waiting for this moment since the counsellor tricked him into talking about the shooting. She'd set a trap and made him say things that weren't true. 'They're a waste of time and money, in my opinion,' he said.

'Miranda disagrees. She thinks you're making some progress.'

It's another trap. Don't utter a word.

'Did you hear me?' Cable asked.

He nodded slowly. *They're in it together. Like a pair of witches.*

'That's good news, isn't it?'

Another nod. Nothing more.

'Are you feeling all right?' Cable asked. 'You're acting awfully odd.'

'I'm fine.'

'So you keep saying.'

Reece leaned forward in his seat. 'But now my shrink's saying the same thing.'

'*Making progress*, remember? Let's not get too far ahead of ourselves.'

'Can I go now?'

Cable nodded. 'Oh, there *is* one other thing before you do. The hospital wants you over there for a chat with the Board. Reassurance that their staff are safe coming and going from work.'

'When?'

'This afternoon. Three o'clock, to be exact.'

Reece's shoulders rounded. 'Can't you do it? I was hoping to knock off early today.'

'Believe me, I would if I could.'

'And there's no one else? No one at all?'

'You're leading the investigation.'

Reece got up, muttering obscenities, this time allowed as far as the office door before Cable stopped him again.

She put the bottle of aspirin to her lips and shook a couple out onto her tongue. 'And *please* Brân – best behaviour.'

Chapter 58

Reece was mumbling to himself as he passed through the incident room. Mostly about having to get across to the hospital and meet with people there.

'I've made a start on tracing the son,' Ginge told him. 'But it's heavy going to be honest. Mrs Gantry had only one child: a boy born in nineteen sixty-two at the Cardiff Royal Infirmary. Six years later, he's put up for adoption. The records after that are a bit shaky. Non-existent in some respects.' He chuckled. 'There were no high-tech servers to store it on back in the Dark Ages.'

'I know,' Reece said. 'Having lived through some of that time period myself.'

Ginge avoided eye contact and instead concentrated on his computer screen. 'Looks like the boy was in and out of foster homes for a while. I'm having to rely on more recent scans of paper records where I can find them. Often, they're not fully completed. Some are illegible. There might be something here to suggest he was taken in by another family member.'

Jenkins came away from her desk. 'Keep digging. If that's true, then whoever it was might lead us to his present whereabouts.'

'Unless they've died after all this time,' Ginge said.

'How long ago do you think the sixties were?' Reece asked, swiping a hand at the ducking newbie. He turned to Jenkins. 'Abandonment might make the son resentful of women?'

She looked less than convinced. 'Mother figures maybe. But what's his issue with the likes of Poppy Jones?'

Reece loosened the knot of his tie. 'Don't know. I was thinking out loud.'

'Did the boy keep the Gantry name?' Jenkins asked.

'Only into his teens,' Ginge answered. 'But then we lose all trace of him at the age of twenty.'

'He could have changed it to hide a past he was embarrassed about.'

'There's no record of that in any of the registers I've had access to.'

'Keep looking.' She watched Reece head over to his office and take his car keys off the desk. 'Going out?'

He checked his watch. 'Hospital. You go find a magistrate and get us a search warrant for the mother's place.'

'On what grounds?'

'I don't know. Think on your feet. Lie if you have to.'

'Boss!' Jenkins slumped onto a vacant chair in the corner of the room. 'I'm on a final written warning as it is.'

'Tell them we're worried about her. That we've reason to believe her life might be in danger. Embellish it for God's sake. You know how it goes.'

CHAPTER 59

Reece waited in a hospital boardroom that smelled of polish and musty old men. There was a table running along the room's centre; a pull-down projector screen hanging from the ceiling at one end of it. He stirred his coffee, listening to the chair express his sorrow over the tragic *passing* of three of the organisation's employees.

Others present in the room included the executive director of nursing, the medical director, and a stern-looking woman from the Deanery. On Reece's insistence, Dr Richard Wellman was there in his capacity as clinical director for anaesthetics.

'This matter has been truly terrible for all concerned,' said the medical director. Dr Simon Underdown was a short, plump man with a rosy complexion. Reece had him pegged as something of a drinker. Something of an eater, too.

The nursing director, on the other hand, was a thin stick of a woman. Slightly kyphotic, and in dire need of a makeover. 'Chief Inspector, how do you propose to keep our staff safe while you're hunting this beastly man?'

Reece put the thumb end of his fist to his mouth and tried not to laugh at the woman's pretentious manner. 'There's a patrol car passing through the site several times a day, as well as a doubling of our usual on-foot activity.'

'And you consider that sufficient?'

'Given current budget restrictions, it's all I'm going to get,' he said curtly.

'And what about further afield?' the chair asked. 'Both nurses were killed at home, were they not?' He sought confirmation from his colleagues.

Reece nodded with the rest of them. 'Staff should be encouraged to travel in pairs. In larger groups, when able.'

'Do you have any idea who you're looking for?' Underdown asked. 'I read you've been trying to trace the owner of a silver Volvo.'

'We're following up on several leads.' Reece let his gaze settle on each of them in turn. 'I'm willing to believe the killer works here at the hospital.'

The director of nursing almost slid off her seat. 'Good Lord. You can't be serious?'

'Security of drugs on that theatre suite is lax,' Reece said. 'Both women were injected with a paralysing agent before they were left to asphyxiate and die.'

The chair's brow furrowed like ripples in wet sand. 'There was nothing in the press about that.'

'And that's how it's staying,' Reece said. 'Kept within these four walls.'

The chair turned side-on. 'Richard, what's your opinion on this?'

Wellman was calm in his response. 'I've already explained to the chief inspector why certain medications must remain available throughout the entire course of a surgical list.' He shrugged. 'Besides, who's to say it didn't originate from a neighbouring hospital, or local veterinary practice?'

'A fair point,' said the medical director, looking decidedly less troubled all of a sudden. 'It could quite easily have come from elsewhere.'

'From a handful of places at most,' Reece said. 'I'm sticking with my gut feeling.'

The woman from the Deanery opened a file on the table in front of her. 'Harlan Miller was stabbed. Where's the link to the others?'

'I can't go into the specifics of each individual case,' Reece said, 'other than to say we believe all three deaths are connected.'

The woman leaned to look down the table at Wellman. 'Miller was doing audit work for you. It says so on his placement record. Did he ever mention being mixed up in anything unsavoury?'

Reece was on his feet. He rounded the table and stopped only when he got behind the anaesthetist's chair. 'You said you'd never heard of Harlan Miller.'

'You caught me on the street, Chief Inspector. And in passing, barked a name.' Wellman stared straight ahead as he spoke. 'Had you shown me a photograph, then perhaps I'd have had a fighting chance of placing him.'

'And now we've jogged your memory, is there anything else you can remember about him?'

'Nothing at all.'

Reece went closer and whispered: 'In what year were you born?'

Chapter 60

Jenkins had positioned a pair of uniforms in the field behind Mrs Gantry's house, in case anyone made a run for it. With her in the unmarked car were Ginge, and two constables who looked like they'd rather be in bed at such an early hour. It was still a few minutes before six in the morning, the day after she'd embellished the shit out of her story at the local magistrates' court.

In the car behind them were four more uniforms; each wearing protective over-vests and BWVs – body-worn video cameras.

The vehicles sped up the gravel drive on Jenkins's command, spewing chippings into the untended flower borders. When they slid to a halt outside the house, Jenkins was first to get out. She marched towards the front door with Ginge in close pursuit. This part of the job always gave her a buzz. The uncertainty of what might happen next was exhilarating.

She banged on the front door and shouted: 'Police,' identifying them to potential occupants and threats alike. 'Open up.' Peering through a small panel of glass, she saw no movement. The door took another hammering. She shouted again. This time, louder. One of the waiting uniforms was summoned forward. 'Use the *Big Red Key*,' Jenkins said, authorising the officer to smash through the door with the heavy length of steel he carried two-handed.

Metal struck against wood three times, and came off victorious, as was always the case.

They were greeted in the cold hallway by air that carried an odd odour. At first, Jenkins didn't recognise it. She sniffed, and called on stored memories to help her out. It wasn't from cooking. Something else altogether. 'You take upstairs,' she told Ginge. 'I'll make a start down here.'

At the end of the hallway was a glass door that opened into a narrow living room, itself divided into two distinct areas. The bit near the front window was more formal and contained a reading chair, lamp, and writing bureau. At the opposite end of the room was a television set, sofa, and a small dining table with chairs.

Jenkins pushed her hands into a pair of blue latex-free gloves and started her search over by the window. She checked behind the reading chair. Lifted its cushioned seat and found nothing. The front of the bureau came down like a medieval drawbridge to reveal a red-leather writing surface lined like a road map from years of use.

Running a hand over it, she wondered what stories the indentations might share if able. She left the red leather to its secrets and moved to a neat letter-rack, checking the address on each envelope before carefully removing the contents to skim read. There were bills, mostly. A television licence and an overdue reminder for an appointment with an optometrist.

On the wall above the bureau was a large print of a hunting scene. A man dressed in a green tunic with matching hat stood upright in the stirrups of his giant steed, blowing into a long and curved horn. A pack of dogs were already unleashed, keen on the scent of the fleeing hare. Jenkins found herself instantly despising the man and all that he and his kind represented.

In the magazine rack next to the log-burner was a copy of the Radio Times and a couple of newspapers. She checked the date on the most recent one.

The tiled mantelpiece was free of both clutter and dust. Everything in the room had the appearance of having been meticulously cleaned. She frowned, her detective mind working overtime.

The kitchen kettle was empty and cold. Not a pot or dish out of place. No teaspoon or butter knife resting in the aluminium sink. The cupboards contained half-sized cans of beans, and corned beef, among other things. There were tea towels in the drawers and instruction booklets for the white goods on show.

She went to the bottom of the stairs. 'Found anything of interest?'

'Not a sausage,' Ginge called back.

She joined him on the landing. 'It's all very neat and tidy.'

'Not a bit like my gaff,' he said. 'More like a show home, this.'

'That's what I thought.'

'Does that bother you?'

'Can't you smell it?' she asked. 'Bleach.'

'Weak,' Ginge said. 'But it's definitely there.'

'Everything in this house has been cleaned to within an inch of its life.'

'Like someone's trying to hide something.'

She nodded. 'And it goes well beyond the realms of the owner being house proud, given the outside looks nothing like this.'

'What are you going to do?' Ginge asked.

Jenkins was already descending the stairs. 'I'm going to get Sioned Williams to search this place with a fine-toothed comb.'

CHAPTER 61

REECE ENTERED THE BUSY pub in Brecon and heard, rather than saw, his mate Yanto shouting at the television in the back room. He ordered a couple of pints from the bar and made his way in. 'There you go,' he said, lowering them onto the table.

The farmer shifted position and looked past him as though he wasn't there.

Reece gave his foot a playful kick. 'You're not still pissed off with me, you miserable sod?'

'You shouldn't have left me on that roof.' Yanto shook his head and ran a huge hand through a mop of tight black curls. 'Taking the piss, that was.'

Reece tried not to laugh. 'I got called back to Cardiff. There's been a couple of murders. Three actually. You must have seen it on the news?'

'You need to sort out your priorities.' Yanto wagged a dirty finger at him. 'Half the week it took me to finish that roof.'

'And I'm very grateful. Look, I've bought you a pint.'

'Half the week.' Yanto took the glass and downed a good two-thirds of its contents in one go. 'The sheep have been running riot with me gone. Turning cartwheels, they are, up in that top field.'

Reece could hold back no longer, and belly-laughed. 'Ah, I love you,' he said when able. 'You're the best mate I ever had.'

Yanto folded his arms across his chest and sank into the fireside armchair. 'Fuck off.'

'I mean it.'

'And I do.'

Reece stood. 'Fancy another pint?'

'You're buying all afternoon,' Yanto told him. '*All* afternoon, I said.'

'Do you think we'll do it?' Reece asked when he got back with the drinks, and two packets of crisps dangling from his teeth.

'It's the Grand Slam.' Yanto pumped the air with his fist. 'Against the English an' all.'

'I know, but we're up against a decent team.'

'The *Grand Slam*.' Yanto's words were delivered with a deep growl. He was on his feet, climbing onto a chair, both arms held high above his head. '*Oggy. Oggy. Oggy,*' he shouted at the top of his voice. '*Oi. Oi. Oi,*' came the resounding reply from all inside the pub.

'Get down.' The woman behind the bar was making her way towards the hinged door in the countertop. 'If I have to come over there,' she warned.

Yanto was back on his arse without uttering a word in protest. Despite the farmer being the hardest man Reece had ever known, he wouldn't have been foolish enough to bet on him in a one-on-one with the pub's landlady.

'How much do I owe you for the roof?' Reece asked.

Yanto shook his head. 'Leave it be.'

'I mean it. Let me pay you for a few day's labour at the very least.'

The farmer looked horrified. 'Butties don't pay for helping each other out.' He finished what was left of the first pint and sank half the second in one swift gulp. 'You've gone soft now you're a city boy. Forgotten your roots, you have.'

'What are you talking about?'

'Poncey suits and ties messing with your head. You've started thinking you're one of them.'

Reece was wearing a red rugby shirt and faded jeans, like most other people in the pub. 'Huh?'

Yanto leaned towards him. 'Remember when we were little kids playing on those mountains out there? Rain, sunshine, or snow. It didn't matter to us.'

'And your point?'

Yanto gestured towards one of the panelled windows. 'They've got paratroopers and SAS training on it now. *SAS*,' he repeated in a higher tone.

'Meaning?'

'That was our playground. We're made of tougher stuff round here. City people are soft. Got everything handed to them on a plate.' He sat back in his chair, his sermon almost over. 'Give 'em to me, they want to. I'd whip the lazy bastards into shape.'

'I'm sure you would.'

'I'm telling you, Brân. There's—'

'Hang on,' Reece said, silencing him. 'I need to take this call.'

Yanto hung his head. 'Here we go again.'

Reece crossed the pub, pushing through hordes of people singing *Mae Hen Wlad Fy Nhadau – Old Land of my Fathers*. He had no chance of hearing anything else until he got to the car park outside. 'Colonel,' he said, near breathless with palpitations.

'Chief Inspector. Buongiorno—good afternoon—to you.'

'Do you have something to tell me?' Reece asked, unable to contain himself.

Colonel Gianfranco Totti of the Carabinieri, in Rome, cleared his throat. 'There have been developments in the case regarding your late wife. I have something important to tell you.'

Chapter 62

Reece felt like he was in a dream. A good dream for a change. One in which the Italian police were bringing the whole terrible event to something near closure. 'And you're confident it's the right man you have in custody?' he asked once the colonel was finished.

Totti said he was, and went to explain the legal process of his country.

'So your equivalent of our magistrates' court after the weekend?' Reece said.

With their telephone conversation over, he'd walked out of the car park, not knowing where he was going. He was in a daze and needed time alone to clear his head. When eventually he returned, it was with no idea of how long he'd been gone.

'We won the Grand Slam!' Yanto kept shouting at him. 'Where've you been?'

Someone grabbed Reece's arm and spun him around while they danced a jig. 'Outside.' He turned to face the doorway. 'I've been on the phone to Italy.'

'I thought you'd buggered off back to Cardiff.'

'They've got him.' Reece was shaking. Crying. 'The Italian police have caught Anwen's killer.'

CHAPTER 63

REECE WOKE UP IN a bathtub containing no water or soapy bubbles, and wasn't at all sure where he was. He let his eyes get used to the dark. That didn't help. His mouth was dry and his head was pounding. There was the sound of snoring nearby. 'Yanto, is that you?'

'Huh?'

'Where the hell are we?'

Yanto sat up and promptly struck his head against the underside of the washbasin. After a fair amount of loud swearing, he got to his feet and opened the blinds. 'In my bathroom,' he said, looking as confused as Reece.

'Why?'

'Didn't we win the Grand Slam yesterday?' The farmer was slowly piecing things together. He put his mouth under the cold water tap and took a long and noisy drink. Then he splashed water on his face and stood still for a good ten seconds or more before moving again.

Reece watched him. 'Did I get a phone call from Rome, or was that a dream?'

'I don't think we were dreaming,' Yanto said. 'Did we stay for the lock-in?'

Reece swallowed and fought the urge to throw up. 'I think we might have done.'

There was the sound of pans knocking against the stove downstairs. 'What time is it?' Yanto asked, reaching for the handle of the bathroom door.

'Twenty-five past ten.'

'In the morning?'

'I think so.'

'Aw bollocks. I was supposed to be taking Ceirios shopping by nine.'

'She'll be all right,' Reece said, stepping out of the bathtub. He grabbed for the wall, his legs objecting to a night of being tucked underneath him.

'You go downstairs first and butter her up,' Yanto said.

Reece grinned. It made his head hurt. 'You make her sound like a piece of toast.'

Yanto pushed him through the open door. 'Go on. She likes you.'

Reece paused on the landing. 'Look who's gone soft now?'

Chapter 64

Yanto took Reece back to his cottage in a white Land Rover Defender that shook and rattled along the tramlines of churned dirt track. It was almost noon. Sunday in the middle of March. 'What are your plans for the afternoon?' he asked with a wide yawn. 'Sleep off that thick head of yours, if you've any sense.'

Reece looked through the windscreen at the mountains beyond. 'I've got something to tell Anwen and Idris.'

'You're not going up Pen y Fan in this weather,' the farmer said, flicking the wipers to full-on. 'It's blowing a gale out there.'

'I'll be careful. I know the route like the back of my hand.'

'Brân—'

'I'm not one of those weekend warriors,' Reece argued. 'I'll be all right. Trust me.'

'I'm coming with you.'

'No, you're not.' He lay his hand on Yanto's knee. 'I'll be fine. Stop mothering me.'

They drove another mile or so in silence, except for the rain drumming on the roof and the grunt of the Defender's engine as its wheels spun in the mud before getting traction and propelling them onward.

'Look at this rain,' Yanto said, still sounding seriously concerned. 'The cloud base is low and there'll be plenty of snow and ice up there.'

'We're built of tougher stuff, remember? Those were your words.'

'You're gonna get yourself killed. Why not wait until tomorrow?'

Reece got out and held onto a door that fought to tear off its hinges and fly away. 'If I die, Anwen and Idris will be there to show me the way home.'

Chapter 65

Jenkins pushed on the iron gate and stood aside to let Cara Frost enter first. 'I can't believe you've never been to Roath Park,' she said, raising the umbrella over both their heads.

Frost ducked and waited for her to unsnag it from the top of the railings. 'I've only lived and worked in Cardiff for six months or so.'

'It's a lovely city,' Jenkins said, turning to keep the boating lake on their left as they set off on a circuit around it. 'Although I'm probably being biased.'

'First impressions are definitely positive,' Frost replied, looping their arms together. 'Looks like it has everything I need right here.'

'What was it like growing up in Guernsey?' Jenkins asked. 'I used to watch re-runs of that detective series when I was a kid. *Oh*, what was it called again?' She snapped her fingers, trying to remember.

'Bergerac?'

'That's the one.'

Frost shook her head. 'That was set on Jersey.'

'I remember now. Blue seas and summer all year long.'

'Not all year.' Frost repositioned the umbrella so they could catch sight of the way ahead. 'And you grew up here in sunny Cardiff.'

Jenkins giggled. Happy for the first time in a long while. 'I'm an Ely girl,' she said sheepishly. 'But don't let that put you off.'

'You'll have to educate me.'

'Ely's nothing like Guernsey.' Jenkins paused for thought. 'A person can go one of two ways coming from my neck of the woods.' She paused a second time. 'I suppose that's true wherever people come from.'

'And you chose the police over the dark side?'

'I can't remember wanting to do anything else.'

'Because of something you saw or experienced as a child?'

'Not that I remember.' Jenkins slowed to a halt close to the water's edge. She toed a small stone before tapping it over the side with a *plink* sound. She looked for another. 'My father was a policeman back in Jamaica. He told me stories—little girl versions, obviously—and that had me sold from a young age.' *Plink* went another stone into the lake.

'Is he still there now?'

'He came to Cardiff in the seventies, met Mum, and had little ol' me.'

'Did he join the South Wales Police when he got here?'

There were no more stones to be found. 'Diabetes did for his toes. He became a lay-preacher instead.' Jenkins looked across to the boathouse on the other side of the lake, where the pigeons were doing their dance on the roof. She tried to flush all thoughts of Belle Gillighan from her mind – something that was easier said than done. 'Dad thought it was God's sign for him to follow another path in life.'

'I didn't have you down as the religious type,' Frost said.

'I'm not. I went along with it because it made him happy. Each to their own, I always say.'

'Very noble of you.' Frost leaned closer and planted a kiss on her temple.

Jenkins went back to watching the birds and thought she heard someone call her name. There was a woman standing close to the boathouse. Was she looking at them? It was difficult to tell. Cara Frost tugged her arm. 'Sorry. What?'

'I asked if your father still worked at the church?'

The woman was nowhere to be seen when Jenkins next looked. She checked up and down the lake. Then the area near the memorial lighthouse. 'He's dead. Had a heart attack a few years back. Mum still helps there a couple of days a week. It's good for her to get out.'

Frost raised the collar of her coat and fastened the top button. 'Do you see her much?'

'Not as often as I should.' Not since she'd been back at work, certainly. Had she even told her mother that she *was* back? She couldn't recall and made a firm promise to do it that night.

'I'm enjoying getting to know you better,' Frost said, steering them towards an empty bench. 'We've been out only a handful of times since this began.'

Jenkins lowered her head and voice. 'It's me.' She picked at the edge of her thumbnail. 'Belle left scars that don't heal anywhere near as quickly as the physical ones did.'

Chapter 66

Yanto wasn't wrong in his assessment of the day's weather. Just getting from the cottage to the foot of the mountain had been an astonishing feat of endurance. Pounding through puddles and mud, Reece had been mid-shin, and a lot deeper at times. He pulled at handfuls of bracken, using anything he could to make his way through the battering wind.

Hail fell like glass marbles, sending him to seek shelter next to a large, craggy rock. He curled into the foetal position and made himself small while falling ice struck rock with the clinking sound of a stonemason's chisel.

His wet-weather gear did a sterling job of keeping him dry and warm, though a bit more beard coverage would have been a good thing. He waited for the worst of it to pass before setting off again, zig-zagging as though negotiating a field of scattered land mines.

At times, he sought to duck beneath the wind and avoid it. Now and again, he stood tall and let it push him on his way.

Heading south west, he passed the Cwar Mawr quarry a short distance in. He knew he had, even though he couldn't properly see it. The rain had eased a little. Or was it a case of him getting used to it? His trail shoes gripped the silty ground, slipping only when they contacted a flat and well-trodden rock on the path.

He pushed on, bent at the waist, and found himself rehearsing his speech over and over in his head. Should he build up to the punchline slowly, adding an air of suspense to the situation? Or was it better to blurt it out as soon as he got there? It didn't matter. The important thing was they'd caught and arrested Anwen's killer after all this time.

Further on, the weather was easing. It wasn't his imagination. Things changed quickly up there on the mountain, and today, it was shifting from awful to something far better. It was a sign of his own improving mental health. He'd tell Miranda Beven at their next counselling session that he was no longer in need of her shrinkery-dinkery. She wouldn't believe him of course. Neither would the chief super.

When he arrived at the snow-covered summit, he instantly forgot most of the speech he'd practised on the way up and threw himself to the ground in a flood of tears. 'They've got him,' he sobbed, clawing at the compacted snow with gloved hands. 'Anwen. Idris. Do you hear me?'

They spoke for a long while. He, in the mother tongue. They, as whispers carried on the winter winds.

Now that some of the cloud cover had shifted, he could see Llyn Cwm Llwch—Dust Valley Lake—way off in the distance. But no matter how hard he tried, there was no sign of the fairies said to inhabit the mythical island at its mid-point.

He made his way over the other side of the summit. Along Corn Ddu—Pen y Fan's slightly shorter sister—and down to where the Tommy Jones obelisk stood alone. He stopped to pay his respects to the dead five-year-old. Removed his woolly hat and read the tribute carved in the rock, as he always did. 'Sleep tight, little-un,' he said, before continuing his way down the mountain.

Chapter 67

It was a little after 7:30pm when Reece heard a car pull up outside his cottage in Brecon. He rose from his chair and opened the curtains wide enough to see what was going on. At first, the stark white light from the headlamps blinded him. The driver shut them off, leaving halos of a softer glow hanging in the air before all went dark again.

When the door opened and the occupant got out, he recognised the man immediately. Tapping on the window, he told Twm Pryce to make his way round to the kitchen entrance at the side of the property.

'What's up?' Reece asked.

The pathologist looked troubled and entered without answering.

Reece shut the door behind them and followed him in. 'Twm? Are you okay?'

Pryce stopped next to the kitchen table. 'You've been baking.'

'Having a go at some bread.' Reece nodded towards a notebook lying open on the kitchen table. 'Tried my hand at a traditional lamb cawl while I was at it.' He stepped aside, giving the pathologist an unhindered view of the pot on the stove. 'Anwen had recipes for all sorts. Are you hungry?'

Pryce removed his jacket and driving gloves. 'Not really.'

Reece could tell the man was famished. 'I was about to have another bowl.' That wasn't true. 'It would be nice to have some company for once.'

Pryce took a seat at the table. 'A small one then.'

'What's this about?' Reece asked, serving a full bowl of cawl and a chunk of bread torn from the warm loaf. 'I'm surprised you found me way out in the sticks. You've not been to the cottage before, have you?'

Pryce shook his head. 'My first time. The wonders of satnav.'

'This place shows up on it?' Reece was genuinely amazed. 'Jenkins reckons I've got it on my phone somewhere. Or a version of it.'

'And if you spent your money instead of hoarding it all, you'd have it in your car as well.'

Reece made a face that meant he wouldn't be getting it anytime soon. 'All those things do is encourage drivers to fiddle and take their attention off the road. Bloody death traps if you ask me.'

'And you poking at the innards of your dashboard with a screwdriver is perfectly safe?'

Reece rested his spoon next to his bowl. 'Twm, why *did* you come here tonight?'

The pathologist raised a bushy eyebrow, his own spoon left to support itself in the thick mix of steaming liquid and vegetables. 'I fear I might have missed something recently – during a post-mortem on a young woman.' He rescued the drowning spoon and used it to stir his evening meal. 'She was only twenty-three and didn't have a thing wrong with her that I could find.' He ran the spoon through a few slow circuits of the bowl and added: 'She was a nurse at the hospital.'

Reece's chair creaked beneath him as he shifted position. 'When is it we're talking about?'

'Only a couple of weeks ago.'

The detective smelled blood. 'What do you think you missed?'

'I did all the usual tox screens, of course. But not for Suxamethonium Chloride, or any of its metabolites. Why would I?'

'But now you wish you had done?'

Pryce took a deep breath and pushed the bowl away. 'Cara told me about the cases she's been working on. And that got me thinking.'

Chapter 68

Reece finished what he had to say and awaited the chief super's response. It didn't take long for him to get an answer.

Cable looked horrified. 'Not a hope in hell. You'd have to be absolutely bonkers to think I'd see it any other way.' She massaged her temples and dropped her chin onto her chest. 'Can you even imagine what ACC Harris would have to say about this?'

Reece didn't give a damn what the man thought, and was on his feet, refusing to sit down again when he was told to do so. 'We'll let the girl rot and not know then, shall we? Is that what you want?'

Cable poked her head halfway across the desk. 'And you think leaving her to rest is any worse than us digging her up to realise you're wrong?' The chief super's voice was loud enough to attract the attention of her personal assistant outside. The woman stared for a while before going back to her work.

Reece paced like a guard on patrol. 'The family deserves to know either way. There's justice to be served.' He leaned on the desk, and with a deep breath, brought things down a level. 'All I'm saying is, we can't leave her there and wonder if she might have been another victim.'

Cable pinched the bridge of her nose between finger and thumb. 'You've given me a nosebleed.'

'Put your head back.' Reece demonstrated. 'And pinch your nose just there.'

She glared at him and spoke through gritted teeth. 'Don't!'

'Just trying to help.'

Cable used a paper tissue to wipe blood spots from the surface of her desk. 'Oh, you're *trying* all right.'

'She was twenty-three,' Reece continued. 'Little more than a kid. Would you be happy with that on your conscience?'

Cable tore a handful of tissues from a square box and shoved them to her face. 'You're going to be the death of me, I swear.'

'That's a yes, then?' He pushed the telephone towards her and waited where he was until she picked it up.

She turned the swivel chair one hundred and eighty degrees so she couldn't see him. Then jammed a finger in her free ear so she couldn't hear him. 'They warned me about you before I came here. Even back in London, they know who you are.'

Reece pulled a face and edged away.

'Most people said I was crazy to even consider coming anywhere near this place. Anywhere near *you*, especially.' When she turned round again, he was already gone.

Reece was in his office eating a cheese and pickle sandwich with salt and vinegar crisps when Cable found him. 'How did it go with the ACC?' he asked.

'Billy Creed,' she said with wide-open arms.

It wasn't the answer he was expecting, and it threw him momentarily. 'What about him?'

'His lawyer has been on to the Executive Office. My phoning ACC Harris saved him the bother of a telephone call here.'

Reece held the crisp packet above his head and shook the remaining crumbs into his open mouth. 'Is this about Pete Hall's disappearance?'

'Among other things.'

He scrunched the empty crisp packet and lobbed it towards the bin. It opened mid-air and fell well short of its intended target. 'I promised the man's wife I'd look into it. You know that already.'

'I told you not to go within a mile of Creed.'

Reece turned away and spoke into his hand.

'What did you say?'

'It's always the same. No matter who's in charge, I'm always told to stay away from Creed.'

'Meaning?'

'It's almost as though someone's looking out for him. Watching his back.'

Cable almost toppled over. 'I hope you're not implying that something improper is going on?'

'I'm saying you're getting in the way of me doing my job. Your predecessor was the same. And his before him. It's a fact.'

Cable wiped new spots of blood from the lapels of her blouse. 'If you're incapable of obeying orders, I'll have you chained to a desk until the day you draw your pension.' She swung open the door and stood there waiting. *'Out!'*

Reece stayed where he was and pointed at the ceiling. 'You're in the wrong office, ma'am. Yours is upstairs.'

Chapter 69

Richard Wellman returned his teacup to its saucer. 'I knew as soon as Mother opened the front door. Isn't that remarkable after all these years?'

Whatever Miranda Beven's view, her face gave nothing away. 'And did she recognise you?'

'I believe she did.'

'You sound unsure?'

'Not at all. You see, Mother isn't the welcoming type. *Cold* is how I'd describe her.'

'And why do you think that is?'

Wellman looked away, his mood quickly souring. *Because she's a self-centred bitch.* Composing himself, he said: 'I'm not sure. You'd have to ask her.'

'Might it be because—?'

'I've already said I don't know.' His tone had changed and when he next paid the counsellor any attention, it was with a stony stare. Beven only half-smiled. He could see her lips trembling. *She's scared.* The experience was new and excited him. A hefty dose of Suxamethonium Chloride had prevented the others exhibiting such overt signs of fear. This here was different and turned him on.

But then, *she* was different. Was well dressed. No chest or thighs on show. No flaunting her wares in public. He studied her hands: the fourth finger on the left one specifically. She was married. Had no Facebook account. He'd already checked. *I'll let you live, Miranda. But do be careful to never anger me like that again.* 'Please, continue.'

Beven wiped her hands on her trousers. 'Could we go back to that recent meeting with your mother?'

Wellman nodded slowly. 'We can.'

'Thank you. When you went inside the house, did your mother's attitude towards you change?'

You mean when I throttled her until she shit herself? He took a moment before answering. 'There was no change at all. Just business chit-chat about how reliable a Volvo is, and that I was getting the vehicle for well under its market value.'

'That must have hurt. Perhaps you'd be willing to share some of those feelings with me?'

Be careful, Miranda. You're pushing buttons you should stay well clear of. 'I hated her for it.'

'Hated your mother, or women in general?'

Oh, you're good. Very fucking good. Wellman fussed with his red bow tie. 'I don't hate women as a group. Only those who act like shameless whores.' He stopped himself, aware he'd already said too much? The word was carved into the flabby flesh of Sandra Coles's chest. He couldn't recall if the newspapers had mentioned that fact. *Miranda is staring. She knows what you've done.*

Beven stood to collect their cups and saucers. 'I think we'll bring today's session to an end.'

He caught her wrist as she reached for his teacup. Let his eyes wander over her slim figure and full lips. Something was changing within him. He liked it.

'Dr Wellman, let go please.' She fought against his tight grip. 'I said let go of my arm.'

He released her and watched her rub an area of reddening skin. 'As you wish.'

She went to the other side of the room, keeping maximum separation from him. 'I want you to leave.'

He got up and made his way towards her, his polished shoes scuffing along the varnished surface of the wooden floor. He flexed his fingers while searching for a suitable squeeze-point on her slim neck. 'We're nowhere near finished,' he said, now almost within an arm's length of her.

A loud knock at the door made them both jump. Beven checked her watch. 'My twelve o'clock appointment is early,' she said with ill-disguised relief.

Wellman replied with the coldest of goodbyes. As he descended the stairs of the building, he was still sexually aroused. *Time to look up Smiler, the student nurse. I've got something new planned for that one.*

Chapter 70

'Who let *you* in here?' Reece said, entering his office to find Maggie Kavanagh sat behind his desk, filing her nails. He'd been gone for only twenty minutes – talking rugby with George, the desk sergeant, downstairs.

Kavanagh looked up. Her hands held out in front of her like a praying mantis. 'Charming. Is that any way to behave when an old friend pays you a visit?'

'And you've been smoking.' He went to the window and opened it. 'What have I told you about that?'

'I might have had a cheeky one,' she said with a wet cough. 'But I left the door open. No harm done, lovie.'

Reece poked his head through the office door. *'Ginge!'*

'Yes, boss.'

He pointed at the newspaper reporter. 'Is this your doing?'

Ginge looked like he wasn't sure what to say, and stood rooted to the spot. When Kavanagh nodded, he said: 'Maggie told me she had an appointment with you.'

Reece spun on his heels. 'What appointment?'

Another wet cough. 'It was more of an open invitation.'

He shooed her from behind the desk, but didn't take the seat himself. 'When?'

'In the pub the other night. At Jenkins's drinks. You said I could pop round for a chat any time I wanted.'

'No, I didn't.'

'Never mind that. I'm told you've linked the deaths of Poppy Jones and Sandra Cole.'

Reece looked at Ginge, who shook his head in complete denial.

'It wasn't him,' Kavanagh said, pulling a chair away from the far wall. She dragged it nearer the desk and went to sit down. 'I got the news from one of Cole's neighbours.'

Reece tried to take the chair from her, but gave up when she slapped his hand. 'I'm not in the mood for this,' he said.

'You never are.'

'Maggie—'

'I want an exclusive.' Kavanagh took a cigarette from its packet and dry-smoked it. 'An exclusive, or I'll run a story on what I have so far.'

'You've got sod all,' Reece said, dropping into his swivel chair. 'And that's the way it's staying.'

'You're investigating the recent deaths of three hospital staff, and over the weekend, raided the home of a Mrs Molly Gantry. You're now looking for her son in connection with that silver Volvo you mentioned at the press conference.' Kavanagh took another dry puff of her cigarette and winked. 'How's that, for starters?'

Reece's jaw fell open. 'How the—?'

'Money talks, Brân. *You* know how the world works.'

He removed his tie and wound it around a clenched fist. 'You listen to me. If I find that anyone at this station has been talking to—'

'Dry your powder,' she told him. 'I can get you what you need on the Gantry woman. Everything there is to know and more.'

'Ginge is doing just fine on his own.'

Kavanagh inhaled deeply on the unlit cigarette. 'Two heads are better than one.'

Reece leaned an elbow on the armrest of the chair and put his knuckles—wrap an' all—to his teeth. 'Okay,' he said with a deep sigh. 'But these are the rules of engagement...'

Chapter 71

Wellman found Smiler in the more compact of two coffee rooms on the Main Theatre corridor. Lounging on a sofa opposite an anaesthetic trainee. Twirling a curl of black hair with her finger.

The trainee stood when the clinical director entered; made his excuses and left without as much as a backward glance for his admirer.

Smiler turned her attention to the new arrival and went back to playing with her hair. 'Hello, Dr Wellman,' she said with a voice that carried a husky rasp.

See how easily she shifts from one to the other of us? There's no doubting her being a bona fide whore. 'I didn't catch your name last time,' he said, craning his neck to get a better look.

'Skye,' she replied, raising the name badge towards him.

She made me look at the swell of her breasts. She could easily have told me without doing that. 'What a lovely name.'

'Thank you. Can I get you a coffee?' Skye asked. 'I was about to make one for myself.'

She's trying to keep me here. Doesn't want me racing off like that pea-brained trainee did. 'Stay where you are. I'll do the honours,' he said. 'Milk and sugar?'

'Just milk, thanks. I'm sweet enough,' she joked. People came and went. But not Skye.

Wellman checked the time. 'I thought they let you students out long before now?'

'I'll be going soon,' she told him. 'Just psyching myself up first.'

He frowned. 'For what?'

'I left my car over on Heath Park, behind the hospital.' She glanced at the windows and the cloak of impenetrable darkness beyond. 'There wasn't a space anywhere closer.'

'You're waiting for company like the police advised you to?'

'That's just it. There isn't any. I'm the only student on duty here this evening.'

'Tell you what,' Wellman said, waving his coffee mug at her. 'I'll chaperon you over there. Then perhaps you'd be kind enough to drop me back at my car? It's in the multi-storey.'

'You'd do that?'

'Sure. Why not? Look at the size of me,' he said, rising on his toes to well over six feet in height. 'No prowler is going to mess with this.'

'Definitely not.' Smiler was smiling. 'Thank you so much.'

'On one condition, though. We can't let anybody see us leave the hospital together.' Skye looked wary for a moment. Wellman came closer and whispered: 'I've a reputation for being something of a miserable so-and-so.' He winked and stepped away.

'Ah, right.' Skye tapped her nose. 'I get you.'

Wellman grinned. *You'd be the first. Even sweet Miranda is struggling.*

CHAPTER 72

THEY MET AGAIN NEAR a chain-link fence running parallel with the wooded area of Heath Park fields. The car park was little more than fifty metres beyond. 'I can see why you were nervous to walk alone,' Wellman said, unable to believe his luck.

'It's the shortest route across,' Skye told him. 'There's a hole in the fence next to that tree.' She led the way and stuck her leg through when they got there. 'Are you sure you're okay with this?'

It was darker on the side of the woods. And silent except for the noise of their feet on fallen leaves and brittle stick. 'It's no problem at all.'

Skye ducked beneath a low-hanging branch and held it to one side. 'I'm going to get you something nice as a thank you.'

'The pleasure's all mine.' He hoped that hadn't come across as sounding sleazy.

'And your secret's safe with me. Don't you worry about that.'

Whyever would I worry? I'm the last person you'll ever speak to. In fact, you should get as much talking done as you possibly can. Right now. Before it's too late.

'Dr Wellman?' Skye turned in all directions but couldn't see him. 'Stop messing. You're scaring me.'

He took the syringe from his coat pocket and held it behind his back as he rounded the trunk of a towering oak. 'It isn't nearly as easy getting through this when you're my height. You were saying?'

'For a minute then I—*Ouch!*' Skye put a hand to her shoulder. 'What was that?' She rubbed the area with a circular motion. 'It feels like I was stung by a bee.'

'Not at this time of night. Or this time of year.' Wellman shook his head. 'A sharp thorn is more likely. Probably got inside your coat when we went through those bushes back there?'

Skye lowered her hand to her side. 'I've come over a bit weird, actually.'

He hadn't brought the Schimmelbusch mask with him. Hadn't yet replaced the bottle of Sevoflurane broken in Coco's kitchen. It had taken a full thirty minutes with doors and windows open to get rid of all traces of the smell. 'Weird,' he whispered. 'In what way?'

'It's hard to explain. I don't feel right.' She was slurring her words and swaying unsteadily on her feet.

Wellman put an arm around her. 'It wasn't a bee sting. A thorn, neither.' The whore had gone into the woods at night. All alone with a man more than twice her age. He held the needle between his finger and thumb and let the syringe swing like a pendulum. 'It was this.'

'What have you done?' That's what she tried to say. He filled in the blanks.

'I'm making the world a better place. Not that you'll understand.'

'You killed those women.' She attempted a scream but didn't come anywhere close.

Wellman had timed the revelation just right. *Practice makes perfect,* as the saying went. Or something like that. It would be only a matter of seconds before she fully succumbed to the effects of the drug. 'Can you outrun me?' he asked. 'A young slip of a thing like you should be able to.'

'Please,' was the last word Skye spoke.

'I'll give you a ten-second head start,' he said, prodding her in the small of the back. 'One.' He watched her stagger off into the darkness, taking two steps sideways for every step she managed straight ahead. He closed his eyes and listened. She wouldn't get far. When he heard her fall to the ground, he followed like a viper locating its prey. When he got there, he stood astride her twitching body and undid the front of his trousers.

Chapter 73

'We need to stop meeting like this,' Jenkins said, standing next to the half-naked corpse of a young woman. 'People are going to start talking about us.' It was a lame opening line, but then again, there wasn't much else to say. She noted the crude chest carving. 'Looks like the same killer.'

Sioned Williams got up off the floor, circles of black mud staining the knees of her coveralls. 'He raped her this time,' she said, pointing to smears of blood on the woman's inner thigh. 'You were right about the level of violence escalating with each attack.' She wrote her identifiers on the outside of an evidence bag before handing it to another member of her team. 'What the hell is he going to do to his next victim?'

Jenkins had no idea and didn't want to think that far ahead. 'Did he leave a specimen?'

'Used a condom,' Williams said. 'And took it away with him.'

Jenkins's eyes wandered from the breast-carving to more red lettering, this time on the young woman's bare abdomen. 'What does it say?' she asked, angling her head to get a better look.

Williams squatted. 'There's a number four. Here,' she said, using a finger to write in the air above the carving. 'That says *OF*, I think.'

Jenkins moved side-on to the body and squinted to see if that helped. 'And the squiggly thing?'

'I'd say it was a question mark. Meaning: four of how many, perhaps?'

Reece poked his head through the tent flap, his gaze drawn to the lifeless body lying on the hard ground. The young woman's limbs were perfectly straight, as though her killer had carefully posed her after death. Some of her clothing was scattered next to her: a shoe, jeans and underwear. He'd seen a coat on the wet grass outside marked with a yellow cone.

'He's started playing games with us,' Jenkins said, pointing out the additional knife-work. She looked perplexed. 'But it says four, not three.'

'There *are* four.' He told them about Twm Pryce's visit, his request to exhume Megan Lewis, and ACC Harris's refusal to entertain any such thing. Reaching beneath his coveralls, he patted himself down until he'd located his phone. Then he turned his back on his audience and went at Chief Superintendent Cable without warning – shouting about how ACC Harris was wrong to refuse his request. He hung up mid-sentence and kicked at the air. 'Fucking idiots!' he hissed, searching for somewhere to launch the handset without it hitting someone. 'You two finish up here.'

Jenkins followed him outside. 'And you're going *where?*'

Reece marched straight ahead. 'It's best you don't know.'

Chapter 74

Reece pulled up outside a red-brick bungalow with a white garage door. On a rectangular plate next to the front window, it read: 1 Park Place – the address Twm Pryce had given him. He'd already spoken with the coroner, something the chief super and ACC Harris knew nothing about. There were things the dead girl's family needed to know, and he wasn't willing to let the bureaucrats at police headquarters get in the way.

With a great deal of apprehension, he got out of the car and made his way up the crazy-paved garden path. He didn't need to knock when he got to the door, watched as he was by two sad faces on the other side of the glass. One disappeared, only to reappear in the doorway a few moments later.

With introductions over, he went inside, unsure of how to get started with such a grim tale. How to tell the grieving parents that an exhumation would be undertaken with or without their consent. Life as they'd previously known it was over, and what news he'd brought them would undoubtedly cause immeasurable levels of pain.

Friends and family would already have encouraged them to move on, repeating well-intentioned comments like: *Megan wouldn't have wanted you to be like this.* How the hell could anyone know what the dead wanted? He'd heard it all himself following Anwen's death. They could stick their advice, as far as he was concerned.

He regretted not having brought the Family Liaison Officers with him. Those FLOs were worth their weight in gold at times like these.

'There's sugar in the bowl.' Mrs Lewis placed a plastic tray on the kitchen table. It was of the type found in school canteens and motorway service stations: dark brown and devoid of any discernible pattern. 'Biscuits just there,' she said, pointing to a small plate. Her eyes showed the telltale signs of immeasurable grief, her hands shaking enough to spill a small amount of coffee from two of the three floral mugs.

Reece rescued his from the puddle and stirred in two sugars. He took a sip and began what he'd come for. 'There's no easy way for me to say this.' He put the mug down and reached for Mrs Lewis's hand. 'I've every reason to believe Megan was murdered.' He tightened his grip when the woman tried to pull away. Stood and put an arm around her shoulder when she fell apart. If he cried with her, he knew he wouldn't stop. 'I'll catch the man who did this,' he said, composing himself. 'I give you my word.' He went back to his chair and sat down. 'But I need you to listen to what I have to say.'

'No way,' Mr Lewis said, once Reece had outlined his earlier conversation with the coroner. 'You're not doing that. Not to our Megan.'

'I can imagine how—'

The woman reached for another handful of paper tissues. 'You're trained to say such things. You've no idea how we feel. How could you?'

Reece let it pass. There was no point in him going over the same old ground every time someone said something similar. It never helped. 'The coroner had to be informed of the new findings,' he explained. 'I had no choice in notifying him.'

'Get out of our house.' Mr Lewis stood, his chair toppling onto the tiled floor with a cracking sound. He made no effort to reach for it and stopped Reece when he tried.

Chapter 75

'She's waiting upstairs,' George said. 'And spitting piss when I saw her last.'

Reece slowed as he walked through the foyer of the Cardiff Bay police station. 'Who is?'

'The chief super. Not just her, but the ACC went up there a little while ago.' The desk sergeant rolled his eyes. 'What've you been up to this time?'

Reece stopped at the door at the foot of the stairs. *'Me?'* They both laughed. Then he was gone, taking the steps two at a time.

'The chief super wants to see you,' Ginge said on first sight of him. 'Looked a bit miffed, too.'

'Is that fresh coffee?' Reece asked, using a finger to clean his mug.

'Didn't you hear me, boss? The chief super's waiting upstairs.'

'Of course I did. But that doesn't mean I have to go sprinting up there like some first-year schoolkid. That lot aren't like us,' Reece said, settling on the edge of Ginge's desk. He plunged the same finger into his coffee and chased something that might have been a fruit fly around the surface of it. 'They're not proper coppers.'

'I don't get you?'

'They've all got degrees,' Reece said. 'And act like it's something to be proud of.'

'I've got a degree.' Ginge did look proud. 'In History and Fine Art.'

Reece put the mug and its drowning fly to one side and got up off the desk. 'And I bet Billy Creed and his kind are shitting themselves because of that.' He made his way across the incident room. 'Upstairs, you said? Both of them?'

Reece could see them through the glass of Cable's office window. She was seated and leaning on her elbows. Harris was prowling nearby like a hungry lion. 'How are you doing?' Reece said, passing the PA's desk.

'You can't go in there yet,' she replied. 'Chief Superintendent Cable asked that you take a seat over there when you arrived.' She pointed towards a line-up of what might have been IKEA furniture, in greys and oranges mostly.

Reece didn't stop. 'This'll speed things up.'

The woman chased after him. 'Chief Inspector, I—'

He caught hold of the door handle and opened it in one noisy movement. Harris was still in mid-sentence. 'Afternoon both,' Reece said, cutting him off.

Cable looked up from where she was. Then at the PA who stood tugging the DCI's sleeve.

'It wasn't her fault,' Reece admitted.

'That will be all,' Cable told the flustered PA.

'Close the door,' Harris said, 'and sit down.'

'I'd rather stand, if it's all the same with you, sir?'

The ACC ran a hand over his Brylcreemed mullet. 'I don't give a flying fuck what you'd rather do. Park your arse on that chair. *Now!'*

Reece sat. He took a pen from a pot on the desk and tapped out a tune on his knee. Harris glared at him, insisting he stop. Reece put the pen away in the jacket pocket of his suit. He looked at them both in turn. 'I'm sensing there's a problem.'

His comment was directed at Cable, but it was Harris who answered first. 'There's a problem, all right.' He came closer, shaking with rage. He bent at the waist and stared deep into the detective's eyes. 'And I'm looking at it.'

Reece tried not to laugh in the man's face. 'Has this got anything to do with the exhumation order?'

'You know damn well it has. Didn't I make it explicitly clear we were doing no such thing?' Harris straightened. 'There's no reason to exhume that poor girl. She's already had a post-mortem carried out by the most senior forensic pathologist available to us.'

Reece let his head fall to one side. Did he really have to go through this again? 'That would be the very same man who came out to Brecon on the weekend to tell me he'd likely made a mistake? That's right,' he said when Harris glanced at Cable. 'Twm Pryce wants this second post-mortem as much as I do.'

Harris took a couple of steps rearwards. 'What?'

'The chief super tried telling you this morning, sir.' Reece nodded. 'I got the impression you were more concerned about my dealings with Billy Creed and weren't listening properly.'

The combover got more attention. The area in front of Cable's desk walked in both directions. 'But an exhumation of all things...'

'I have to agree with my officer,' Cable said, getting to her feet. 'With the case developing so rapidly, DCI Reece was right to inform the coroner and family.'

Harris snatched his service hat from a hook on the wall. 'Sort this mess out,' he said, looking at neither of them as he left.

When they were alone, Reece whistled. 'That was a bit tense. Thanks for backing me.'

Cable slammed the office door shut. 'Stay where you are. I haven't started on you yet.'

Chapter 76

Ffion Morgan waited in one of the hospital's outpatient rooms. She wasn't there to witness another post-mortem examination, but could have done with a vomit bowl, nonetheless.

She was shaking and couldn't stop. Even Josh's strong arm around her shoulders did little to make her feel safe. She'd have swapped this experience for anything, including a full day downstairs with the dead.

The word itself sent her mind into overdrive. Wouldn't that be her anytime soon? A statistic. Another hopeless victim of the mutated BRCA genes.

She listened to names called by a short nurse dressed in green scrubs; women vacating their seats with the same look of fear on their faces. Some came back to wait for who only knew what. Others, she never set eyes on again.

When the nurse called Morgan's name, her legs refused to move. She looked for help from Josh. Where the hell was that vomit bowl? And what on earth was she doing in a place like this at her age?

She'd done this walk so many times before. But only in the darkest of her nightmares. She'd get to the consulting room, the attending doctor doing their best to maintain eye contact. Morgan knew what they were about to say before she'd even sat down. A sentence of death would be passed. She'd be told how little time she had remaining and that she should get her life affairs in order. It was nobody's fault. Some people got dealt a bad deck. Plain and simple. Hers was pretty shitty by most standards. 'You don't have to come in with me,' she told Josh. 'There's no need for you to listen to any of this.'

He held her tightly and kissed her before speaking. 'This is you and me together. Soulmates, no matter what.'

A nurse took them into a room that was smaller than Morgan had expected for such things. It was very white, except for a black examination couch pushed against the far wall. The doctor was sitting side-on at a wooden desk, no doubt rehearsing his awkward speech.

Morgan saw no box of tissues.

'Take a seat,' the doctor said after checking who Josh was. He wasted no time and hit her with it, ready or not. 'It's good news,' he said with a wide smile. 'You've got the all clear.'

'What? Did you just say I'm okay? I don't have cancer?'

'The biopsies showed no sign of malignancy. We'll keep a close eye on you, obviously. Because of your family history.'

Morgan heard little more after that. She bent at the waist, sobbing. Josh wasn't much better. She sat up straight, suddenly worried. 'Are you sure you've got the right patient? I mean, you read about this sort of thing all the time, don't you? About how they give a patient their results and then a few weeks later—'

The doctor rested his hand on hers. 'You don't have breast cancer.'

Morgan got up and walked about the cubicle. Everything was a blur. 'Oh, my God.' She laughed. Then cried some more. Vomiting came last of the three.

'Someone's gonna sleep well tonight,' the nurse in green scrubs said, before leaving in search of a mop and bucket.

Chapter 77

Jenkins had waited for Reece to return from the chief super's office before giving him the news. She didn't dare ask how it had gone up there, but given the sour look on his face, it had been no walk in the park. 'The forensic sweep on the Gantry house came up empty.'

He accepted the lukewarm coffee, but didn't as yet take a sip. 'And you found no correspondence from the son? No letters, photographs, nothing at all?'

'Zilch, except for a diary that Ginge has been checking through this morning.'

'Find anything?' Reece asked over his shoulder.

'It might be nothing,' Ginge replied. 'But the initials *FB* crop up regularly. Could be some reference to Facebook, I suppose.' He shrugged, accepting he might be clutching at straws.

'Okay. I want Molly Gantry's name and picture splashed across all media outlets,' Reece said. 'Television and newspapers. And get the local radio stations involved. Someone's going to recognise this woman if she's been out and about recently. The son might have been with her.'

'If she's alive, that is,' Jenkins said. 'There's nothing to suggest she's in any way involved, and might even be a victim if this is down to childhood abandonment.'

'True,' Reece said, checking his watch. 'Did we get a match on those rogue fibres found on Sandra Cole's clothing?'

Sioned Williams shook her head. 'Only that they came from a black jogging suit. Common to a dozen or more retail outlets you could take your pick from. And there were no prints on the knife, or anything else we tested. I'm thinking we might have run a blank on this one.'

'He's a careful so-and-so,' Reece said.

Williams agreed. 'Forensically aware.'

'What does that tell us about him, Agent Starling?' Reece's question was aimed at Jenkins; a jokey response to her previous admission of interest in profiling techniques.

She gave him her best sod-off look, but answered anyway. 'That he's likely to be a high-functioning individual.'

'Employed?'

'Look, boss, I've no formal training in any of this, and could be completely off-piste with everything I'm saying.'

'Humour me,' Reece said. 'Do you think he's employed?'

Jenkins took a deep breath. 'I'd imagine so. He's likely to mix in professional circles, yet be awkward around women and relationships. That might spill over into his private life as well.'

'Not married then?'

She hunched her shoulders under the effort of her answer. 'Some serial killers hold down perfectly normal relationships: wife, kids, the lot. Others are loners, or outcasts even.' She approached the evidence board and trailed a finger over a few of the photographs pinned to it. 'Poppy Jones's murder was made to look like she'd died of natural causes. And if you're right, Megan Lewis's too.'

'Meaning?'

'That their deaths were personal to the killer and not meant for a wider audience.'

Ginge smacked his lips. 'There was no attempt to hide what he'd done to Sandra Cole and Skye Dean.'

'He's lost his focus,' Jenkins said. 'He'd have started out with a clear-cut reason for what he's doing. Something that would have made sense to him, if not to most normal people. As his mental health deteriorates, he's becoming less able to control himself. Take Poppy, for example. She was paralysed. He could have done anything he wanted to her, but didn't. Maybe he was forced to act violently towards Sandra Cole and got a kick out of it. It was only a matter of time then before he combined control, violence, and sex as a method of killing.'

Ginge was following along as best he could. 'But surely his behaviour at work would change too. Wouldn't he stick out like a sore thumb there?'

Jenkins only half-nodded. 'Until now, his professional and private lives are likely to have been kept very much separate. I'd imagine he's been functioning at a high level of competence still.'

'Might that be changing?' Reece asked.

Jenkins thought long and hard before answering. 'If it is, then let's hope no one picks him up on it. Because if those lines blur, then he won't think twice about dealing with them in the only way he knows how.'

Chapter 78

Reece was dreaming. This time of graveyards and not the cobbled streets of Rome. There was a dull knocking sound coming from the underside of the coffin lid. *Knock, knock, knock,* it went for all to hear. But no one did, except him. He rolled onto his other side, listening to the young woman's voice pleading for help. 'There it is again,' he said.

Megan Lewis's mother pointed a finger in warning.

The dour-faced vicar and all those present shook their heads.

Reece went nearer the gaping hole in the ground. 'Are you deaf?' Again, he got no response. 'It's her. Megan's alive and trying to get out.'

The pallbearers and grieving family watched in silence.

And then the vicar started up again.

Knock, knock, knock.

'If you don't let her out, then I will,' Reece warned.

ACC Harris pushed through the crowd, a Brylcreemed combover stuck to his head like a shiny cowpat. 'What do you think you're playing at?' he demanded to know. 'You're for it this time.'

Reece looked to Chief Superintendent Cable. She was there too. 'You'll stick up for me, won't you?'

'Go home,' she answered. 'You're not needed here.' There was laughter with that. Everyone mocking him in their own way.

'Fuck you!' Reece shouted, now standing on the edge of the hole. 'Especially *you,*' he told the vicar. 'Idris always said you were a pompous old sod.' Harris reached for him but slipped and fell to the floor, his combover flopping onto his reddened face. Reece wondered how best to get down there. Into the hole. How flimsy that coffin lid might be under his full weight. He didn't want to go crashing through it and injure the poor girl.

'Jump,' Megan called, as though aware of what he was trying to accomplish. *'I've moved to one side now the drug has worn off.'*

'I'm coming,' Reece said, taking a small landslide of earth and grit with him. He was careful to step only on the outer edges of the coffin when he got there. 'You're going to be safe now.' He was busy releasing the first of six thumbscrews when something hit him square on his back. He thought it might have started raining again. But no, this was something far heavier. 'What the hell are you doing?' he asked, raising an arm against the shower of falling earth.

Harris peered into the hole. 'You were warned.'

Cable came alongside and nodded. 'If only you'd listened for once.'

Then it was the vicar's turn. He made the sign of the cross and walked away.

Reece dropped to his knees and worked the last of the creaking thumbscrews loose. 'Look!' he shouted, and lifted the lid of the coffin. 'Do you believe me now?'

'That's not my daughter,' Mr Lewis said.

His wife appeared only a moment later. 'Not her at all.'

'What?' Reece shook his head and turned away from them. He put a hand to his mouth and froze. The girl wasn't alive. And the parents were correct: it wasn't Megan Lewis.

Anwen stared at him. Or would have done had the holes in her face contained eyeballs and not dirt and worms. Her lips were retracted from yellowed teeth, held that way in something of a sinister grin. She was grabbing at his leg. Gripping hold of his trousers.

An engine started up on the ground above. The sound of a mini-digger momentarily taking Reece's mind off the rotting corpse. 'I'm still in here,' he called to the digger's driver. 'Get me out.' He pulled his leg free of his dead wife's grip and tried to climb the wall of the grave. But instead of the hole being the regulation three to four feet deep, it was twice that depth and sinking fast.

A bell tolled in the distance. Loud and slow.

Was it for him?

Did they think he was dead?

He jerked himself out of the dream and opened an eye. Just one at first. Then released his grip on the pillow and grabbed for his phone—4.10am—the start of a new day. He threw his legs over the side of the bed and waited for the rest of him to catch up before getting to his feet.

It would have to be a short run this morning. In less than two hours time, he was due at the local cemetery.

CHAPTER 79

THEY WERE THERE TO exhume Megan Lewis's body. It was just after 6.00am and still dark. A thick frost had settled overnight and clung to the leading edges of the headstones like a sprinkling of silver glitter.

Reece went in search of the man from the local authority. In his peripheral vision he saw a line of waiting cars, including a black Jag carrying Harris, Cable, and the dead girl's parents. Even from that distance, their anger and contempt for him was clear to see.

What he was doing wasn't for his own benefit. Theirs, neither. This was for Megan. Their daughter. If she'd been murdered—and he was as sure as he could be that she had—then she deserved justice like anyone else. Someone had to pay for prematurely ending her young life, and for tearing apart what looked to be a normal, loving family. He nodded at them, but didn't go over to talk.

'I'm Detective Chief Inspector Reece,' he told the man from the council, and produced formal identification when asked.

'Geoffrey Squire.' The red-nosed man stamped his feet and blew on his hands. 'Another ten minutes or so before we go digging for treasure.'

Reece leaned in close and spoke into Squire's ear. 'You might want to show some respect, or you and me are going to fall out.'

Squire stiffened. 'I didn't mean anything by it. A bit of harmless fun, that's all.'

'How old are you?'

'I don't see what that's got to do with—'

Reece caught and pinched the man's elbow. 'It was a simple enough question.'

'Forty-five.'

'Wife and kids?'

'No.'

Reece let go. 'Thought not.'

Despite the early hour, there was already a heavy press presence on the peripheries. Not that the journalists and camera crews would have seen much, given the grave was shrouded by a large white tent. Stood outside the flimsy structure were four men: two leaning on dirty shovels, the others sharing a smoke while bemoaning the state of the cold ground.

The man from the council checked his watch and announced: 'It's time to begin.' He glanced at Reece, as though seeking approval for his choice of words. When he got none, he produced a clipboard and set about checking details against those contained on the licence. 'To which mortuary will the remains be taken?' he asked, when most of the blank bits had been completed with dates, times, and signatures.

'The University Hospital, in Cardiff,' Reece told him.

'Says here, you'll be re-interring the body later today.' Squire looked up from his paperwork. 'That's very unusual.'

'I don't want this going on for a second longer than it needs to,' Reece said.

'Fair enough.' Another date and signature were added to the collection. 'Today it is then.'

Once the vicar—not the one from the previous night's dream—was done with prayers, the two men with shovels stepped forward and broke the ground. Even from within the tent, the sound of digging disturbed the resident crows, sending them into a frenzy of morning conversation. It took almost 20 minutes for them to get down to where Megan Lewis rested; until shovel struck wood. There was a large pile of earth set to one side of the grave, and a green carpet opposite, waiting for the coffin to be raised. Next to the flap of the tent was a much larger casket that would protect the fragile cargo during its short journey across the city by private ambulance.

When Reece started back to his car, the black Jag was nowhere to be seen.

Chapter 80

By the time Reece got over to the mortuary, the outer casket was already open, Megan Lewis's coffin resting on a wheeled trolley next to an empty extraction table. There was a hive of activity on the other side of the glass screen, most of it led by Dr Cara Frost. She was talking. Gesticulating. Issuing instructions, though as yet, had not flicked the switch that would enable onlookers in the gallery to hear a word of what she said.

Standing next to Reece was Twm Pryce. The man looked as though the weight of the world was resting on his shoulders. 'What a terrible thing,' he said, watching them lift Megan out of the coffin and position her for examination.

Some in the cutting room reacted to the noxious odour that came with her and turned their noses away. Not so Cara Frost, who took both control and the head end.

Pryce ran a handful of fingers through neat, silvered hair, watching them unwrap her. 'I'm going to resign when this is over. Regardless of the outcome.'

Reece's head snapped up and towards the pathologist. 'Why would you want to do that?'

'Because I'm losing my touch.' Pryce pointed. 'Look at Cara. I was once like her: youthful and as keen as they come.'

'You couldn't have known about the paralysing drug. No one could.'

'Cara did.'

'Because of a hunch. Nothing more.'

'And that's my point. A little while ago, that would have been me.' Pryce went closer to the glass. 'I've made up my mind. It's been coming a while.'

'What will you do?' Reece asked.

'Days off are for fishing. Same as they always were.'

'Not all day, every day.'

'I'll keep the evenings for drinking good whisky in Brecon.' He smiled. Or at least attempted to. 'That's if you're willing to spend any more time with a useless old codger?'

Reece shoved his hands in his pockets. 'You know you're welcome whenever you want. But retirement—' He puffed his cheeks.

'When will *you* go?' Pryce asked.

Reece was surprised by the question. 'The sharks are circling,' he answered tiredly. 'Cable really went for me yesterday. And Harris thinks I'm—'

'A brilliant detective. The best he's ever known,' Pryce interrupted. 'Said so himself.'

'Maybe it is time for you to go,' Reece said with a laugh. 'You've gone barking mad.'

'It's as true as I'm standing before you,' the pathologist insisted. 'Harris has no issue with your competence.'

'He's got one hell of a way of showing it.'

For a moment, Pryce looked as though he was struggling for the right words. 'Get yourself well.' He reached for Reece's arm. 'That's their concern.'

Reece pulled away and increased the distance between the two of them. 'Did they put you up to this? You, of all people.'

'I'm speaking as a friend.'

'I'm fine, Twm. The Italians nailing Anwen's killer has put me in a much better place these past few days.'

'You *are* still going to counselling?'

'For what it's worth.'

'Glad to hear it.'

Reece turned to the glass. 'Will you give it a rest now? Looks like they're just about ready to start.'

Chapter 81

Richard Wellman was at home watching the early evening news. The feature headline stated that the police now believed there to be four, not three, victims of the same killer, though they neglected to disclose what had led them to that conclusion.

The newsreader told the public that the first victim's name was Megan Lewis: a twenty-three-year-old nurse—yada, yada—working at the University Hospital in Cardiff.

Wellman closed his eyes and recalled his final moments with the *Prototype*.

He'd rolled off the bed and stood over Megan while she lay there dying, her eyes pleading with him to share more air. 'Don't be frightened,' he'd said. 'I'm going to be here with you all the way.'

Megan didn't gasp.

Nor did she struggle.

She simply went a darker shade of blue. Then died.

The television images were of the exterior of a white tent set against grey headstones and distant hills. There were people stood nearby. One of them looked over his shoulder and stared into the camera. It was the policeman. The detective. DCI Reece.

Wellman tapped an empty wine glass against his teeth, unwilling to blink until Reece looked away. 'So, you think you know what's going on here?'

The reporter went on to explain to the morons at home what exhumation meant. Why it had been applied for. And how the family must have been feeling as they watched on, helplessly.

A right fucking expert, if ever there was one.

But would they find traces of Suxamethonium Chloride this late on?

Did it matter either way? He'd be giving them plenty more victims. The pretty counsellor on Cathedral Road, for one. She knew way too much. Was slowly but surely piecing it all together. And the medical director at the hospital. If *he* probed any deeper than he already was, then there were plans for him, too.

Wellman drummed his fingers on the armrest of his chair, a worrying thought suddenly crossing his mind. Were they all in this together? It was the medical director who'd sent him to the counsellor. And she, in turn, was in cahoots with the detective. They were setting a trap. It was obvious. Why had he been so slow in realising they were all taking him for a ride?

He rose from the chair and made his way upstairs with the back of his hand pressed to his nose. He pulled his shirt-collar across the lower half of his face and opened the bedroom door. Gagging, he spat on the carpet. 'Mother, it's time I got you buried.'

Chapter 82

Mother peeked through an eight-inch gap in the zipper of a hospital body bag. Just her face and a few well-fed maggots. The mattress she lay on took pride of place in the centre of the bedroom floor, safely contained within its original sealed sheet of clear plastic.

Wellman had been careful to take up the carpet beforehand and store it in the spare room. The same was true of the furniture.

He stooped over the thick black bag, coughing and gagging with every stinking breath his body forced him to take. 'It needn't have ended like this,' he said, pulling the metal zipper closed to its end-point. 'All you had to do was love and bring me up as the son I am.'

He fetched a roll of packing-tape and a pair of long scissors from a drawer in the other room, a few wayward maggots crunching underfoot as he went.

Wrestling the black bag onto a separate sheet of clear plastic laid out on the boarded floor, he rolled it and its grisly contents side-to-side as he wrapped it. A full ten minutes of sweaty labour was what it took to get Mother looking like an insect at a spider-feast. Leaning back on his haunches, exhausted and out of breath, he let the tape and scissors fall onto the boards next to him.

It was done. Mother was ready to go. And not a moment too soon.

Wellman got up off the floor and threw open the bedroom window, coughing and gulping lungfuls of fresh air. He didn't dare stay there long, concerned an insomniac neighbour might see him and ask questions the next time they met.

He didn't like being forced to act. Mistakes were more likely when one's actions were influenced by others. But the detective was already closer than the anaesthetist would have liked, and that was an unnecessary distraction.

Grasping what might have been Mother's ankles, he dragged her across the bedroom floor and out onto more sheeting that continued all the way to the front door. He pondered how best to get her downstairs with the minimum of fuss. In the end, he put a foot against her head and pushed, sending her on her way like a gruesome tobogganist.

He followed, careful not to slip and do himself a serious injury. Now came the risky task of getting Mother bundled into the back of his car and buried some place suitable.

Chapter 83

Back at the Midnight Club, Billy Creed was busy doling out punishment. Jimmy Chin stood in front of the office door, blocking all possible means of escape for Kyle Cartwright. The younger man ducked and dived, all the while spitting blood and pleading for his life.

The veins in the gangster's neck bulged beneath his tattooed skin. 'I told you to torch it.'

'We did, Billy. I swear.' That got him a hard palm-slap to the earlobe. *'Fuck!* I've gone deaf.'

Creed lunged. 'It don't matter. You don't listen even when they're working.'

'We took that van up the coast road and put a match to—'

Another slap. More screaming. 'Do you know how many cameras they've got round there?'

'Not where we was. Nobody saw us,' Cartwright lied. The rolled-up newspaper caught him square on the bridge of the nose, showering Jimmy Chin with a fine spray of blood.

'Security saw you.'

'What security?'

Creed unrolled the newspaper and went straight to the page in question, tossing the others onto the floor. 'See if you can't win first prize for guessing who this pair are.' The black-and-white image was smeared with fresh blood, and showed a large van with flames spewing out the windows of its front cabin. A smaller vehicle—one with *Security* written up its side in bold lettering—waited a safe distance away. 'Recognise them yet?' Creed asked, punching a hole through Albino Ron's head. He grabbed Cartwright by the back of the neck and slammed him against the tabletop with enough force to split the wood. He reached for his walking cane, rubbing his knee with his free hand.

Cartwright cowered and tried to roll away. 'No, Billy. Please.'

Creed put the pointy end of the cane against the younger man's left eyelid. 'Tell me that machete didn't survive the fire.'

Cartwright's hand trembled next to the cane, not daring to touch it. 'It'll be all burned up, Billy. I knows it will.'

'I'm letting you off lightly this time,' Creed said in a friendlier tone. 'On account of you being Denny's brother.'

LIAM HANSON

Kyle Cartwright made the fateful error of relaxing his guard. When his eyeball popped, he screamed like a cat caught beneath a moving car.

Chapter 84

Wellman's car turned in a full-circle almost, at a small roundabout on the outskirts of Llandaff. He went past the BBC Wales studios, heading for Llantrisant Road and a rendezvous with a shallow grave and one hundred and fifty pounds of rotting flesh.

The houses were fewer the further he drove away from the city; pavements and street lamps swapped for thorny hedgerows and near-impenetrable darkness. It wasn't far off midnight, a thick cloud-base hanging low over Cardiff like some invading alien lifeform. It was picking to rain. Wasn't it always?

There was very little traffic on the roads thanks to the late hour. A few taxis, the odd car, and the last buses on their way back from town.

He was beginning to relax when he saw a police patrol car parked up at a junction just ahead. A BMW estate model. He scanned his dashboard. Lights on - check. Not speeding - check. Insurance and MOT - all good. He drove on, not daring to look at the driver as he went past. The police car pulled out behind him, its occupants in conversation. The officer in the passenger seat was checking something on what looked to be an iPad-type device.

Wellman drew a hand along the angle of his jawline. They were searching his details. Looking for reasons to pull him over. Just as well he hadn't taken the Volvo from the lock-up. He banged the steering wheel and swore for his own benefit.

The blue lights came on behind him.

No siren as yet.

He indicated left and let his car roll to a full stop next to a raised banking, the vehicle leaning slightly towards the road. He was unlatching the seatbelt and deciding what to say when they pulled around him, accelerating towards the Danescourt roundabout and out of sight.

A short distance further on, he came to a new housing development – if dozens of quick-build dwellings blighting an otherwise beautiful stretch of wild landscape could be referred to as such.

Opposite was a farm gate, and a sign tied to a leaning fencepost with *Private. Keep Out*, daubed in a hand-painted red scrawl. There were runs in the paint that made it look as though the lettering was bleeding. Wholly appropriate given the circumstances. He was in and out of the car for the shortest of hops, closing the gate before driving off up the lane.

He'd previously walked this particular stretch of track as part of a ramblers' party many years ago, and from what he could see in the darkness, the area looked to have changed little. The trees were taller. The hedgerows fuller. But all in all, it wasn't too dissimilar given the passage of time.

He took the arcing bend slowly, headlights off, his eyes not yet fully accustomed to the darkness. The car rocked on its squeaking suspension, deep potholes testing the mettle of the front shock absorbers. There was a turn further along on the left, if memory served him correctly, leading to a dense circle of trees in a dip in the road. He wasn't wrong, and less than a minute later drove into the thick of it, two wheels coming close to slipping into a water-filled ditch.

He braked to a full stop. Then reversed into a space between the trees, before getting out to open the boot. Mother didn't smell anywhere near as bad wrapped in plastic sheeting, but was a tight fit for his small Japanese hatchback.

The moon made a skittish appearance from behind its cover of cloud, prompting an owl to hoot nearby. With a torch and shovel in hand, he went in search of a suitable burial site, leaving Mother to amuse herself.

It wasn't long before he found an area of softer ground. A bonus was the accumulation of water running off the adjacent fields. People would walk around it if they came in this direction, favouring a drier and less muddy area instead.

When the spade hit a small rock, the noise travelled across the land like a gunshot. He waited with his shoulders hunched, listening for voices, watching for movement. When sure it was safe to do so, he started up with the digging again.

Dumping Mother into the narrow boot of his car had been a much simpler task than getting her out. The plastic sheeting threatened to tear apart when he tugged at it. Shaking with an uncontrollable rage, he took his fists to her, pummelling something that started off firm but soon went to soft mush under his unforgiving onslaught. Gripping the bumper of the car, he leaned his weight on it until the lactic acid burn in his shoulders had passed. He was dripping with sweat and close to vomiting.

There was a dent in the sheeting where he'd thumped it: enough of one for him to get a better grip and pull Mother more upright. It was then a case of getting his hands round the back and pulling her towards him. She came up and over the high point of the loading bay in an arcing motion, falling to the floor at his feet with what sounded like something snapping, or coming apart.

The first couple of metres of ground were peppered with small stones, some of which tore slits in the plastic sheeting as he pulled Mother towards her grave. Once on the wet grass, she slid more easily towards the mound of earth and gaping hole.

Chapter 85

Reece stared through the glass of the one-way window. 'What do you make of him?'

Dr Richard Wellman sat alone in the interview room, his attention alternating between the hands on an expensive wristwatch and the battleship-grey walls of the near-silent environment. He was alone: no legal representation required when one agrees to *pop in and answer a couple of quick questions.*

'Shifty,' Jenkins answered. 'Can't put my finger on it, but something about the man doesn't sit right.'

'I know what you mean.'

'And with him being an anaesthetist and all.' She clucked her tongue.

'That was a spot of luck,' Reece said. 'Ginge knowing the crew who pulled him over last night.'

Jenkins read through the officers' report. 'They came across him twice. Well after midnight and driving like he was being overly careful.'

Reece leaned over her shoulder, trying to get a better view of the paperwork. 'What got them asking about the spade in the boot?'

'They got bad vibes, like we did.'

Reece pointed. 'Says here the spade and his footwear had fresh dirt on them. Like he'd only just been digging.'

'After midnight? Nothing weird there.'

'Nothing at all.' Reece swallowed the remainder of his water and tossed the plastic cup into an open bin. 'Shall we go and find out what he's been up to?'

Jenkins was already on her way. 'Try stopping me.'

Chapter 86

Their meeting was informal, and as such, would not be recorded. Reece sat down and waited for Jenkins to get comfortable in her seat.

'I'll be writing to the police commissioner,' Wellman said before anyone else had spoken. 'This is beginning to feel like harassment.'

Reece folded his arms. 'You came here of your own free will. Meaning, you can walk out anytime you want.'

Wellman glanced at the clock. 'Five minutes and no more.'

'Fine by me.'

Jenkins fired the first shot. 'Why did you tell DCI Reece you didn't know Harlan Miller?'

The anaesthetist pushed the table away from him and stood, looking to Reece for an explanation. 'This is old ground, Chief Inspector.'

Reece said nothing while he repositioned the table.

Jenkins raised her hands in apology. 'Okay, I'll stick with the events of last night. Where were you going at one in the morning?'

Wellman lowered himself slowly. 'I was on my way home. I'd been working in my office at the hospital, if you must know.'

'At *that* hour?'

'Insomnia is a terrible thing.'

Reece nodded to himself, and wouldn't have argued with a word of that.

'You were stopped near Danescourt,' Jenkins said.

'Something else I'll be bringing up with the police commissioner.'

'Your car was seen on that same stretch of road well over an hour earlier.'

'And that's a crime?'

'No, but it would raise suspicion.'

'Of what?'

'Your motive for being there?'

Wellman leaned to read the ID badge on Jenkins's lanyard. 'What did you say your name was?'

She gave him her rank and surname only. 'And what *were* you doing there?' She interrupted when he answered. 'Or should my question be: where and why had you been digging at that time of night?' She put the patrol crew's report on the desk in front of her and spun it around. 'This says your clothing and boots were stained with fresh mud. There was also a dirty spade in the back of your car.'

Silence.

'And you still maintain you were at the hospital, working in your office?'

More silence. The same stony stare.

'Doctor, what aren't you telling us?'

Wellman stood again, and for a moment looked like he might say or do something. Instead, he turned his back on the detectives and left without making a fuss.

Jenkins leaned into Reece. 'Are you thinking what I'm thinking?'

Chapter 87

Detective Constable Ffion Morgan stood in Reece's office doorway looking nervous. 'Ginge said you wanted to see me.'

Reece lowered his pen and shut the file he was working on. 'Come in and close the door.'

'Am I in trouble?'

He smiled warmly and pointed to a chair. 'Relax, it's just a chat I've been meaning to have with you.'

Morgan took a seat and patted the trousers of her charcoal-grey suit. 'Okay.'

'You must have been under a lot of stress lately, what with the—' He nodded at her chest.

'The breast lump, you mean?'

'Yeah. A tough time for you and Josh.'

'The scariest days of my life.' She blinked rapidly. 'I couldn't have done it without him. Or Jenks, for that matter.'

'But it's sorted now? You got the all clear?'

'That's what they told me.' Morgan folded her hands in her lap. 'Something like this brings everything in life into perspective, doesn't it? Shows us how easily loved ones can be snapped away.' Her head came up suddenly. 'Sorry. I didn't mean to—'

When he looked away, he sensed she was still watching him. 'I know you didn't.'

'What was Anwen like?'

Reece lifted a silver photo frame and stared at it. 'Beautiful, inside and out.' He handed it over. 'Practically perfect, as Mary Poppins would say.'

'She's very pretty.' Morgan blushed a deep crimson but didn't correct her use of present tense. 'I've been wanting to tell you how sorry I am for your loss, but—'

Reece drew a sharp intake of air, interrupting her. 'But I'm a moody old bastard, aren't I?'

'You certainly have your moments.' She let out the briefest of giggles. 'But you've always got our backs, no matter how bad things get. That's why all of us would willingly go down fighting with you.'

He wasn't sure how best to respond to that. 'I wanted you to know my door is always open.'

'Understood.'

'And if you need any time off at all...'

Morgan shook her head. 'Without work to occupy my mind, I'd have gone nuts with the worry.'

He could relate to that.

'Was there anything else, boss?'

'I don't think so. Not unless—'

Morgan checked the office door was closed. 'I'm not sure you're going to like this, but I've had this idea I wanted to run by you.'

CHAPTER 88

REECE USED A PLASTIC fork to poke at a staff canteen lemon cheesecake.

'Shame we never got to ask if he knew Molly Gantry,' Jenkins said. 'I reckon that would really have put the cat among the pigeons.'

'It's still half-frozen.' Reece tapped the top of his dessert like it was the shell of a hard-boiled egg. 'Three bloody quid they charged me for this.'

'Take it back and ask for another one.'

He pushed the plate away and put his fork down. 'It'll defrost in a bit.'

Jenkins picked at the crust and nibbled on it. 'Do you think he could have been burying another victim last night?'

Reece pulled the plate back towards him and used his hands to form a protective barrier around it. 'He hasn't done anything like that before. The killer, I mean.'

'True, but Sandra Cole was the first victim to meet a violent end. Skye Dean was the first to be sexually assaulted. Maybe burying his victims is his newest MO?'

'Burying them *alive?*' Several heads turned on the nearest tables. Reece waited until the onlookers had gone back to their food. 'I suppose it would have the same effect as paralysing their breathing muscles.'

'Exactly. A slow and horrible death.'

Reece gave his cheesecake another go. It was marginally better. 'That's a very scary thought.'

'Do you buy the *working in his office* thing?'

Reece shook his head. 'But how would we prove he wasn't?'

'Local traffic cameras would show where he went. And I assume there'd be some record of him logging onto the hospital intranet, as part of their security.'

'Him not being at work doesn't automatically mean he was up to no good elsewhere? That's how the CPS would see it.'

'True. But it does give us cause to ask him why he's been lying to us.'

There was a lot Reece wanted to ask Dr Richard Wellman, and would have done had he not walked out on them so early on. 'Ginge says there's been no activity on Molly Gantry's bank account for the best part of a month. No sightings of her, either.'

Jenkins leaned on her elbows. 'Maybe that's why he was out digging last night. Got worried with all the media interest and us asking questions, and moved her body – permanently?'

'It's possible, I suppose. We still don't have any solid evidence in support of him being our perp, though.' When Reece next dug into his cheesecake, the crust broke apart, showering the table with pieces of biscuit. 'Shit!'

'Bloody hell.' Jenkins picked crumbs off her sleeve. Then she snatched the plate away from him before he could stop her. 'Safer there,' she said, moving it again when he grabbed for it. 'Right, so how do we catch him out, supposing he *is* our killer?'

Reece was eyeing an advert for homemade apple pie and custard he'd already decided to try next time he was in the canteen. 'Funny you should ask that.'

'Funny as in, *ha, ha?*'

'You be the judge.' He spent the next minute or so repeating what Ffion Morgan had suggested.

Jenkins looked like she was about to choke. 'Bait? You can't be serious? She's only just had a major health scare.'

'That's what *I* told her. Stop having a go at me.'

'You're not going to let her do it. No way.'

'Where are you going now?' Reece got up and followed. 'Hey, I'm talking to you.'

Chapter 89

Chief Superintendent Cable was at the far end of the canteen, talking with DI Adams and some other people. She broke away from their conversation and headed towards Reece. He saw her coming and beat a quick retreat, zig-zagging between the tables and chairs until he reached the exit. When he got upstairs, he found Jenkins in front of the evidence board, staring at photographs of the known victims.

Harlan Miller's was to one side of the others. She repositioned it next to Poppy Jones's. 'You're here because of something you know.'

Reece came to a halt behind her. 'What was that?'

She turned, startled. 'I meant what I said. Ffion's not up to this.'

Morgan entered the room at that moment, hunting for somewhere to put a tray of coffees. 'Cheers for the vote of no confidence. And there's me thinking you and I were mates.'

'We are. It came out wrong,' Jenkins said. 'This killer is a clever bastard, and I'm not letting anyone put you in danger.' She rubbed the front of her neck. 'I've been there, and it wasn't my idea of fun.'

Morgan handed over two of the coffees. 'Don't forget that I'm a trained killer.' She chopped the air with her free hand. 'Bruce Ffi, remember?'

'This isn't a video game,' Jenkins said with a snap to her voice. 'You don't get up off your arse and press *reset*. If this guy gets close enough to stick you with that drug, then it's over. Kaput. Dead.'

Morgan looked ready to argue, but didn't because Chief Superintendent Cable had entered the room. 'Ma'am.'

'What was that about downstairs?' she asked Reece.

'A misunderstanding.'

'That's not how it looked to the rest of us.' Cable turned to Morgan. 'Are you involved in whatever's going on here?'

'Ffion wants to play honeytrap to the killer,' Jenkins said. 'It's a crazy idea.'

'I'll be all right, ma'am,' Morgan insisted. 'There'll be plenty of backup. Besides, I do martial arts.'

'Not anymore,' Jenkins was quick to point out.

'It's not something you forget when you've done it for as long as I did.'

'Tell me more,' Cable said.

Reece answered his phone when it rang. 'Maggie, this isn't a good time.'

Kavanagh cleared her throat. 'That conversation we had in your office the other day.'

'Maggie, can we—?'

'You're going to want to hear this,' the reporter told him between bouts of coughing.

With their brief conversation over, Reece went straight to his office for his jacket and car keys.

'We're not finished here,' Cable said, watching him head out onto the landing.

'We are for now,' he called over his shoulder. 'Jenkins, you're coming with me.'

Chapter 90

Simon Underdown—medical director—was both annoyed and flustered. Annoyed, because Reece had summoned him from an important board meeting. Flustered, because of the direction their conversation was rapidly travelling in. 'I didn't act alone,' he said defensively. 'I took advice from the relevant people in human resources and occupational health.'

'But you must have been concerned he'd pose a real risk to vulnerable women in his care?' Reece was astounded by the other man's poor judgement. 'Especially after everything that happened in Brussels.'

The medical director double took. 'How could you possibly know anything of that? The matter was dealt with in the strictest confidence.'

'Swept under the carpet more like.' Maggie Kavanagh had fully briefed Reece on every detail known to her. He chose not to divulge his source. 'That jolly in Brussels: tell us what you know about that.'

Underwood blinked like he might have been on the verge of having an epileptic fit. 'It was no *jolly*, Chief Inspector. That was a highly regarded international conference.'

Reece guffawed. 'But matey-boy went wandering, didn't he?'

'Sleepwalking.'

'If you say so. Found his way into the bedroom of a young pharmaceutical rep. She woke up with him standing over her and screamed the place down.'

Underwood waved his hand dismissively. 'Hotel security accepted Richard's explanation. And the woman in question was happy to move on. There was no harm done.'

'I bet your expenses sheet didn't show the backhander you paid to keep her quiet?'

Underwood's complexion was blood red. 'I don't like your attitude, Chief Inspector.'

'And *I* don't like people withholding information relevant to a murder investigation. So, unless you want my team crawling over this hospital like flies on shit, you're going to tell me everything I need to know about Dr Richard Wellman.'

Underwood went to a filing cabinet, returning with a thin folder made from blue card. He dropped it onto his desk and sat down. 'We sent Richard for counselling as part of the Employee Wellbeing Scheme. His psychological downturn was related to a recent bereavement in the family.'

'The Mother?' Reece asked.

'An aunt, I believe.' Underwood peered over the top of his spectacles. 'Richard wasn't the same after she died. Had a bit of a breakdown, but refused to take time off work. He wanted to keep himself busy, you understand.'

Reece pointed at the file. 'I want a copy of that.'

'Not without going through the proper channels.' Underwood closed the cover and put a hand on top of it. 'Good day, Chief Inspector.'

Chapter 91

'I'll drive,' Reece said, getting into his battered Peugeot.

Jenkins slammed the passenger-side door three times before the lock would properly engage. 'Are we bringing Wellman in?'

'Not yet. What we have so far wouldn't pass the CPS threshold test.'

'You could give it a punt. You never know.'

Reece turned the key in the ignition and revved the engine until he was sure it wouldn't cut out on him. 'We need something tangible to link him to those murders.'

Jenkins waited while he fiddled with the radio. Once done, he left the short screwdriver poking out of the dashboard like a spare gearstick. 'I can't imagine him being stupid enough to keep his gear at home.'

'There's only one way to know for sure,' Reece said, pulling away from the parking space to begin a slow circuit of the hospital.

'Do you think we'll find a magistrate willing to sign a search warrant?'

He glanced at her and clucked his tongue. 'That's where you come in.'

Jenkins slumped in her seat. 'Aw, boss. Not again.'

'Stop whinging. Tell them it was an order.' Reece gripped the steering wheel two-handed and shifted position on the worn seat. 'Actually, it is. I'm ordering you to get us a search warrant, however you manage it. Happier now?'

'Not really.'

'Tough. That's what's happening.'

They passed Harlan Miller's place of death. The CSI tent was long gone, the bloodstains on the tarmac floor washed away by frequent deluges of cold rain. Short lengths of blue-and-white crime scene tape hung limply from the cemetery railings. A yellow square next to it displayed a date and time, appealing for witnesses to the *Serious Incident.*

Jenkins nodded in the sign's direction. 'Wellman up for that as well, do you think?'

Reece kept his eyes on the road. 'You said yourself, back in the Incident Room, Miller could have been killed because of something he knew.'

'Something that made him a threat.'

'Exactly. Put it all in the paperwork for the magistrate.'

Jenkins feigned surprise. 'I'm to include fact as well as fiction?'

'Only if you think it'll help our cause.' They turned down City Road, stop-starting in a busier flow of traffic before pulling to a complete halt behind a parked patrol car.

Jenkins looked in all directions. 'Why have we stopped?'

'Get them to take you back to the station.'

'And you?' she asked, undoing her seatbelt.

Reece gave the radio another poke. 'I'm off to Cathedral Road.'

Chapter 92

Reece closed the office door behind him and walked across the hardwood floor to his chair.

Dr Miranda Beven waited for him to get seated. 'Is this the way it's going to be from now on?'

'I don't get you?'

'We had an appointment yesterday.'

'Did we?' Reece checked for diary entries in the calender app on his phone. 'Are you sure you're not mistaken?'

Beven folded her arms and stared at him like his mother used to when he was a young boy. 'You're incorrigible, Chief Inspector.'

'I'm what?'

'Incapable of being reformed.'

'That's a good thing, isn't it?' He broke out in his best smile and kept it going for as long as he could. 'And the reason you've been telling the chief super I'm practically cured.'

'*Making progress*, is what I said.'

'Still, we're moving in the right direction.'

'We'd be making quicker progress if you gave me a fighting chance, Chief Inspector.'

He sighed. 'When are you going to start calling me Reece, like everyone else?'

'When you stop acting like a petulant adolescent.'

'Ouch.'

Beven took a seat opposite. 'This isn't a game. I run a professional setup here. You're sent to me with a problem. I get to the root of it. Together, we work on the solution. At the end of the process, I tell your employer that you no longer pose a danger to yourself or others. That's how it works.'

'I'm not here to talk about me,' Reece said, fiddling with his tie. 'Not today. Richard Wellman—'

Beven shook her head. 'I've already told you more than once, there's nothing I can divulge about another client.'

'Not even if I said your life was in danger?'

Chapter 93

Reece stopped a few paces short of Jenkins's desk. 'CPS?'

She looked defeated. 'A big fat no is what they said.'

'You told them about our meeting with Underwood? And the conference in Belgium?'

'They were still having none of it. Not without solid evidence.'

'Like another dead nurse, you mean?' Reece wrestled his jacket off and flung it through the open door. 'What planet are they on?'

'Don't shoot the messenger.'

'We're going to try again,' he said, dragging an empty chair up next to her. Jenkins shifted a few inches, giving him more room at the desk. 'Miranda Beven emailed the medical director earlier today—not long after you and me left the hospital—advising him to pull Wellman from all clinical duties with immediate effect.'

'No shit?'

Reece retold what he knew of the wrist-grabbing incident. 'Miranda was scared. Wellman's attitude towards her changed in a split-second. And those FB entries in that diary you and Ginge found at the Gantry house: I think they're a reference to a Freda Beck. He's made his first mistake. We're on to him.'

Jenkins closed her eyes. 'Wait, wait, wait. Make this easy for me. Whose Freda Beck?'

'Wellman's aunt: the family member who rescued him from foster care and brought him up as her own. He mentioned her during one of his counselling sessions.'

'Okay. But why would Molly Gantry write this other woman's initials in her diary?'

'Because the two of them were in contact.' Reece had the diary with him and was thumbing through its pages. 'Frequently, if the number of entries in here is anything to go by.'

'You think Wellman killed them both when he found out?'

Reece shook his head. 'I doubt he would have mentioned the aunt's name if that were the case. I think he's still in the dark about them meeting up.'

'Are you going to tell him?'

'Not yet. Get Ginge to find the most recent address for Freda Beck. And where she's buried.'

'Another exhumation?'

'More of a bargaining chip.' He stood. 'You coming for coffee?'

'I'm good here, thanks.'

'I know that look. What's wrong?'

Jenkins picked at her thumb nail. 'I still can't believe you're putting Ffion out on the streets tonight.'

Chapter 94

Richard Wellman shuffled on the threshold of his office doorway, irritated by the late intrusion. He was dressed in a long raincoat buttoned to the collar, with a leather satchel hanging from his shoulder. 'I was about to leave for home. It's been a long and frustrating day,' he said, checking the corridor in both directions.

'Could we go back inside?' Simon Underwood's tone was professional rather than friendly. 'This shouldn't take very long, but we do need to talk.'

Wellman re-entered the office and lobbed a heavy bunch of keys onto his desk. When he offered a chair, it was without turning to face the medical director.

Underwood cleared his throat. 'The police were here earlier today. Detective Chief Inspector Reece. He knows about Brussels. About you and what happened with that girl in the hotel bedroom.'

Wellman's fists tightened inside his coat pockets. 'Impossible.'

'Someone must have said something.' Looking up quickly, Underwood added: 'Not me. The girl perhaps?'

Wellman rose and fell on the balls of his feet. 'There was a silence clause attached to that settlement figure. She wouldn't risk having to hand back the money.'

Underwood nodded in agreement. 'I suppose not.'

'What's really on your mind?' Wellman asked. 'This is a conversation that could easily have been conducted over the telephone.'

Underwood ran a finger along the inside of his collar. 'How long have you and I known each other?'

'Best if you get straight to the point.'

'Yes. *Erm*. Well, I've received an email from Miranda Beven. She's following it up with a formal report, but, *erm,* she's raised concerns regarding your mental wellbeing.'

'I see.'

'You do? Oh good. She believes you require more specialist help than she has to offer.'

'A psychiatrist?'

Underwood looked away. 'Yes, that's right.'

'And what do *you* think, Simon? Do you also have concerns?'

The medical director took a deep breath before answering. 'I'm left with no alternative but to remove you from all clinical duties with immediate effect.'

CHAPTER 95

SIMON UNDERWOOD APPEARED MORE confident now he had it out in the open. 'I'm going to speak with the board first thing in the morning and recommend we put you on an indefinite period of sick leave.' He patted Wellman's shoulder. 'It's in your best interests. You do understand?'

'Are the other board members aware of this email from Miranda Beven?'

'Not as yet. It's too late in the day.' Underwood looked set to leave. 'Oh, yes. I've been meaning to ask: you didn't intend to mislead DCI Reece with the date of birth you gave, did you?' When he bent to collect his coat and case, Wellman brought the brass lamp-stand down on the back of his head. There was a dull thud and a cracking sound as the skull gave way under the weight of the blow. The medical director hit the floor with sprawling limbs, cerebrospinal fluid already trickling from his ears and nostrils. Wellman stepped over him as he convulsed and Cheyne-Stoked his last few breaths.

There were cardboard boxes and filing cabinets in the small annexe room. Behind which were a pair of green painted doors hiding pipework running from the bathrooms and toilets on the next floor up. In one of the cabinet drawers were a couple of spare body bags, kept there for a job such as this. The spilled brain fluid smelled worse than a wet dog.

The job of getting the dead man hidden wasn't a simple one. The cleaning staff would soon be in, and Wellman insisting they vacuum around a leaking corpse was probably going a step beyond the call of duty.

He shoved the boxes to one side and emptied a few of the cabinet drawers before pulling the complete units away from the wall. Taking the body bag by its foot-end, he dragged Underwood from his resting place in front of the office desk to the open green doors. There was plenty of space between the pipes, and the black bag would ensure the stench of decomposition would be safely sealed away for some time to come. In the unlikely event that any noxious gases did escape, it could be blamed on the botched plumbing as usual.

No one would be any the wiser for months. Years even. And by then, Wellman would have long since moved his old friend to an alternative location. Perhaps have him share a grave with Mother. Even in death, the whore would likely relish the male company.

The knock at the office door startled him. It shouldn't have, given he'd been expecting it. The rattle of keys had him move quickly. 'One moment,' he called.

'Sorry, Doc. I thought the room was empty.' The young man was dressed in a maroon-coloured uniform that came close to matching the birthmark beneath his right eye. His cleaning trolley was already wedged between the open door and its scratched frame.

'I told you to wait.' Wellman squatted to lift the lamp off the floor. 'I tripped on the lead and knocked it over,' he said, placing the brass stand in its empty space on the desk.

'There's blood on your shirt,' said Jordan Patterson. 'Did you cut yourself when you fell?'

Chapter 96

Patterson took his cleaning trolley up to the fourth floor and cupped a hand over his mouth and phone while he spoke. 'Come on, Zoe. Talk to me.'

'Piss off, Jordan. Do us all a favour and jump under a bus.' The line went dead.

He dialled a second time. 'Listen to me. *Please.*'

'I'm warning you. I'll tell the police.'

He was agitated and turning in circles. 'There's some weird shit going on at the hospital and I need your help.'

'It's no bed of roses back home.' Zoe's tone was deeply sarcastic. 'We've got two bedrooms sealed off and a couple of policemen stood on the front and back doorsteps.'

He heard her speak to someone else. 'That's not where you are now?' There were several background sounds familiar to him. The racking of pool balls. The jukebox in the corner of the room with its volume cycling up and down mid-song without human command to do so. And the fire door banging against the brick wall as smokers went outside for a sneaky cigarette. He knew exactly where she was.

'It's none of your business where I am.'

'Why won't Lowri answer my calls since the police spoke to her the other day?'

'Because she's scared of you. We all are.'

'I didn't kill anybody. I swear. Do you think those detectives would have let me go if they thought I had?'

A brief pause. 'I don't know what to think anymore. Everything's gone crazy.'

'You and me both.' Patterson checked the corridor. He went to the stairwell leading to the third floor and opened the door. There was nobody hiding there. No one eavesdropping. He let it close and went back to his cleaning trolley. 'What was the name of that doctor who used to spook Poppy? The one who was always staring at her.'

'I don't know. Why?'

'Was it a *Wellman?*' He'd read the plaque on the office door. 'It was something like that, wasn't it?'

'Maybe. Jordan, if you think he's involved, go to the police and let them know.'

'I will,' he said with another check of the corridor. 'But there's something I need to do first.'

Chapter 97

Wellman entered the medical director's office using a key taken from the dead man's coat pocket. There would be no one waiting at home for Simon Underwood. Nobody fussing as early evening wandered into the territory of late night. Like himself, Underwood wasn't married.

He sat down and booted up a computer that was as painfully slow as every other he'd used in the organisation. Thousands of hours wasted per annum by staff waiting for the spinning orb to morph into something more useful. He knew the login and password by heart, having inputted it on several occasions when acting up while Underwood was sick, or on holiday. It hadn't changed. Good old Simon: predictable as ever. Microsoft Outlook loaded a mix of read and unread emails that announced their arrival with rapid-fire pinging sounds.

Dr Miranda Beven. There it was. Using the mail client's search facility, he gathered all correspondence between Underwood and the counsellor. *You two have been busy.* He read the content and didn't like what he saw. Especially the bit where Beven advised that he be removed from all clinical duties pending a full psychiatric review.

It was *her* fault. She was no longer innocent.

He deleted all references to himself, then emptied the deleted folder. Next, he checked for evidence that any of the mail had already been forwarded to the chair of the organisation. It hadn't. Not that he could see.

Finally, he set an out of office alert, and left.

CHAPTER 98

THERE WAS LESS THAN an hour to go until midnight and Morgan's lone walk through the dark suburbs of Cardiff.

'We should have stuck Harris in a skirt and heels and been done with it,' Reece said, annoyed that the ACC had given the idea his full approval. It was true that Harlan Miller's parents had been kicking up a fuss, but what they were about to embark on would never work, even with the most dim-witted of killers, which theirs wasn't.

A magistrate had already signed Reece's new application to search Wellman's house, rendering the honeytrap sting unnecessary. But hey-ho, the warrant wouldn't be served until the following morning, when most of the team would be knackered and well past their best.

'I'll be all right,' Morgan kept saying before they left her in the hospital concourse, awaiting the order to get going. There were plain-clothes officers positioned at strategic waypoints, lying in wait as backup if required. Morgan would stick to the route and had a two-way radio in her bag. Would could possibly go wrong?

The only potential fly in the ointment was a fifty-metre stretch of dipping pavement sitting in something of a radio blind spot. Concerned, Reece had reluctantly conceded they had no feasible alternative, this area being the killer's patch.

Jenkins was waiting in the front passenger seat of the pool car, warming her hands on the vehicle's air blower. 'I've got a bad feeling about this.'

'You and me both,' Reece said. 'That's why we won't be letting her out of our sight.'

'Apart from that stretch where we lose all contact with her, you mean?'

Reece depressed the *talk* button on his radio. 'Last chance to change your mind.'

'I'm all set to go,' Morgan told him.

'Okay then.' Reece glanced at Jenkins. 'We'll be with you all the way.'

Chapter 99

There was a brief burst of static from Reece's radio, followed by something he didn't catch. 'Say that again.'

'I'm turning off Allensbank Road,' Morgan said. 'There's someone approaching on my side of the pavement. Do you want me to cross, or keep going for now?'

'That's *your* call. But be careful.'

'They don't look big enough to be Wellman. Hard to be sure, though. He's downhill from where I am.'

'Cross,' Reece said. 'Let's see what he does.'

'He's crossing with me.' There was a nervous edge to Morgan's voice that hadn't been there only a moment earlier. 'He's reaching into his pocket.'

Jenkins shifted in her seat and buckled up, ready for the chase.

Reece spoke into the shoulder radio: 'Say the word and we're there.'

'He's got something in his hand now. It's small. I can't make it out.'

'Cross again if you need to. Don't let him get close.'

There was a long period of worrying silence.

'Why isn't she answering?' Jenkins asked.

'Ffion?' The tension in Reece's voice was unmistakable.

'Start the engine,' Jenkins said. 'We can't take the risk.'

'Ffion. Answer me.' Reece again.

Radio static. Then: 'He wanted a light for a cigarette.' Morgan was back online. 'He was harmless enough. A bit drunk, but—'

'Has he gone?'

'Yep. Making his way up the hill.'

Jenkins whistled through her teeth. 'Don't do that to me.'

'You can't be far from the blind spot now,' Reece said. 'Maintain radio contact for as long as you can.'

'Send her another way,' Jenkins insisted. 'She doesn't have to go down there.'

Reece wished he could agree. 'This is where several women reported being followed.'

'I know that, but—'

'She'll be okay,' Reece said, the fingers of his free hand crossed and hidden from sight at his side.

Chapter 100

Jordan Patterson hadn't made it over to the hospital social club in time. When he did get there, the place was already locked up and dark, Zoe nowhere to be seen. He knew the route she'd take home. People were creatures of habit.

He broke into a slow jog once clear of the hospital boundary and made his way down Allensbank Road. It was picking to rain, and he had no coat. He drew the hood of his sweatshirt over his head and saw her as soon as he took a right turn into the next street.

Not wanting to call out and risk her contacting the police before he got close, he sped up, shortening the distance between them – no thought given to how she'd react to him bounding out of the darkness.

'Does anyone see her?' Reece asked.

'I don't like this,' Jenkins said. 'She has to be out the other side by now.' She tapped the handbrake. 'We need to go.'

Reece was about to respond when he was interrupted by a loud scream coming from the adjacent street. 'Go, go, go,' he said, giving his team the command they'd been waiting for. He started the engine, and without fastening his seatbelt, screeched off onto the other side of the road in a wide arc.

Jenkins pointed at a couple wrestling against the wall of a nearby house. 'There they are.'

'That's not Ffion,' Reece said, yanking the handbrake with a loud grating sound. He pushed the door open and leapt out of the car, leaving the engine running. Taking the man by the collar, he swung him around and cocked a tightly clenched fist, ready to deliver the first blow if necessary.

The attacker let go of the woman and covered up for the impending strike to his face.

The front door of the nearest house opened to reveal a burly man wearing little more than a bushy beard and Bart Simpson boxer shorts. He stepped onto the wet pavement wearing sliders and came in their direction like a bear making a break from the trees. 'Fuck off,' he shouted, hitching a thumb at the struggling pair.

'We're police officers,' Reece said, for the benefit of all those present. The brief lapse in concentration was enough to allow Jordan Patterson to pull free and scarper. 'Stop!' Reece shouted, breaking into a sprint.

'You've woken the kids,' the bearded man called after him. 'I'm gonna beat the shit out of both of you when you come back for that car.' He reached through the open window and removed the keys from the ignition.

'Give me those.' Jenkins snatched for them. 'If you know what's good for you—' She reached beneath her stab-vest and produced ID. 'You stay where you are,' she told Zoe when she made a move to get away.

Reece knew he was in a one-horse race. Jordan Patterson might have had close to three decades on him in terms of age, but the younger man wouldn't be winning tonight. The detective pumped his arms and brought his knees up high with every stride, the speed and endurance built from his daily runs paying off in bucketloads. He was catching up. 'I told you to stop.'

Patterson didn't and went racing across the road without first looking for oncoming traffic. Reece followed with the same level of disregard for his own safety.

There were more calls for the younger man to give himself up. A uniform waited ahead, waving his arms as though marshalling an aircraft onto its stand. Fat lot of good that was going to be.

Reece dived, tapping Patterson's ankle with a firm hand. Patterson went down hard against the wing of a parked car. Reece was the slower of the two to react, but by then it was all over. The waving uniform had him. 'You're nicked,' Reece panted, staring up at a starry sky with the flat of his back resting in a pavement puddle.

Reece bathed a pair of scuffed knees in a bowl of warm water and TCP solution he'd found in the police surgeon's room downstairs.

'Not the result we were hoping for,' Jenkins said, watching him mend himself.

'My trousers are ruined,' he replied, showing her the gaping holes in the knees. His face lit up with a wide smile. 'Did you see that tackle?' He slapped a hand against the desk, spilling water from the makeshift bowl. 'If ever Wales find themselves short of a fullback...' He sat up straight and whistled.

'The wing mirror of that BMW is totally knackered,' Jenkins said, spoiling his moment of glory. 'No cheap fix there.'

'I'll put a claim in for the car and my trousers at the same time.' He rolled them into a ball and tossed them across the room, watching them land on top of the bin. He sat for a while in his underpants and wet shirt, staring at the clock. 'There's not much point in us going home. The raid on Wellman's house happens in only a few hours from now.'

'Never mind that,' Jenkins said. 'Go find something to hide the budgie smugglers before you get yourself arrested.'

Reece let his knees be and got up with a stoop and a groan. He crossed the Incident Room looking like a half-dressed toddler. 'There should be something to wear in the custody suite. Even if it's only a pair of those grey joggers they hand out to every waif and stray dragged in here.'

'You can't go downstairs looking like that,' Jenkins said, following him out onto the landing.

'Stop fussing,' he called over his shoulder. 'There's never anyone about at this time of night.'

Chapter 101

That wasn't true. There were plenty of people about the station. Even at that ungodly hour. Cleaners for one. Most of them speaking in broken English when Reece trudged by, flashing half-moons of white arse-cheek as he went down the corridor.

'Don't ask,' was all they got in response to their giggles. He used the stairs. Most people were lazy. He'd likely come across no one else. When he got through the door on the ground floor, there was uproar going on at the front desk.

He recognised one of two women immediately: the wife of the missing CCTV engineer. She was drunk and had already called the desk sergeant the C-word on at least two occasions that Reece had heard for himself.

Kath Hall's embarrassed friend was doing her best to drag her away.

Hall turned, as though suddenly aware someone was watching. She looked Reece up and down. 'And what the fuck have you been up to?' She came towards him; all teeth, spit, and sharp fingernails. 'Not looking for my Pete's killer, that's for sure.'

Reece raised an arm to fend her off. 'Hang on,' he said, under a deluge of flailing fists. 'Let me explain.' By the time he got her to an interview room, she was apologetic and tearful.

'I didn't mean to react like that.' Hall was shaking and spoke in rapid bursts. 'I can't sleep. Can't eat. Not knowing what they did to Pete is driving me round the bend.'

Reece nodded. 'We've been a bit thin on the ground lately. You must have seen the news?'

'Poor women.' Hall blew her nose in a paper hanky. 'Who would do such a thing? And to nurses, of all people?'

Reece had since sourced a pair of jogging bottoms that were at least one size too tight. He squirmed, trying to get comfortable. 'You've still not heard from your husband?'

'He's *dead!* That gangster did for him.' Kath Hall turned to her companion. 'Didn't he?' The woman nodded. 'See? Sharon thinks so too.'

'I need evidence,' Reece said. 'As much as I'd like to, I can't bring Billy Creed in on what's little more than a hunch.'

Hall reached into her coat pocket and handed him a folded sheet of paper. 'I've been going through Pete's online diary. On the day he went missing, he was supposed to meet BC at a local snooker club. That's what it says there in the five o'clock slot. BC—Billy Creed—that good enough for you?'

Chief Superintendent Cable wouldn't think so. 'I'll look into it.'

'That's what you said last time.'

'I will. You have my word.'

'When?' Hall was crying again, and gripped a thick wad of paper hankies in her fist. 'Once I've waved enough money at a television camera?'

'That wasn't my idea.'

'If you won't do it for me and Pete, then do it for our kids.'

Reece recognised the signs of desperation, having experienced most of them himself. 'I'll need something personal of your husband's. A toothbrush or comb we can get DNA off.'

Chapter 102

Reece was the first to wake. He opened an eye and wondered where he was. His brain caught up a few moments later. The office wall clock claimed it was just before five in the morning, and given the heavy blanket of darkness all around, he had no reason to doubt it.

The others were asleep at their desks—a disciplinary offence ordinarily—a late finish to the Pete Hall discussion, leaving little time for anyone to return home before the early start at Dr Wellman's house.

Morgan had mentioned nothing to Josh about her acting as prowler-bait. They were busy preparing for a morning raid. That's all he needed to know.

Jenkins had dropped into her chair with a loud yawn. She'd been snoring noisily ever since, her jacket pulled up and over her head.

Ginge had jumped at the chance of looking into the case of the disappearing CCTV man, and couldn't thank the DCI enough.

Reece gave the coffee pot a brief swill under the tap, returning to the Incident Room after filling the machine with a fresh load. Someone broke wind: Jenkins, the likely culprit. She shifted position and repeated the offence. Reece smirked and stood watching them sleep like a proud father checking on the kids before turning in for the night. They were becoming a great team. Even the wet-behind-the-ears newbie was showing promise. He was lucky to have them and knew it. Using a couple of spoons in an empty glass, he walked the length and breadth of the room shaking it like an improvised school bell.

'Jesus Christ.' Jenkins pulled the jacket tighter to her head. 'I've only just dropped off.'

Ginge was up and out of his chair like a sprinter off the blocks. 'Morning, boss.'

Reece tossed twenty quid at him. 'Go see how many bacon rolls you can get for that.'

'Ginge!' Jenkins screamed when he switched the lights on in search of a missing shoe. 'I'll staple your hands to the wall, you do that again.' She reached across her desk and waved the stapler at him. *'Lights!'*

'It can't be morning already?' Morgan raised her head off the desk and wiped dried dribble from the corner of her mouth. 'Not yet.'

Reece was busy clearing the surface of an unoccupied desk, getting it ready for when breakfast arrived.

Ginge appeared in the open doorway not fifteen minutes later, a bulging carrier bag banging against his thigh. 'I had enough money for ten. Doris gave us an extra one for free. Something about you having a frozen cheesecake the other day. So that's eleven in total.'

Jenkins glared at him. 'Where's the orange juice?'

Ginge peered into the bag. Then at Reece. 'You wanted juice as well?'

Jenkins pointed at the door. Ginge was on his way again. This time accompanied by a round of loud laughter. 'Get back in here.' Jenkins stretched like a fireside cat. 'I was messing, you daft sod.'

Morgan stood, still wearing the clothing from the previous night's outing. 'I can't go looking like this. I need a shower and clean clothes.'

'You're going on a raid,' Reece told her. 'Not out on the bloody pull.'

Chapter 103

Reece closed the door to the interview room. 'Sleep well?'

Jordan Patterson looked up. 'This is bullshit and you know it.' He angled his head towards the duty solicitor. 'That's why I'm saying nothing until he tells me to.'

Reece took a seat on the opposite side of the table. 'Morning Giles.'

Patterson slumped in his chair and forced a hand down the front of his joggers. 'You two know each other? That's marvellous, that is.'

Reece pressed the red button on the DIR machine and waited until it had gone quiet. 'For the recording, could you confirm you've spoken to no one about the events of yesterday – myself included.'

Patterson rolled his eyes. 'Just me and my shadow in that cell. Who do you think I've been talking to?'

'Answer yes or no.'

'No, obviously.'

'Why were you following Zoe last night?'

'What did *she* tell you?'

Reece said nothing and waited patiently. Most people couldn't resist the urge to fill an awkward silence when nervous, often incriminating themselves. Jordan Patterson was no different from the average man.

'I wanted to talk,' he said.

'About what?'

'Things.'

Reece glanced at the solicitor when he got no further explanation. 'You're on an assault charge, Jordan. Keeping quiet won't impress the magistrate.'

'Grabbing hold of someone isn't assault.'

'I think Giles here will tell you it is.' The brief nodded on cue. 'What was so important you had to pin a woman against the wall so she couldn't run away?'

'Nothing.'

'Come on. Let's get this over and done with.'

Patterson stared at the wall. He scratched his head. Wiped the back of his hand across his mouth. Looked away. Then refocused on Reece. 'There's a doctor at the hospital. Poppy didn't like him. Said he was creepy. All I wanted last night was to ask Zoe what she knew about him.'

'What does this doctor look like?' Reece asked, his interest piqued. 'Did Poppy ever give you a description?'

'Never mind that. I can give you his name.'

Chapter 104

Jenkins served the search warrant and waited for Wellman to step aside. 'You'll find everything is in order, Doctor.'

'What the hell are you playing at?' he said, refusing to get out of her way.

'We're here to search these premises for evidence linking you to a Mrs Molly Gantry.' The intention was to first establish a connection between the anaesthetist and the woman thought to be his mother, and in so-doing, the Volvo. Next, place the car at the scene of at least one murder and see how things progressed from there.

'This is preposterous.'

'Stand back, please.'

'You can't come—'

'In you go,' Jenkins told a line of waiting uniforms. There was no need for the *Big Red Key* on this occasion. They pushed past the man in the tartan dressing gown and filed down the hallway before splitting into smaller teams. Some went through to the living room. Others climbed the carpeted stairs. Each team calling out when the rooms they were responsible for had been systematically cleared.

The CSI contingent stayed where they were for the time being, waiting to be told the place was safe enough to enter.

Wellman went to follow the last of the uniforms inside. 'I've already told you. I'd never heard the Gantry woman's name before you started asking questions about her.'

Jenkins blocked his way. 'If there's anything you need from the house, someone will get it once we're finished.' He stared into her eyes with a level of contempt that sent a cold shiver coursing through her. 'Move away.' She repeated the command. Louder this time.

Wellman blinked and reluctantly gave her more room. 'I'm working at the hospital this morning. My briefcase. My clothing.'

She shook her head. 'I'm afraid not. I'll need you to accompany me to the station.'

'What?'

Reece had phoned only minutes earlier, instructing her to bring Wellman in, kicking and screaming if necessary. 'There have been several developments in the Poppy Jones case,' Jenkins said.

'And what's that got to do with me?'

She was almost ready to go. 'You'll be told soon enough.'

LIAM HANSON

'Have it your own way.' Wellman put up no fight. He simply leaned over and whispered in her ear. 'You *will* regret this.'

CHAPTER 105

REECE WAS KILLING TIME in his office while waiting for Jenkins's return. He'd organised Jordan Patterson's release with the firm instruction for him to stay clear of Zoe and the other members of the household.

Meanwhile, Ginge was on a roll. Linking fingerprints found on the inside of the partly burned-out van, to one Kyle Cartwright. Another twenty minutes spent digging around in various police databases told him that not only was Cartwright a violent offender—but surprise, surprise—was also a known associate of Billy Creed. 'Boss.'

Reece came as far as the doorway. 'What is it?'

'You'll want to see this.' Ginge took the laptop with him, balancing it on the inside of his left arm. The screen blinked and went blank. 'It shouldn't be doing that,' he said, tapping keys in what appeared to be a random order.

Reece screwed his eyes shut. 'Can't you just tell me what you've found?'

'There was a van torched near the Welsh Water plant the other night. It made the local paper.' Ginge got the laptop booted up again and scrolled to the online version of the story. 'Kyle Cartwright,' he said, pointing at the screen. 'And Ronnie Jones.'

Reece nodded. 'What's your point?'

'There was a machete and what looked like bloodstained rags found in the back of it.' Ginge showed an image of a blade placed alongside a scale of measurement. The metal was tarnished with colours ranging from black through to light blue and yellow. Its wooden handle had been completely destroyed, leaving only a short shank of metal that would have slotted into it. The blade itself had a pronounced back-bow, bent that way by the intense heat of the blaze. 'Forensics found evidence of what might be organic tissue along the cutting edge. It's burned up pretty bad and they're not hopeful of extracting any useful DNA from it.'

'How does any of this help us nail Wellman?' Reece scratched his head, wondering if he'd missed something. 'Or are you suggesting he used the machete to dispose of the Gantry woman?'

'Oh, this has nothing to do with Dr Wellman or Molly Gantry. There was another set of prints pulled off that van, and they don't belong to Cartwright or Jones.'

Reece pinched the bridge of his nose. 'Ginge, unless you hurry up and get to the point, I'm going to throw you and your laptop out of that sodding window.'

'Sorry, boss. Pete Hall. That's who I reckon these prints might belong to.'

Reece thought about that. Cartwright and Jones were associates of Billy Creed. Kyle Cartwright was Denny Cartwright's younger brother. And Pete Hall had done work on Creed's security cameras, if his wife was right. He slapped Ginge on the back. 'We'll make a detective out of you yet. Can you chase up that toothbrush and comb?'

'Already have, boss. Sioned Williams is taking DNA off them as we speak.'

Chapter 106

The troops were filing in as Reece arrived at the custody suite. Jenkins was issuing orders as she led the way. 'We're not charging him as yet,' he heard her tell the desk sergeant. 'Just holding him for questioning while we complete a forensic sweep at this address.' She handed the sergeant the necessary paperwork and waited for him to read through and sign it.

'How did he take the early wake-up call?' Reece asked when he got her to one side.

'Wasn't too happy. Even threatened me at one point. I think he meant he was going to contact the big wigs and report me.'

'We've got him rattled, then?'

'First time I've seen him properly flustered.' Jenkins's attention was taken by new activity in the corridor. She watched over Reece's shoulder. 'You letting that one go already?'

Jordan Patterson was being led from his cell. Wellman did a double-take on sight of him, the sudden change in his body language speaking volumes.

'Give me a second, will you?' Reece said, walking off. He stepped in front of Patterson when he thought the younger man might try something. 'You remember what I told you. Leave this to us.'

Patterson called across the custody area. 'Oi, you. I know what you were up to yesterday. No fucking good, that's what.'

Reece pulled him to one side. 'What are you talking about?'

'Nothing. Get your hands off me.'

'Jordan, I'll nick you if I have to.'

Patterson pulled himself free and marched towards the exit. 'Get away from me!' he shouted when Reece went after him. 'Just leave me the fuck alone.'

When Reece got back to the custody desk, they'd finished booking Wellman in.

'You want coffee before we start the interviews?' Jenkins asked.

'Coffee sounds good.'

'Can I meet you there?' She waved her phone at him. 'I've found Charlie somewhere warm and dry to live. I just need to dot the i's and cross the t's.'

Reece frowned. 'Charlie?'

'The homeless guy who found Miller's phone.' She was walking away and dialling at the same time. 'One more call to the Veteran's Association should do it.'

'Don't be long,' Reece told her. 'We've another busy day ahead of us.'

Chapter 107

'You know how it goes,' Reece said, before reeling off the preliminaries. 'So,' he continued, 'here we are again, Doctor.'

Wellman's solicitor was an insipid-looking man. Downtrodden and down at the mouth. Reece imagined him wearing cardigans and slippers at home, answering to an overpowering woman named Madge, or suchlike. Reece instinctively knew he wouldn't like the man even before he'd uttered his first words.

'My client has a right to know why his home was ransacked this morning, and why you've brought him here for questioning.'

Reece turned his attention to Jenkins. 'Have you been out ransacking again?'

She raised both hands in denial. 'Not me, boss. I don't think we're allowed to do that sort of thing anymore. Sounds like it might be fun, though.'

'It wasn't her,' Reece told the brief.

The man went bright red. 'I'll be reporting your flippant behaviour to the police and crime commissioner.'

'I think he's already snowed under,' Reece told him.

The solicitor went a shade closer to puce and repeated his earlier comment about his client's legal entitlements.

'Jordan Patterson,' Reece said, pretty much ignoring him.

'Is that a question?'

Reece wondered if the man had an issue with untreated high blood pressure. 'I couldn't help noticing Dr Wellman's response to seeing Patterson downstairs. The sooner he tells me what's going on between them, the sooner we can all go home.'

Wellman stared straight ahead. At Jenkins mostly, even though it was Reece asking the majority of the questions. 'I've never seen him before now.'

'That's not true.' Reece reclined in his seat. 'And it got me wondering how you'd know the ex-boyfriend of Poppy Jones.'

Wellman leaned sideways and whispered something in Insipid's ear. He got a nod in return, and only then did he answer. 'I've seen him at the hospital, obviously, but wasn't aware of his name.'

'Where have we heard that one before?' Jenkins asked. 'Jordan Patterson. Harlan Miller. There's a common theme emerging here.'

She ignored the icy stare. 'What was it Patterson caught you doing yesterday?'

'He's just a cleaner,' Wellman said through gritted teeth. 'Why would you listen to anything he has to say?'

'You *do* know him then?'

'I've seen him with his mop and bucket.'

'And you think less of him because of that?'

Wellman scoffed, but said nothing.

'The upstairs of your house smells peculiarly like Molly Gantry's,' Jenkins said. 'Both of you use unnecessary quantities of bleach. That a family trait?' she asked.

It was Insipid's turn to lean in close, after which he got to his feet, prompting Wellman to do likewise. 'Let's end this pointless charade, shall we? Do you have anything with which to hold or charge my client?' He waited. 'Is that a yes or a no?'

Chapter 108

Jordan Patterson had already joined most of the dots and didn't like the picture he was seeing. He'd chosen to mention nothing to the police about the doctor's blood spattered shirt. In a moment of anger, he'd almost let slip, but stopped himself in the nick of time. He wanted no one poking around that office—especially DCI Reece—not until he'd had a good look in there himself.

'I didn't know you were working today.' The woman leaned on the handle of her cleaning trolley, causing it to lurch to one side. Dirty water swished about in a bucket, some of it spilling onto the floor. She took a mop and dabbed half-heartedly at the puddle.

'I'm on an extra shift,' Patterson said. 'Came here to give you a quick coffee break before I go home.'

'Bullshit. You're up to no good, by the looks of it.' The woman snapped her fingers and chuckled to herself.

Patterson kept his lie going. 'There's no one else free for another hour, at least. Take it or leave it.'

The woman handed him a bunch of keys. 'If you're on the rob, then I wants a pack of twenty for keeping my mouth shut.' With that, she was gone, waddling along the corridor on insteps that were worn away like wedges.

Patterson waited until she was fully out of sight before making off with the trolley. There were so many doors and corridors that it would have been easy for him to get confused and end up in the wrong block. Or on the wrong floor. After a fair amount of searching, he came across the nameplate of Dr Richard Wellman. Turning the key in the lock, he let himself in.

Wellman was on his way back to the hospital, wrestling with the city traffic as much as he was with his thoughts. The female detective had got so far under his skin that he'd almost reached across the table and throttled her. Fortunately for all concerned, they'd not been left alone together.

There would be a time for that at a later date.

The detective had tried baiting him, claiming that Aunt Freda and Mother had been in regular contact with one another. He'd refused to believe a word of it, right up to the point when the smug bitch tossed photocopies of diary entries onto the desk in front of him.

There were dates. Times. Venues they'd chosen to meet in.

Detective *Bitch* had taunted him with a grin. For that alone, she'd die if their paths ever again crossed.

He'd sat in silence, processing all he'd seen and heard, stating: 'No comment,' over and over, like some fucking imbecile.

Aunt Freda had deceived him. *She*, of all people. Even on her deathbed, she'd said nothing of her meetings with Mother.

He banged a clenched fist against the steering wheel. It wasn't supposed to be like this. It should have been simple. Young whores succumbing to death by natural causes. Instead, he had bodies coming out of his ears. Old. Young. One hidden in a cupboard at work. Even his own mother rotting in the woods off Llantrisant Road.

The wheel got another hammering.

Just as well the hospital was only five to ten minutes away.

CHAPTER 109

PATTERSON WANDERED THE EMPTY office, not knowing what he was looking for. It had seemed like a good idea when he left the police station. Now, not so much. He continued his search, hoping that something might catch his eye.

It looked like any other office he'd seen or cleaned. It smelled a bit odd. He remembered that from his first visit. He ran a hand along the upright stem of the lamp. There was a slight bend in the metal; a dent in the dome. He picked at a crusty deposit on the underside and rubbed it between his finger and thumb. Old blood.

The doctor would have him believe it was his own. Unlikely. Tripping and injuring himself on that part of the ornament would have been next to impossible to do. The blood belonged to someone else. Who that was, Patterson had no way of knowing.

There were filing cabinets in a small annexe room. Each of them competing for space with a forest of cardboard boxes. He lifted the lid off one such box and peered inside. It was full of old papers and files, and smelled as though it hadn't been opened in years. He checked two others and found the same. He closed the lids before trying the nearest filing cabinet.

More paperwork. Some dates on the files were from ten, even twenty years earlier. A few were older than that.

He opened and closed the drawers in quick succession. All except one. He pulled at it with so much force the entire cabinet rocked on its front end, shifting a few inches forward with a hollow sounding bang. He froze, his breath held, waiting for the occupants of the office next door to come and knock on the door. Nobody did. He slid the cabinet back into place. These things were easy to get into and rarely required the correct key. Something similar in size and shape would do the trick.

He'd left the pile of master keys on the trolley in the other room. Checking through the bunch, he made his choice. On the first attempt, the key refused to turn in the slot. He removed it, put it in his mouth and wet it with saliva. He tried again. Bingo. He was in.

The drawer was empty, except for a laptop kept inside a canvass shoulder bag. He had no time to fire the thing up. Had little clue how to, in fact. But he knew a man who'd be only too willing to help. With the drawer locked, he dropped the laptop into the net bin hanging from his trolley and covered it with paper towels and a dirty mop head.

He'd only just unlocked the office door to let himself out when the silhouette of the doctor appeared on the other side of the frosted glass.

Chapter 110

Reece pushed a clear evidence bag across the table. 'Recognise that?' Even with two good eyes, Kyle Cartwright might have struggled. An oval-shaped cup of plastic over the left one made it all the more difficult. 'Pick it up if you need to. It's yours after all.'

'Says who?'

'These.' Reece took two photographs from a large envelope and lay them next to the warped machete blade. 'Did Billy Creed tell you to torch the van and get rid of evidence?'

Cartwright fiddled with a piece of tape that had broken free of his cheek and plastic cup. 'I ain't saying nothing.'

'There's you and Ronnie Jones turning up in the van; putting a match to it; doing a runner when security arrived. Then there's these.' Reece produced a few more photographs and fanned them out on the tabletop. 'I'd say those rags had blood on them.' What he wasn't freely admitting—because Cartwright hadn't yet asked—was the lack of DNA evidence linking him to anything other than the abandoned van.

Temperatures would have risen to somewhere around three hundred and fifty degrees centigrade for the metal blade to have warped the way it did. With DNA denaturing at half that, they were on a hiding to nothing. Still, there was no harm in him giving it a try. Reece put one last photograph out in front of him. 'And all because of this man.'

Cartwright gave Pete Hall's smiling face little more than a cursory glance. 'Never seen him before.'

'Stop playing games, Kyle. Billy Creed had you kill him.'

Cartwright shook his head. 'You can't prove that. You can't prove nothing.'

'What did Billy do with Ronnie Jones?' Reece asked. 'Only, we can't find him anywhere.'

Despite Cartwright lacking his dead brother's imposing bulk, there was still an air of menace about him. 'No *fucking* comment.'

'Billy believes everything that leaks out of this station,' Reece said. 'He's so paranoid that if I planted a seed in his head, it wouldn't be long before he's kicking yours like a football.'

Cartwright shifted uneasily in his seat. A loud knock at the door silenced him before he could respond to the ill-disguised threat.

It was Morgan. 'Boss, I need a word outside.'

'Now? Can't it wait until we're finished here?'

'There's a phone call from someone in Rome. They said it's important they speak to you.'

Reece paused the DIR with no further explanation and left the room in a hurry.

Once he'd finished the long and difficult phone call with Colonel Gianfranco Totti, he was numb and unsure of what to do next. Anwen's killer had hanged himself while in police custody. The man had taken the coward's way out, unwilling to face up to the consequences of his actions.

Such things happened in justice systems all over the world. And in one police station where Reece had previously worked. But that made it no less painful to bear. His beautiful wife deserved far better.

He'd wandered the building after that; Chief Superintendent Cable finding him in bits on her way out. She'd tried to take him to a quiet office for tea and sympathy. Reece didn't want her pity. He'd wanted Anwen's killer to rot in jail. To be scared for his life every day. To be set upon in the showers and shanked with a knife fashioned from an old toothbrush. Instead, the man had gone out on his own terms.

There was only one thing left to do. Without returning to the interview room to pick up his jacket, he marched through the foyer, oblivious to the desk sergeant's repeated attempts to get his attention. Out into the cold and dark night he went, headed for the Cardiff Bay barrage and the swollen sea.

Chapter 111

Jordan Patterson was lucky to be alive. The doctor had known he was up to no good in that office – that he wasn't there to give it an early spring clean. They'd stared at one another for what seemed like an eternity, neither of them moving until Wellman caught him by the arm and tried to force him back inside.

It was only the appearance of two middle-aged men wearing blue theatre scrubs and paper hats that gave him the opportunity to escape. The men nodded as they went by, exchanging courteous greetings with the anaesthetist. Patterson pushed through the doorway and followed them down the corridor, making sure he wasn't being followed.

When the two surgeons stopped to call the lift, he rescued the laptop from the depths of his trolley's net bin and scarpered for the exit with it clutched under his arm.

He'd then taken the stolen laptop to the local snooker hall, where he found Cleaver and several other shady characters wiling away the hours in semi-darkness. 'Can you open it?' he asked hopefully. The darkness was punctuated with numerous rectangular islands of green baize. Patterson wasn't of the era when men from the local docks and coal yards had snuck in for a frame or three before going home to their wives and kids. Those were the days when curtains of cigarette smoke had made it almost impossible to get a clear sight of the other end of the table, let alone the far side of the room. 'Look,' he said, losing patience. 'If *you* can't, then I'll go find someone who can.'

'Like who?' Cleaver asked. "There's no one else with my level of skills.' He wobbled his eyebrows and cracked his knuckles theatrically. Then he tapped away at the keyboard.

Patterson checked nobody was watching. Billy Creed was prowling near the till, preoccupied with something else. 'Hurry up.'

'What's on here, anyway?' Cleaver looked suddenly worried. 'Not kiddie-porn?'

'What sort of question's that?'

Cleaver raised a hand in apology. 'Only asking.'

'Well, don't.' Patterson had one eye on the gangster, who was now walking a man between the tables by a fistful of dirty white dreadlocks. 'That sort of talk can get you killed in this place.'

'What *is* on it?'

'I don't know.'

'So what's your interest?'

'I'll know when I see it.'

'How?'

Patterson stood. Then he sat down again. 'You're doing my head in. Just open the sodding thing.'

'Already have.' Cleaver handed back the laptop. 'Security on these things is absolutely shocking,' he said with a loud snort. 'I'd consider making a complaint to the manufacturer if it wasn't for the fact I make a damn good living as a hacker.'

There was a scuffle and raised voices coming from the opposite end of the room. Creed had Albino Ron pinned to the table with a snooker cue pressed to his throat. Patterson could hear the gangster asking for the whereabouts of Kyle Cartwright. Patterson knew the name—had been in school with Kyle—but hadn't been stupid enough to go anywhere near him.

'You two!'

Patterson kept his head down and didn't dare make eye contact.

The voice was more threatening the second time round. 'I'm talking to you.' Patterson raised his head only long enough to let Creed know he was listening. 'You've got to the count of ten to make yourselves scarce.'

Albino Ron's wrists had been bag-tied to the pockets at the near end of the table, his head hanging free over its wooden edge. Creed stood loading snooker balls into a football sock.

Patterson went running for the door. No desire to witness what horrors were about to be inflicted on the struggling man.

Chapter 112

Wellman realised the laptop was missing within minutes of him entering the office. There were no prizes for guessing the culprit's identity. He'd virtually caught the thief red-handed.

The detective had the cleaner doing his dirty work. He remembered seeing them in conversation together in the corridor at the police station. They'd made a show of pretending to argue; the cleaner doing a splendid job of racing off in a contrived strop.

Wellman had already deleted the device's search history. Emptied all temporary folders and stored caches. But the police would use forensic software to trawl the hard drive in search of incriminating evidence. And issue his Internet Service Provider with warrants for information relating to his browsing habits. He'd been careless. Too sure he'd never be considered a suspect.

The thought festered like an open sore. He punched the empty cabinet in a fit of rage, leaving a fist-sized dent in the drawer's front.

Someone knocked on his office door a few moments later. 'Richard, are you okay in there?' The woman sounded concerned. Do-gooders always did.

He answered without moving from where he was. 'One of the cabinet drawers got stuck. Had to give it a kick to free it up.'

'I'm next door for another five or ten minutes, if you need me.'

'That won't be necessary.' Wellman lowered his voice to a whisper. 'Not unless you're offering to hold the cleaner down while I gut him.'

Chapter 113

Cleaver had used modified freeware downloaded from the internet to retrieve much of the laptop's deleted history. That cost Patterson a burger, fries, and Coca Cola. Mostly because they'd needed an active, and free, Wi-Fi connection to get it done.

They'd soon found references to Poppy's Facebook account, the doctor having browsed it on several occasions. There were similar finds relating to other women. Megan Lewis featured prominently. *The* Megan Lewis: the one exhumed in the spotlight of news crews.

There was already sufficient evidence for him to hand over to the police. But Cleaver had found something else on that laptop. Information that intrigued Patterson enough to have him visit Cardiff's docklands to take a look for himself.

It was beyond cold on the quayside when he got there. March hadn't yet fully shaken off winter and all he had on was his regulation cleaners' tunic and trousers. Those and a thin black hoodie.

Homeless people were crawling in and out from under the container units further along the dock. A few stopped to warm themselves near basket fires, their grubby faces lit up in tones of orange. All drank cheap booze from bottles, numbing the memories of whatever had put them in such a place.

Patterson blew on his hands and set about breaking into the lock-up. The mechanism wasn't the type used on the filing cabinet back at the doctor's office. This was a padlock that ordinarily required a round key. But it was also a cheap Chinese copy of the real deal, meaning it was next to useless.

Using a technique borrowed from countless hours of watching YouTube videos, he made short work of it; the mechanism popping open in his hands. The door itself was of the up-and-over kind, and squealed loudly when he set it in motion. He stopped to check no one was coming and left the door in the open position when he went inside.

It was dark. Cramped. The bulk of the available space filled with what looked to be a vehicle hidden beneath a grey tarpaulin.

Squatting, he lifted the nearest edge, revealing a kerbed hubcap and a Volvo badge. He shifted position and lifted the tarp fully away from the wheel arch and front wing. The bodywork was painted silver and pockmarked with rust spots that were bubbled and flaking in places. It was the car the police were looking for. While there'd been no mention of the Volvo on the laptop, the doctor had made extensive use of Google Maps in that area, accurately pinpointing his main focus of interest.

Patterson jumped when a noise outside caught him off guard. It sounded like shoes scuffing across hardened concrete. He went to the open door and stuck his head through the gap, his breath condensing on the cold and salty air. He couldn't see anyone, and apart from the occasional bat flapping by, was fairly sure he was still alone.

He'd seen enough and squeezed round the back of the vehicle while talking into his phone. 'I want to speak to someone on the Poppy Jones case.' It was a tight space. He breathed in to give himself more room. 'Reece. Isn't that his name?' He waited while the woman on the other end explained that there was no one from the team available before morning. He was now wedged between the wall and the Volvo's rear bumper. 'Can you take a message, then?' he asked, trying to rotate his leg free. 'And give it to him when he comes in.'

There it was again: the same noise he'd heard only a few minutes earlier. He pushed up on tip-toe, figuring that might help unstick his knee. It didn't.

'Where's my laptop?' The figure stood in the open doorway—tall and wide—clutching something in both hands.

'You killed Poppy,' was all Patterson could think to say.

Wellman poured fluid from a bottle into what looked like a mask lined with wadding.

'I've told the police.' Patterson tried to escape as Wellman edged around the side of the car. 'They're on their way. Be here in a few minutes.'

The anaesthetist laughed off the claim and reached a long arm. 'You're lying,' he said, pressing the mask against Patterson's thrashing face with enough force to pin his head against the block wall. 'Breathe. Make it easy on yourself.'

Patterson swung punches but couldn't reach the taller man. His fists banged against forearms that refused to relent. He was getting sleepy. Every thirsty gulp of air propelling him ever closer towards a certain death.

And then he was gone. Enveloped in total darkness.

When he came to, he was lying face up on the Volvo's bonnet, spreadeagled and unable to move. He tried to breathe but couldn't manage that either. The doctor was leaning over him with his fingers pressed to the side of his neck. He was counting time using the wristwatch on his other hand.

'Three minutes and thirty-seven seconds is how long it took Poppy to die.'

The world was caving in on all sides. There was no white light. No robed figure beckoning him forward with a kindly smile. He was way beyond help and knew it.

The doctor spoke one last time. 'I think you'll fall short of Poppy's valiant performance by a good ten to fifteen seconds.'

Chapter 114

There was no shortage of empty parking spaces outside the Norwegian Church at such a late hour. Not that Reece needed one. He'd travelled the short distance from the police station on foot. Walked along James Street before turning right at the Millennium Centre for the quayside.

There must have been a concert on. The pavements were awash with people dressed for an evening out. Some hailed taxis. Others used phones to check their rides home were on the way. He could hear their excited conversations as he pushed through the crowd.

He'd seen flyers for Elvis Costello and the Imposters over the previous weeks: on lampposts, billboards, and the table in the station foyer. *Oliver's Army* had been a decent enough song in its day. He'd give Costello his due on that. But try as he did, he couldn't think of much else of theirs he liked.

The whitewashed church dated back to the days of the Industrial Revolution. A place of worship for Norwegian sailors when Cardiff's Docks had been the world's greatest exporter of coal. For Reece, it had become his thinking place since Anwen's death. Somewhere he went when he needed to talk things through with her. In life, he'd never have shared such details of the day job, for no other reason than to shield her from the awful things people did to one another. But now she knew first-hand, and there was sod all he could do to change that.

Opposite the church, and well beyond the protection of the tidal barrage system, was a storm leaving Weston-super-Mare, its course set for the shores of South-East Wales. It would race inland, gathering speed before running out of puff somewhere in the mountains.

It wasn't raining yet. But it wouldn't be long before it was.

He walked alongside the man-made lake, navigating by the lights of the barrage ahead and those of the city behind him. He could think of nothing but the dead man in Rome. The murderer. The coward. The *bastard!* He imagined him swinging from what would likely have been a belt gone unnoticed by an incompetent custody officer.

He squatted to pick up a couple of flat stones. Did it by feel alone. They were smooth and icy cold. Like Anwen's skin when he'd kissed her for the last time at the mortuary. He threw the first of the stones, counting the splashes as it skimmed the water in the darkness. 'A triple,' he said proudly.

"Throw one for me," he heard her say. *"Make it a good one."*

He cocked his arm and sent another stone on its way, counting 'One. Two. Three. Four. A quadrupler, if there's such a word.' He looked skywards. 'Have you and Idris been practising up there?' The image of Anwen and her father reunited made him weep. Still, he'd be joining them very soon.

He wiped his eyes and walked further on, stopping to stand above one of five sluice gates that were each capable of allowing over a quarter of a million litres of water per second to flow through. He stood listening to the thunderous roar, completely mesmerised by the awesome draw of it.

The wind was picking up; the approaching storm announcing itself to the people of Wales with the loudest of war cries.

He raised himself onto one of the higher railings and was surprisingly calm for what he was about to do. Gripping an upright of cold steel, he hung over the bubbling torrent. 'I can't do this anymore,' he said, readying himself for the final drop.

Amid the crashing noise of sluice-gate water was a sudden clap of thunder. This one bringing with it a glorious lightning show high above the pointed spire of the Norwegian Church.

It caught him unawares.

Had him stop what he was doing and refocus.

Anwen was sending him back to the world of the living.

Telling him this wasn't his time to die.

Chapter 115

The sudden explosion of thunder made Richard Wellman jump. The frequent streaks of lightning were blinding in their intensity. And the rain was of a kind he'd rarely seen the likes of. It fell vertically to form wide puddles and fast-flowing streams. It got in through the flat roof of the lock-up, soaking the walls and dripping onto the lifeless face of the thieving cleaner.

But now wasn't the time to stand around like an open-mouthed tourist gawping at the spectacle. He had the laptop back in his possession, giving him the upper hand over the police. There was nothing else he could think of linking him to any of the crimes.

DCI Reece and his team knew about Aunt Freda. But so what? Wellman had cleaned her house thoroughly before selling it to a couple of newlyweds who'd then systematically gutted it. When he'd last checked, the place looked as though it had been struck by a stray missile. Nothing to worry about there.

Thoughts of Aunt Freda angered him. Why would she have been in regular contact with Mother for all this time? And why had she kept such information to herself?

They'd played him for a fool. Were undoubtedly in it together, and had been ever since he was a child. He swung a muddy boot at the bumper of the Volvo. *'Bitches!'*

It took him more than ten minutes to drag the cleaner off the bonnet of the car and stuff him in the driver's seat. Wellman wasn't a young man and was exhausted with the effort. He leaned on the metalwork and took a few more minutes to catch his breath before pulling the dusty tarpaulin back into place.

On his journey out of the city's docklands, he saw a lone man making his way along the lakeside path, hunched at the shoulders and soaked to the skin. Just another down-and-out.

Chapter 116

Reece whimpered in his sleep, thrashing about as though emerging from a drunken stupor. Tonight's dream differed from all the rest. Anwen was there, of course. And in danger, as was always the case. But Rome wasn't the venue, and the scooter-riders were nowhere to be seen.

He had no choice but to follow along and watch events play out.

He was at work—in the dream—and had phoned home earlier in the evening to let Anwen know he'd be late. The team was about to close one of the biggest cases of his career and make Cardiff a safer place for women.

Though he knew the killer's identity, the CPS wanted additional evidence that would hold up to legal challenge in the highest courts of the land. Yet the longer they left Wellman free to roam the city streets, the more likely it was he'd strike again.

"We've got the green light," Jenkins said, bursting into the incident room. *"The CPS is on board with us throwing the book at him. Let's go, go, go."*

Reece saw himself taking the stairs to the ground floor. The others took the lift. When he got to the foyer, Jenkins and the rest of them were nowhere to be seen. *"Where are they?"* he asked George, the desk sergeant.

"You're too late, Brân. They left hours ago."

How could that be? Reece shifted in his sleep, rolling onto his other side and immediately back again.

When he checked outside, the entire car park was gone. Tarmac replaced by an expanse of undulating fields. There were snow-covered mountains in the distance. All nonsense, he knew. There should have been streets, flats, and houses.

He saw a man striding across the field, making his way towards a white cottage carrying what must have been a needle and syringe. The man stopped to hold the syringe to the light and made a show of tapping it – expelling air bubbles. When Reece tried to race after him, he found himself back outside the police station in Cardiff Bay.

He took his phone and called Jenkins's number. She didn't answer. He spoke regardless. *"Our man's gone to Brecon. Anwen's his next victim."* He put the phone away and searched his pockets. Where were his car keys? Where was the car park? What the fuck was going on?

LIAM HANSON

He had no usable phone. No car. He'd run instead. It was fifty-something miles door to door. He raced along the pavement, soon finding himself quayside. *"Which way to Brecon?"* he asked a man selling boat trips from a lopsided kiosk. *"This is a police emergency."*

"It'll be quicker if I take you," the man said, starting an outboard motor with a single pull of a short cord.

The speedboat weaved in and out of the busy road traffic, banking sharply as it negotiated a series of roundabouts. When they went the wrong way on the dual carriageway, Reece pointed and said: *"We should have turned there."*

The bald speedboat driver laughed and blew cigar smoke at him.

Reece caught a waft of patchouli oil in the mix. *"You!"*

Billy Creed grinned. *"Don't look so worried, Copper. The doctor will take good care of her."*

Chapter 117

George stuck an arm through the window at the front desk and waved a folded piece of paper at Jenkins as she went by. 'This came in for your lot overnight. I haven't seen the DCI as yet, so you best have it.'

She stopped and took the slip from him. 'What is it?'

George shrugged. 'Another crank caller, I bet. Switchboard's been inundated with them ever since that Yank flashed his cash on camera.'

Jenkins wasn't properly listening and read the note to herself. 'Did anyone respond?'

'Were they supposed to?' George called after her as she made for the lifts. If he said any more than that, she didn't hear him. When she burst into the incident room, she was out of breath and able to speak in clipped sentences only. 'Where's the boss? Have you seen him?'

Chief Superintendent Cable stepped out of Reece's office, a look of worry etched on her face.

'What's wrong?' Jenkins asked.

'Did you speak to him last night?'

Jenkins looked from Cable to Morgan to Ginge. Then at the empty office. 'Please tell me he hasn't—'

'We don't know,' Cable said, beating the others to it.

Ginge explained how Reece had left mid-interview the previous evening.

'He got a call from Rome,' Morgan said.

Cable told them what little Reece had shared with her. 'He was in a terrible state.'

'And you left him on his own?' Jenkins asked.

'He gave me no choice.'

Jenkins turned in a full circle. 'I don't believe what I'm hearing.'

'Do you know where he might be?' Cable again. 'His jacket is on the back of his chair. But his car's gone. We've checked.'

Jenkins tried Reece's number and gave up when he didn't answer after several attempts. She handed the chief super the note George had given her. She needed something to occupy her mind. 'I'd like to follow up on this, ma'am. It might prove useful.'

Cable handed it back after reading it. 'All right. But take a uniform with you. I'm not risking another missing officer.'

Chapter 118

Reece had little idea what made him take a spur-of-the-moment detour to Cathedral Road that morning. The previous night's dream, perhaps? Something about it was still nagging at him: chirping away inside his head like a small bird.

His morning run had failed to get rid of it. And it was still there when he got out of the shower.

He should have been going straight to the police station. First off, to apologise to Ginge. Then, to make Kyle Cartwright spill the beans on Billy Creed's involvement in the Pete Hall disappearance. Cable and Harris could go take a running jump if they thought he wouldn't pursue that angle. Their repeated threats of him finishing his career in a desk job had fallen on deaf ears.

He'd parked his car a few streets away from the Cathedral Road address of Dr Miranda Beven, having been unable to find a space any closer. As soon as he'd started walking, it began raining again. Big fat spots that made wide splatter marks on the cracked paving slabs. He looked to the sky, wondering how there could be any rain left after the previous night's deluge.

When he got nearer Beven's place, he saw the back of a man pulling the front door closed, and recognised him immediately. 'Doctor.'

Wellman turned, the door unlatching and creeping open again by a couple of inches. 'Chief Inspector. What are you doing here?' He looked nervous. Flighty.

'I could ask you the same thing,' Reece said, blocking the anaesthetist's way when he tried to move around him.

Wellman sidestepped onto the shingle border of the garden. 'There's an emergency already on its way to the hospital. Let me pass.'

Reece let him get as far as the pavement. 'Just a minute,' he called, starting down the path. 'I said, wait.'

Wellman glanced at a window on the upper floor of the building. 'You're wanted upstairs.' He stopped to close the gate with a gloved hand. 'I had no time to stay and watch this time.' His face was expressionless. 'What are you waiting for, Chief Inspector? Poor Miranda's brain is turning to mush.'

Reece ran to the front door and shoved it against the wall inside with a clatter of its heavy brass fittings. He paused on the doorstep to speak. 'Your Aunt Freda's the next to be dug up.' He wasn't sure that Wellman could hear him. Didn't know if he'd take the bait.

Chapter 119

Jenkins had given up trying to get hold of Reece and was travelling the short distance to the docklands with a wet-behind-the-ears uniform in tow. Morgan and Ginge had stayed back at the police station, their mission to locate the missing DCI.

The patrol car slipped and skidded in the mud as it crawled down the narrow lane, its young driver coming close to scraping the doors against the walls of passing lock-ups. 'It's this one here,' he said, pulling to a stop alongside number thirteen.

'Unlucky for some.' Jenkins got out and pulled on a broken padlock looped through a ring-and-flap latch. 'Give us a hand with this.' The lock-up door squealed open, sending a large flock of seagulls on their way. She entered, mud squelching over the fabric of her new

Nike trainers. Gripping handfuls of tarpaulin, she pulled it away from the bonnet and windscreen to reveal a silver-coloured Volvo, complete with Jordan Patterson sitting in the driver's seat.

'He's dead, Sarge,' said the uniform, stating the obvious.

Jenkins donned a pair of blue examination gloves and opened the car door. There was no need for a pulse check. Patterson was displaying the classic Q sign of death: his mouth open, tongue lolling to one side.

She went round to the passenger door of the vehicle, glad for once to be slight in stature. The door knocked against the block wall when she leaned in to open the glovebox. Inside was a faded owners' manual and an old-style tax disk. When she rummaged under those, she struck gold. The knife had all the characteristics documented in Harlan Miller's post-mortem report. 'Get this over to the station,' she said, dropping it into a clear plastic tube the uniform had fetched from the patrol car. 'Tell them to send a full crime scene team out here.'

'What about you?' the officer asked. 'I thought we were supposed to stay together?'

'Someone's got to play scene guard until reinforcements arrive,' she told him, while looking for a place to sit. 'It might as well be me this time.'

The patrol car had been gone for only a few minutes when her phone rang in her jacket pocket. 'Boss. Where have you been?'

CHAPTER 120

'Never mind that.' Reece raced up the stairs with his phone pressed to his ear. 'Wellman got to Miranda Beven.'

'Is she dead?'

'I don't know yet.' He hammered on the door to the counsellor's office. 'Send an ambulance over to Cathedral Road.'

'Will do. Where's Wellman now?'

'On his way to the Thornhill Crematorium, if I'm right. Get yourselves over to Freda Beck's burial plot and nick him when he shows. Do you have a key for this?' Reece asked the bemused accountant when he appeared from the office next door.

Miranda Beven was slumped on the couch. Fully clothed but worryingly blue.

He grabbed her under both armpits and pulled her onto the hardwood floor. No time spent on niceties now they were against the clock. The pulse in her neck was slow and weak. She was alive, but only just.

'She's not breathing,' the accountant said.

Reece crouched over the cyanosed face, not knowing if he could keep her alive for the time it would take the ambulance to arrive. He tilted her head and lifted her jaw. There was no respiratory effort. He put his lips to hers, watching her chest rise and fall as he blew into her mouth. Maybe he *could* keep her alive. He wasn't going to give up without trying. Again and again he repeated the manoeuvre, settling into a rhythm that was in sync with his own rapid breathing pattern. He stopped for a moment. 'Go outside and make sure the ambulance knows where we are when it gets here.' He lowered his face to hers. 'Come on, Miranda. Don't you dare die on me.'

Chapter 121

Reece couldn't be absolutely sure that Wellman had taken the bait and gone running to the crematorium. The earlier threat of exhuming Aunt Freda had been an out-and-out lie. There was no obvious reason to suspect she'd succumbed to the same tragic end as the other women. Would the festering thought alone be enough to overwhelm the man and have him act as predicted? Reece certainly hoped so.

It was all over for Wellman now. He'd been caught in the act this time and there was no going back. He'd want to pay his last respects to his dead aunt while he still had the opportunity.

The paralysing agent had worn off eventually, Miranda Beven emerging from the ordeal groggy, but with her higher functions seemingly intact. Once she was in the experienced hands of the paramedic crew, Reece was on his way.

He turned left on the junction at the bottom of Cathedral Road—not waiting for the lights to turn green—across the bridge spanning the swollen River Taff and past the front of the castle. When the little Peugeot hit the speed bumps in the road, his body shook almost as violently as the car did. It felt like someone had connected the steering wheel to a pneumatic drill. Rattling and squeaking loudly, the 205 didn't dare fail him.

He hammered along Manor Way: a long and straight stretch of road that was only a mile or two from his destination. He braked for the changing traffic lights on the busy crossroads. Accelerated away again, once sure that it was safe to do so.

Three or four minutes to go at the very most.

Jenkins had her back to the open door of the lock-up when she first realised she was no longer alone. She turned and couldn't believe what she was seeing. 'Stay where you are.'

Wellman's reaction to finding her there was characteristically matter of fact. 'You didn't think I'd fall for that exhumation nonsense, did you? DCI Reece must take me for a complete fool.'

Jenkins spoke loudly, hoping someone in a neighbouring lock-up might hear and come to investigate. 'You're finished.'

Wellman took a small brown bottle from his pocket and held it up to the light. 'Almost. But not quite.'

Jenkins glanced over the doctor's shoulder, searching for any sign of blue lights coming down the lane. Listening for the sirens of patrol cars in the distance. 'Is that how you did it?' she asked, nodding at the bottle.

'Sevoflurane,' he said, reading its name off the label like it was a vintage wine. 'A wonderful inhalation agent. The more you struggle and hyperventilate, the quicker its rate of onset.'

'Why?' Jenkins asked. 'What did any of those women do to you?'

Wellman took a mask and wadding from his other pocket. 'Nice try.' He came closer. 'I'm going to enjoy watching you die.'

Chapter 122

Reece swung the Peugeot through the double gates of Thornhill Crematorium, accelerating along the winding driveway, past rows of miniature wooden crosses and wreaths of artificial poppies.

People dressed mostly in black turned to stare as he sped by. Some shook their heads. Others waved a weak arm in protest. A man in navy-blue overalls stepped behind the bulk of his mowing machine. Another jumped away from the road; a sweeping brush and shovel still gripped in his hands.

Reece pulled into the busy car park with a squeal of the car's ageing suspension and a grating sound from its handbrake. Leaving the vehicle unlocked, he went in search of the vicar.

The man in question was short and plump, with a purple nose that was much too broad for his pockmarked face. He looked mildly irritated, having been disturbed between funeral services. 'You asked to see me.'

Reece stood beneath a concrete overhang, avoiding a new shower of rain. 'I need to find a burial plot somewhere out there,' he said, turning to survey a couple of hills that were full of them.

'And would this be for yourself, or a family member?'

'I meant the plot is already out there. With someone in it.'

The vicar frowned. 'And might I ask the nature of your enquiry?'

'It's in connection with a murder investigation,' Reece said, conscious that Wellman wouldn't stop long. 'I need to find the plot belonging to a Freda Beck.'

The vicar took him inside and walked with a side-to-side gait that had him look like the needle of a metronome. 'I don't store the details in my head, you understand. We have a records department for such things.' They went to an area of the building that wouldn't have looked out of place in a modern-day business block, where they found a woman feeding paper into a photocopier. She looked up and flashed a well-practised smile. 'Miss Lewis will assist you.' The vicar checked his pocket watch. 'If you'll please excuse me, Chief Inspector, I'm already late for our next appointment.'

Chapter 123

'That's the boss's car,' Morgan told the driver of the high-performance BMW. The Peugeot was parked on the road and partially blocking the route of the arriving hearse. 'Pull up behind it.'

'I can't see Jenks yet,' Ginge said from his seat in the back.

Once on foot, they made way for a large group of mourners coming down the steps. Again, for a separate group that had stopped to read cards attached to rows of floral tributes. Morgan pulled at the collar of her coat, holding it over her head like a makeshift umbrella.

'I've got the boss.' Ginge pointed into the distance. 'Next to the taller monument over there.'

Morgan shielded her eyes from the driving rain and squinted. 'I think you're right. Come on.'

Reece trudged across the exposed landscape, the smooth soles of his shoes slipping and sliding like he was walking on ice. Ahead of him was a marble cross, but no Dr Wellman. He put a hand to his jaw and scratched his wet beard. He checked neighbouring plots, but this was the right grave. It had Freda Beck's name on it.

Making their way towards him were two familiar looking figures. They grabbed at one-another's coat sleeves in repeated attempts to stay upright. One of the accompanying uniforms wasn't so lucky and went down flat on his face.

But still no Dr Wellman.

'Where is he?' Morgan asked once close enough to be heard.

'He should have been here by now,' Reece said. *'Fuck!'* He punched the air in front of him. 'I was sure he'd come.'

'What do we do now?' Ginge asked.

Morgan lowered her head to the worst of the weather. 'Is it worth us checking with the hospital?'

'No, he's gone elsewhere.' Reece shook his head and rubbed his eyes. 'But *where?* is the question.'

Ginge raised his phone. 'Shall I stop Jenks making her way over here?'

'Where is she?' Reece asked.

Morgan told him about the phone call during the night. The note from George. And Jenkins's request of the chief super to let her go to the docks and follow it up herself.

'*Shit.*' Reece's chin dropped onto his chest. 'I know where he is.'

Chapter 124

Wellman hadn't expected to find Jenkins at the lock-up. With police certain to make his arrest within the hour, and his career in ruins, he'd decided to end it all, like his father before him. And in what better place to commit the act than Mother's car? A final middle finger to the woman.

He had two remaining vials of Suxamethonium Chloride in his coat pocket. Both originally intended for himself. There was only one syringe and needle. Not that sharing was an issue, given the terminal circumstances.

The female detective had to die. She'd been disrespectful of him and was obviously a bad person. He was doing society a favour, even if society was too stupid to view it that way.

He flicked one of the vials with a fingernail, fully separating air and solution. His hands were trembling as he drew the drug into the syringe. Thoughts of his own impending death, perhaps. 'Here goes,' he said, holding the needle close to Jenkins's right thigh.

'Itchy's having none of that.'

The voice came from somewhere over Wellman's shoulder and belonged to a dishevelled man standing just outside the doorway of the lock-up. 'This is no business of yours,' he said. 'Go away and I'll let you be.'

There were sirens wailing in the distance. Itchy pointed at the loaded syringe. 'Not until you put that down.'

Wellman came towards him, jabbing the air with his makeshift weapon. 'You'll run if you know what's good for you.'

Itchy removed his dirty coat and tossed it into the lane behind him. Then he folded his shirtsleeves back to his elbows. 'You're going to regret this,' he said, raising both fists in a southpaw boxer's stance. He pulled twice on an imaginary bell cord hanging above his right shoulder. *'Ding. Ding.'*

The first left hook caught Wellman over the liver, forcing venous blood back into his head, almost rendering him unconscious from the outset. As he tottered unsteadily, a right uppercut shifted his jaw sideways, rocking his head, adding to the insult. The second left hook was probably unnecessary, given that he was already falling backwards onto the bonnet of the Volvo.

Jenkins stirred. Disturbed by Wellman landing on top of her. The sirens of the police cars pulling up outside the lock-up got her moving again.

Reece was in one of them, but only until it slid to a full stop. *'Elan!'* he shouted, racing through puddles that were ankle-deep. Jenkins fell into his arms. 'It's over,' he told her. Wellman mumbled something from his position on the floor. Reece kicked the syringe to one side and dangled his cuffs in front of him. 'Are you up to doing the honours?'

Jenkins dropped to straddle the killer. 'Dr Richard Wellman, consider yourself well and truly nicked.'

Chapter 125

THE FOLLOWING DAY

Jenkins was busy cleaning the evidence board with a handful of alcohol wipes, the best part of a month's work reduced to wide swirls of black and red ink. She was humming a tune and happy. 'Charlie's due an award for saving my life.'

Morgan was standing next to her; taking photographs down and piling them on the edge of the nearest desk. 'You've started making a habit of this. Getting to be a right little attention seeker, so you are.'

Jenkins stopped what she was doing. 'That's bollocks and you know it.'

'It was a joke.'

'It had better be.'

Morgan pulled a silly face, quickly diffusing things. 'Seriously though, it was an excellent result all round. The girls, Miller, and Jordan Patterson all cleared up neatly.' It was true. Even the Americans had gone home with an answer to accompany the body of their dead son. The family had spoken with ACC Harris before leaving, asking that he pass on their sincere thanks to DCI Reece and the Cardiff Murder Squad.

Jenkins looked across to the office. Reece was in there, but with the door closed.

'What about Molly Gantry?' Morgan asked, searching for a box big enough to put the crime scene photographs in.

Jenkins cleaned ink off her hands with a couple of paper tissues and some spit. 'Forensics say the soil on that spade is common to lots of places in the area. Let's hope Wellman does the right thing and speaks up. If not, some poor digger driver's going to get a nasty surprise next time a housing development goes up.'

The photographs were packed and labelled for storage. Morgan put the box to one side. 'Kyle Cartwright's prepared to cop full blame for Pete Hall's murder. Creed had nothing to do with it, is what he's insisting.'

'No surprise there. He wouldn't have survived two minutes if he'd turned Queen's evidence.' Jenkins went back to her desk, acknowledging Reece when he emerged from his office.

He wandered over to her with a mug in hand. 'I heard what you said about Molly Gantry. I'm not giving up that easily. We know the patrol car stopped Wellman somewhere on Llantrisant Road. We'll get a cadaver dog to sniff along the route.' Jenkins looked unconvinced. 'I've just come off the phone to the hospital,' Reece said, changing the subject. 'They're letting Miranda home later today.'

Jenkins relieved him of the empty coffee mug. 'That's great news.'

Morgan and Ginge both agreed. 'You saved her life,' Ginge said with all the excitement of a proud son. 'There's no doubting that.'

'When did he stop calling her Dr Beven?' Morgan whispered.

Jenkins winked. 'Watch this space.'

Reece went back to his office and stuck an arm in his suit jacket. 'You two can stay put and finish clearing this lot away.'

'What about me?' Ginge asked.

Reece took a short screwdriver from his pocket and tossed it towards the newbie. 'You'll be needing that.'

'Why? Where are we going?'

Reece was already out on the landing, Ginge following with a lolloping trot. 'The hospital. Can you believe those people? They've only gone and lost the medical director.'

ABOUT THE AUTHOR

Liam Hanson is the crime and thriller pen name of author Andy Roberts. Andy lives in a small rural village in South Wales and is married with two grown-up children. Now the proud owners of a camper van nicknamed 'Griff', Andy and his wife spend most days on the road, searching for new locations to walk Walter, their New Zealand Huntaway.

If you enjoy Andy's work and would like to support him, then please leave a review in the usual places.

To learn of new releases and special offers, you can sign up for his no-spam newsletter, found on his Facebook page: www.facebook.com/liamhansonauthor